# UNDER THE COLD STONES

**A gripping thriller, dark and full of suspense**

## DAN MCNAY

Paperback published by The Book Folks

London, 2017

© Dan McNay

This book is a work of fiction. Names, characters, businesses, organizations, places and events are either the product of the author's imagination or are used fictitiously. Any resemblance to actual persons, living or dead, events or locales is entirely coincidental.

All rights reserved. No part of this publication may be reproduced, stored in retrieval system, copied in any form or by any means, electronic, mechanical, photocopying, recording or otherwise transmitted without written permission from the publisher.

ISBN 978-1-5208-3801-4

www.thebookfolks.com

HAZELTINE PUBLIC LIBRARY
891 BUSTI-SUGAR GROVE ROAD
JAMESTOWN, NY 14701

To Diane Moreau, the love of my life.

# Chapter one

The sky was a brilliant blue over the rows of new corn behind the telephone poles and old fence posts they were passing. The interior of the bus was dim and quiet in comparison. One could be young here. With the folded-up cuffs of your jeans and a ponytail. Daydee had been young here once a long time ago. Somewhere there she played hayseed with a straw in her mouth and one of those round ragged straw hats you got at the county fair. Somewhere there. She looked away. There were only a few others on the bus with her. The lady across the aisle looked about her age, but in a flannel shirt and jeans. No make-up and stringy hair. Daydee felt overdressed. She was being met by her mother's friend, and maybe the lawyer later. She had worn her best skirt and jacket, but now it felt a bit tight for this part of the country. Too much make-up maybe. Were false eyelashes even done in Paris these days?

"Excuse me, darling," she asked the lady. "What kind of crop is that?"

"The soybeans?"

"Oh, well, aren't I stupid."

The lady shrugged.

"Are you going to Paris?" Daydee asked.

"Yeah. You?"

"Yes, my mother just died."

"Really? What is her name?"

"Mary McIntire."

"I knew her. I'm sorry for your loss."

"I wasn't very close to her."

The woman nodded. She had a kind manner. Daydee imagined her atop a tractor. Measuring herself up to her was silly.

"Are you a farmer?" Daydee asked.

"My husband is. He is your mother's sharecropper on the farm, actually."

"Well, it's a small world."

"Paris, Illinois, is a small place. Do you know where you're staying?"

"I have the address in my purse somewhere."

"I can give you directions if you want."

"I'm being met. A Winston somebody."

"Oh, he'll take care of you."

Daydee thought that Winston might have been the name of the football coach at the high school. It had stuck because of the cigarettes her mother smoked. And there she was. Sitting in that overstuffed chair beside the full ashtray. Some stupid thing on the television.

"That looks like shit! Go change!"

And Daydee having stopped, mad, and flipped her the bird. She couldn't help herself. Her mother was a bitch.

"What the fuck!"

Then she would rush out the front door as her mother struggled to get out of the chair.

Thank God she was dead.

There was the yardstick that finally broke on her back the last time her mother tried using it. Daydee had laughed at her despite the stinging welts.

At sixteen, Daydee had snitched three hundred dollars from the coffee can her mother kept in the refrigerator. And carrying a suitcase, she stood on the highway with her thumb out. It was just dumb luck a cop hadn't seen her. The guy who drove the bread truck that delivered to the restaurant where she was a waitress stopped for her. The only question he asked was, where was she off to? Daydee told him New Orleans. He wished her luck when he dropped her at the next little town. No one ever came looking for her.

That was twenty-three years ago.

Two years ago, after drinking too much, she bought a Christmas card at a drugstore and mailed it at the next corner. A couple of cards came. Phone numbers were exchanged but never called. Then Winston called to tell her the bitch had died. There was a will. Life hadn't been easy lately. John was in jail. No one called. She didn't have the heart to start strolling around the hotels at night again.

The lady had said something, but it didn't register. Then she offered her hand.

"My name is Hanna."

Daydee hadn't shaken hands with anyone in God knows how long. John had said she was beginning to touch him like his grandmother used to. She reached over and tried not to be too dainty. Hanna needed some hand lotion.

Outside the fields became scattered farms with long gravel drives, then the yards appeared. Frame houses with brick porches lined the block behind shade trees and sidewalks. No one out and about on a spring morning. Hadn't there been a 'Welcome to Paris' sign? None of it looked familiar. None of it. It could be any little town.

The bus rolled down Main Street and pulled over to stop in front of The Beacon-News building. This she recognized. A green two-story stone building with 'The Beacon-News' in black lettering across the front and forties-looking windows on the second floor. Both women got up. Hanna motioned for her to go first. Was she going to hold the door for her as well? It was a bus, no door to hold. The town smelled like popcorn because of the big cereal factory north of town. She had forgotten. Her heels clicked on the sidewalk. It was so quiet here. There was a little man in overalls waiting beside the bus baggage storage. He had a cotton candy white beard that hid his face. Hanna pecked him on the cheek.

"This is my husband, Sean."

Another handshake. He looked embarrassed.

"I didn't learn your name," Hanna said.

"Deidre," her husband said.

Their bags were pulled out and set on the sidewalk in front of them. Sean picked up his wife's, nodded and walked off to an old pickup truck. Hanna waved and followed him.

The bus left her there. She glanced at her reflection in the window of the newspaper office. Fluffing out her hair, she hoped no one inside noticed her being vain. Her hair was 'to die for'. Thick auburn masses down to the middle of her back and it would take any curl she wanted to give it. The guys would always start by burying their face in it. No sign of Winston. If he was the coach, he had to be in his eighties now. She couldn't picture him. She looked at herself again. The reflection didn't show age, which was nice. The suit was too tight for this little town. She would stop worrying about how she looked. It didn't matter here. She stood there for a long time. It was hot in the sun and she was growing moist under her blouse. A truck came down the street and slowed to take a look at her. She didn't know the driver. She lit a cigarette. Let him gawk, she thought, some excitement in corn country. Well, she couldn't just stand here and melt in the sun. She tossed the cigarette, she was trying to quit anyway, and carried her bag into the newspaper office.

It was dark inside. There was a long counter across the front. And desks. The open door in the back led to the press machinery sitting silently. Everything was wooden and old, unchanged from sixty years ago when it was new.

She fished in her purse for the slip with her mother's address on it.

A man came out of the back. He was tall with wire rim glasses and a boy's haircut of gray hair. Stooped shoulders and a little pot belly made him a little town newspaper guy. You'd know him anywhere.

"Hey, good-looking."

He smiled, taken off guard.

"I was supposed to be picked up, but he hasn't shown up. Can you tell me how to get to this address?"

"It's not too far, down Main for three blocks and then a left. Maybe just a couple blocks after that."

"You mind if I leave my bag with you and come back? It's too heavy to lug that far."

"Not at all." He opened the little gate and brought it behind the counter. "Who was meeting you? I could give them a call."

"All I have is my mother's number, and she just passed on."

"You're Deidre."

"Yes."

"I was a couple of years ahead of you in high school. Everyone thought you were probably dead."

"It hadn't occurred to me that anyone here even noticed that I left."

"Are you kidding?" he asked.

She had to get out of here. She patted his cheek.

"You're sweet. I'll come back in a bit to get it. Thanks."

She lit up another cigarette outside. Was this the way it was going to be? With every man in town knowing her by name? She thought she could just sneak in here and get the money from her mother's estate and leave without getting caught up in anything. She didn't want to be some kind of weird celebrity. With people talking. Men had been looking all of her life, but she was used to being an object with a make-believe name. Tongues didn't wag in New Orleans.

A block further and her feet began to ache and a tiny drip of sweat ran down her neck. She stopped in the shade of a large maple. A cat inching forward on its belly caught her eye. There was a baby bird flapping about in the grass between them. She walked over, shooing the cat away, and took a look. It was a fat little house wren with its mouth open. Above her within reach was a nest with four more gulping air as well. She needed something to scoop it up and put it back without touching it. The mother wouldn't feed it if it didn't smell right, or at least that's what she understood. She just couldn't leave it for the cat's lunch. A car stopped behind her as she looked around for something she could use.

A little old man got out. This had to be Winston.

"Sorry, I'm late. I lost track of the time. Boy, have you turned into a looker."

He shook her hand and his square face and bald head flushed red.

"I shouldn't have said that. I'm sorry."

"No worries, hon. I like being complimented. You have a piece of cardboard?"

She pointed out the baby bird. He went to his car and came back with a brown paper bag. Folding it into a scoop, she managed to pick up the bird, but her jacket wasn't going to let her stretch her arms up high enough. She put it down and took off the jacket to hand it to Winston.

"That's all I'm taking off, hon," she replied to his look.

The bird got home this time. She slipped the jacket back on as they walked to the car. He held the door for her and then climbed behind the wheel, more flushed than before. She touched his arm.

"Take a deep breath, hon."

He obliged her. She told him about her suitcase and he drove back to the newspaper office to retrieve it. Not letting her budge, he ran in and loaded it into the trunk and climbed back in. Then they drove to her mother's apartment building. Sighing, she waited for him to run around and open her door for her as she knew he would.

There were about ten apartments to the building. It was all decked out with phony shutters and white columns. It didn't look very run down at all. Not what she expected. There was a brown 'Manager' sign on the door. The whiff of Chanel #5 inside made her gag.

"Leave the door open, honey. It's stuffy in here."

He dropped the suitcase by the door to the bedroom and handed her the keys.

"Are you alright?" she asked. Why was he still flustered?

"She was an old and dear friend."

"I never heard anyone say anything like that about her."

"You've been gone a long, long time, Deidra."

She started to correct him about the name she was used to, but held her tongue. She didn't want to explain anything right now.

"The lawyer couldn't meet today. He said tomorrow afternoon would fine. How long before you have to go back to New Orleans?"

"I'm not. I closed up shop."

"This town will seem real boring after where you've been."

"Oh, I remember a few wild things about Paris," she smiled.

He looked like a deer about to be run over.

"I got to go. About eight tomorrow morning? I'll pick you up."

"Sure, thanks."

He rushed off. He didn't wave from the car, but he quickly glanced back at her in the doorway, before driving off.

She was glad she didn't tell him her nickname. It would be too hard to explain. Deidra, Deidra, she repeated to herself as if that was going to help. She doubted she would respond in the right way when people here called her by name. And it seemed that a lot of them remembered her. She kicked off her shoes. It was good to be out of them, but the carpet didn't look very clean. It all looked like a grandma apartment: bric-a-brac about, worn furniture with permanently indented seat cushions and that grandma smell. She went around and opened all the windows that would open. At least she died clean. No big blood stains anywhere. The bed was made. Her mother never made her bed.

There were no pictures anywhere. The walls were bare. Had there been any when she was little? The only thing she recalled was a Beatles poster she had on the back of her bedroom door. Well, that was one thing they had in common, sort of. Her mother didn't give a damn. Daydee didn't want her johns to know personal details of what she thought of as her life. There were some framed photos in her Magazine Street apartment, but they were pictures of her or exotic views from some of the trips. And that Gauguin print of him leering at the two native girls. She had left that one behind.

There was some food in the fridge. And whiskey and rum. She started rifling all the drawers and cabinets, looking for any accounting papers and legal documents, and carried everything to the kitchen table. At the bottom of a box, she found a photo album. She stopped to make herself a sandwich and rum and diet coke and sat down to look at it. How long had it been since she had tasted bologna and ketchup on white bread? There she was. As well as her crazy father who had disappeared. Her bike and birthday cake. The cast on her arm at eleven. She wondered if her father ever turned up again. Maybe Winston would know. He had decided to mow the front lawn with no clothes on. Daydee was eight. She tried pleading with him to come inside, she remembered the tears. The neighbors watched, but no one helped. A cop came and handcuffed him and took him away. And that was it. He never came back. Her mother refused to talk about him.

She had put the album aside and was looking through the papers when there was a knock at the door. It was Hanna and her husband.

"Well, hello again." Daydee wasn't sure what to do with them. "Come on in."

They were acting shy.

"Have a seat. Would you like a cool drink? I have some diet soda. Or something stronger?"

They could probably smell the rum. They didn't sit.

"We came with a purpose, Deidre," Hanna said. "I don't know how much you know about your mother's life."

Daydee laughed. "I can imagine."

"You know she married my father a few years ago?"

"No."

"He died about three years ago. He lived here with your mother. When he moved in he brought some things with him that he and my mother had, and I'm interested in maybe getting them from you if you are willing to part with them."

"Ok," Daydee said. She looked around. It all looked like junk. She probably would have given it all to the Goodwill.

"If this isn't a good time, we can come back."

Daydee shook her head, trying not to smile.

"What are you looking for?"

"These lamps were my mother's and the little elephants. And there was a big serving platter that was hand carved."

"Why don't you go through the apartment and gather up what you want."

"You're being too generous," Hanna said.

"Not at all. I would have probably gotten rid of everything. I didn't love my mother. Go for it."

Hanna went into the bedroom with husband in tow. Daydee refilled her drink while they gathered things in the living room. There would be no lamps left and no mirror in the bedroom.

"There's an old mantle clock that belonged to my grandfather, but I didn't see it anywhere. I'd be interested in that too if it turns up."

"Sure."

"So, what do you think?" Sean asked her.

"About what?"

"How about a hundred?"

She hadn't even thought of charging them, but that was about the amount that she had to her name. The extra money would be a big help.

"Sold."

"I can write you a check," Hanna offered.

"Cash would be better."

They checked wallets and came up with sixty.

"I can come back with the rest tomorrow," Sean said.

"Winston is bringing me around to see everything, so I'll see you in the morning I think."

"Shall we leave it here, until it's paid in full?" Hanna asked.

"Don't be silly."

They were quick to start walking it all out to their pickup. Daydee offered towels to wrap the breakables, but Hanna said they were fine. Sean thanked her with another handshake on his last trip out. They waved as they drove off.

"You can't have too many friends," Daydee said out loud at the screen. She had none at all, except John, right now.

She returned to the pile of paper on the table, but her heart wasn't in it. Another drink would do her in. She made it and left it on the coffee table. Going to the bedroom, she rifled the closet for more bed linen and carried it out to make up the couch. She undressed, leaving a pile on the chair. It was cool, but she couldn't tolerate her mother's smell. Arsenio Hall was on. Swinging his fist. She awoke much later, in the middle of the night, with an old grainy black and white movie. She thought she heard something. Getting up with the blanket around her, she peeked at the kitchen. Nothing. She went on to the bedroom. Leaving the windows open was probably stupid.

"Hello?"

They would answer her? She flicked on the light. The room was the way she had left it. Her mother? She pulled open the closet door. All of her clothes. Those would go tomorrow, that would get her out of here.

"You're dead," she said. "You need to go. I wouldn't want to go where you're going, either."

Had she been in her dreams?

"There's not a damn thing you can tell me. And I don't give a fuck."

She turned off the light and closed the door behind her. Her suitcase was sitting there in the living room. She had forgotten to unpack. She crawled back on the couch and hid her face in the blanket. The television talked at her to reassure her. She slept again. Her mother may have floated through again, but when she opened her eyes to the morning, she couldn't recall any of her dreams.

# Chapter two

The sky outside was bright blue and the birds were gossiping. She couldn't remember what time Winston was coming, so she got up right away. She made toast to help her queasy stomach. The blanket slipped off as she carried it back to the couch. All the curtains were open. She wasn't in her second story apartment any more. She hurried around to close them. There wasn't anybody out. Didn't people work for a living here? There was a guy outside the bedroom window walking his dog when she wheeled her suitcase in there to unpack. He waved before she could draw the shades. Bastard. At least pretend you didn't see anything. She threw all of her mother's clothes on the bed and used the hangers for her own things. She'd be wrinkled today. Raking everything off the bathroom counter into the wastebasket, she carried it out to the bed as well. There must be a store where they send you to buy old women things. She showered and did her hair and make-up and tried to tone down. The sweater was good. It would give the boys something to look at while they explained fertilizer. Her skirt was probably too tight. She needed a farm girl sundress. She eyed her mother's shoes and tried them. They were black and fit her. Better an inch than two and a half in the mud. Sensible shoes next – when she went to buy lamps. Back in the bathroom, she wiped off the red lipstick and did a gloss instead.

She was ready to smile at the world. When she opened the front curtains, Winston was out front parking his car. She went out to meet him rather than let him see the shambles she had made of the apartment in one evening. The shoes felt weird and she was short. He jumped out as if to run around and hold the car door again.

"Relax honey, I can get in the car just fine on my own."

"Breakfast?" he asked, pulling out.

"Sure. You make beds, Winston?"

"Oh. Well, I straightened up the place a bit."

"She never made a bed."

Winston smiled.

"Did she have a car?"

"There's a pickup out at the cemetery. Jack has been using it to carry supplies for the upkeep."

"Jack?"

"Jack Evans. He went to high school with you. He played football for me."

There were two boys.

"One was a quarterback and the other was the end." Daydee recalled.

"The school won state two years in a row with those two," Winston said. "I had a little to do with it too."

"Which one was Jack?"

"The tall one. He had blonde hair back then. He's the preacher at the Baptist Church. He does odd jobs around town for extra money. He's been doing the grounds at the cemetery for the last six or seven years."

She thought they were both something back then. But arrogant, they walked on water.

"Edward is a big hot shot lawyer now. He has a hand in running the town and county these days."

Probably not too arrogant now. She imagined them as the type she usually got. A belly, graying hair. Money, but that was about it. No charm left at all. Every one of them with a wife that lost interest long ago.

The restaurant was the one where she had been a waitress on the weekends. She was nervous. All those people in there were probably the same people she had waited on so long ago. There had never been any friends here. Just jealous girls and horny boys. The plates and coffee cups were probably just as chipped. Everyone looked up when they came in. There were a few nods and a couple of hellos from faces she didn't recognize at all. The waitress that came with coffee might have been a girl she had worked with here. It was a guess. She looked older, but Daydee knew better.

"So how are you, darling?" Daydee asked.

There was a look of surprise.

"Same old, same old. So, where you been?"

"New Orleans, most of the time."

"Boy, that must have been something. What are you having?"

They ordered.

"She been here forever?" Daydee asked Winston.

"I've been here forever."

Jack came over to the table. She hadn't noticed him coming in. He was still tall and thin, but his short hair was gray now. Still good looking. Laugh lines around his eyes. A wedding ring. A very big University Class Ring. IU? There was a piece missing from his earlobe, as if someone had taken a small bite out of it. He pulled up a chair and sat with them.

"It's good to have you back," he said. "Winston told us you were coming. Have you had Jesus come into your life?"

Daydee laughed at him.

"Not yet, but today might be the day."

"Well, that's a hopeful attitude. How long before you have to go back?"

"I'm not."

The waitress came back to pour Jack coffee.

"You're not going back to New Orleans?" he asked.

"I thought the estate might take a while to settle. There wasn't anything to keep me down there. Up here, they have good looking preachers. Thought maybe I'd go find Jesus."

"Our doors are always open to sinners. Maybe you could bring this old guy with you."

Winston looked into his coffee.

"Stop by the cemetery. I'll show you the improvements I've made." He eyed Winston. "See you outside for a minute, coach?"

Winston got up and followed him outside. They were soon in a heated discussion outside the front window. A stranger coming in, turned to look back at them. Jack was angry. Not much of a way to keep a secret, she thought. Jack left. Winston stood with his back to the window for a moment, looking up and down the street. He rubbed his forehead before coming back in.

Sean, from yesterday, appeared at the table as soon as Winston sat down again. She hadn't spotted him either when they came in. He stroked his fluffy beard like it was a rabbit's foot. Why do guys with beards do that?

"I brought you the rest of the money," he told her, pulling out his wallet.

Great, she thought, if they don't know, they do now. She wanted to refuse the money, but she really needed it.

"What time are you guys coming by? I have some tractor riding to do."

"Two?" Daydee suggested to both of them.

"Three," Sean said.

Winston nodded.

"Three it is, honey," she said.

Sean blushed and left.

"What was all that about?" she asked Winston.

It took him a moment to understand what she was asking. He looked out the window at where he and Jack had stood.

"Just old business."

"So, you've never been to his church?"

Winston shook his head and tried his eggs. They looked cold.

"I used to go to Mass in New Orleans. Mostly for the show," she told him.

"There's a big Catholic church in town. Maybe you don't remember. I was raised Baptist."

"I was raised Jim Beam myself."

That got a smile out of him. He pushed his plate away and took a piece of toast.

"You ready to go?" he asked.

Winston grabbed a toothpick after paying at the register. Everyone in the restaurant seemed to watch them go out. She didn't look back. She was afraid she would find them all at the window. He was rooting around in his mouth.

"What first?" he asked.

"The cemetery."

\* \* \*

They drove a short distance to the north side of town. There was a wrought iron archway over the entrance. The lettering spelled out 'Paris Memorial Gardens'. Pretty fancy. The whole thing was just a large expanse of lawn. All the markers were flush with the ground. There was a couple of shade trees and some shrubbery for decoration. It all sloped down toward a gravel road that ran across the bottom end. The land across the road was overgrown and covered in trees. There was a concrete bunker with a lot of windows that looked like an office and a big sheet metal shed with one open side. There was a backhoe and a couple of lawn-mowers and shovels and a bunch of other stuff. She didn't know what. There was an old brown pickup parked beside the shed.

It had to be a stick.

She had a Louisiana Driver's License, but she hadn't had a car in years. The johns came to her, or she rode the bus or streetcar. It was much cheaper. You couldn't really park in the Quarter or downtown anyway. Well, everyone would just have to stay out of her way.

They parked in front of the office. Jack wasn't here yet.

"Your mother is over here," Winston said.

They walked over to a new mound of earth.

"Shall I leave you?" Winston said.

"Don't be silly. I didn't love her."

She wandered over to the graves nearby. We are all here, she realized. Her grandmother and grandfather, her great-grandmother and the great-aunt and the great-uncle separately – they were brother and sister. And her father.

"My father came back?"

Winston rubbed his forehead.

"About fifteen years ago. Somebody thought they saw him wandering around out on your farm. Your mother and aunt went out to look for him, but couldn't find him. The sheriff went and looked too. Then there was a fire in the old barn out there and when they got it out, they found him inside, all burned up."

She felt her tears begin to well up. All this time she had imagined him crazy as a loon, wandering the streets somewhere. Like the Magic Bead Lady in the French Quarter. The homeless crazy woman would hit up the shopkeepers with a present of her magic bead and mumble some blessing on the shop and they would give her money. Surviving on the kindness of strangers. And he has been here all this time. She wouldn't let herself cry. What good would it do?

"There was a new young DA in town who decided your mother had probably killed him, so he pressed charges. There was a trial. Edward defended her. She got off. There wasn't any evidence. Why would she kill him anyway? She could have had him locked up as a crazy person. No need to kill anybody."

"Jesus."

Jack pulled up in his pickup. She was thankful for the distraction. They walked back to office where he had parked.

"I think you are just as good looking as you were in high school," she told him.

His eyes jumped at Winston behind her.

"I have a wife and two kids now."

"You have pictures?"

He looked a bit confused, but took his wallet out of his back pocket. He told her their names and ages. The wife was pretty. Daydee oohed.

"Let me show you the office," Jack suggested.

He unlocked it and handed her the keys. They went in. It was a nice cozy room with wood paneling and black file cabinets and two overstuffed chairs before a desk. There were a lot of windows that opened to the expanse of lawn. The customers could sit there in comfort and look out at the peaceful park as they signed the papers. Atop one of the cabinets was Hanna's mantle clock. It was a little crowded with all of them standing. Daydee touched Jack's arm to move around him to open a file drawer and look inside. He jumped out of the way. Winston had followed them in, but then went back outside.

"Your mother ran the business and scheduled everything. She would just call when there was a burial. I'm busy Sundays, so we had them all on Saturday. I don't know much about the paperwork, I'm afraid. I come out once a week and mow, and weed and install markers when they come in."

She touched his arm again to go back to the desk. He jumped again.

"There's no answer phone?"

"Everyone knew to call her at home. You want to see the shed and the equipment?"

"Sure."

She locked the door and kept the keys. She was beside Jack walking down. He made her feel tiny.

"So, what time Sunday?"

"Nine. Winston could bring you."

Winston looked away when she glanced at him. Good. She really had no intention of going.

"I've started buying sod piecemeal to cover the new graves. It makes it look better quicker."

"That sounds like a great idea."

He showed her around the shed and explained what some of the equipment was. She tried the door of the backhoe, but it didn't want to open easily. Jack pulled it open for her.

"I don't use this one. I have my own. It's in town at a job site right now."

She turned and acted off balance and grabbed his arm to steady herself. She knew she was a little too close.

"Well, let's just keep everything as is, until I get it figured out. Ok, hon?"

Jack nodded.

She looked at the keys for something that would fit the truck. He pointed.

"You don't need it?"

"No, I drove figuring you would want the use of it."

"Where next," she asked Winston. "The farm?"

"Sure."

She climbed in her pickup. She wasn't sure about driving with even the low heels she had borrowed so she took them off and put them next to her on the seat. Winston was mumbling something to Jack. She rolled down the window.

"You coming?"

Winston came over to join her.

"You want me to drive?" he asked after he climbed into the passenger's side.

"No."

It started easily enough. She hit the brake and the clutch and tried to shift into first. It grinded. Jack was at the window.

"You have to double clutch it. Every time you change gears, you have to put in the clutch twice. The second time is the charm."

"Good to know."

She tried again. The gears screeched a bit, but the truck jerked forward. She weaved up the drive and came a little close to the archway when she left the grounds.

"I can drive," Winston told her.

She didn't answer. She was scared to death. She hadn't driven a vehicle in four years. The last time was when her client was too soused to get back to the hotel. And that was a fancy rental. Winston was clutching his arm rest.

"You should probably have your shoes on."

She laughed. And ran a stop sign. He hollered directions and asked her to slow down. They were on the highway out of town. This was a blast! Just like when she borrowed her mother's car. She revved it up to the top of second and made it into third. Her hair was going to be a mess from the open window. They came to the driveway for the farm and she took it too fast, one back tire sliding into the ditch, but she recovered. Sean was out by his tractor. She coasted in with the clutch in and wrestled it back into first. When she braked, the engine died.

"I'll practice," she told him.

She tried fixing her hair in the mirror, but it was hopeless. Sean was coming over. She didn't want to make them wait while she sorted the tangles out. There was a contraption hitched to his tractor. And behind that, a pile of gray and blackened lumber. The burnt-out barn. A little distance further was the old Victorian farm house, all boarded up, surrounded by rows of corn. She recalled that there had been a yard with a fence long ago.

"You were lucky to make that turn coming in," Sean said.

"Glad you liked it, Sweetie."

"No, seriously." He was frowning.

"Seriously, I couldn't give a rat's ass what you think of my driving."

Sean looked at Winston.

"He's busy thanking the lord he's still alive," Daydee said.

"Sorry, Miss McIntire. I was concerned about you hurting yourself."

"So, what's going on with the farm?"

She opened the door and slipped her shoes on. She hopped down, shaking out her hair with her fingers.

"You want a tour?"

"What are you getting ready to do?" she asked.

"I'm fertilizing."

"I could go once around with you. I think I remember how to hold on."

"It's not safe. And my wife won't like it when she brings lunch later. I meant a tour in the truck."

"Next time, I guess. You have an old tractor," Daydee said.

"It works just fine."

"So, what you doing with the crops? We're partners now, right?"

"I've planted half soy and half corn. About 180 acres each. I've gotten a futures offer for $7.40 a bushel on the soy that we should probably take. It won't go much higher than that."

"I don't know what that means," she told him.

"It's an offer to buy the crop before it comes out of the ground. Most wait until mid-summer, but that price will go down by then."

"When do we get the money?"

"At harvest, at delivery," he said.

"Let's do it if you think we should."

She got a smile finally.

"Yes, ma'am. I'll bet you a percentage if you want."

She didn't understand what he meant by that, but she guessed it was something guys did. She put out her hand. He wiped his on the seat of his pants before he shook. He pointed at the tractor and left to climb into the seat. She got back into the truck, taking her shoes off again. Winston just looked at them on the seat. Uncle Alec never said boo, but he would take her for a ride around the corn.

\* \* \*

"So, where's the other farm?"

"There's a piece your mother kept. But I think she traded the other farm to Edward for his legal fees when she was on trial."

"Oh." She felt cheated. The other half was her great-grandmother's. She was there a lot when she was a little kid. "Well, let's go look at the ten acres."

She remembered the mantle clock after she turned on the highway.

"You have Sean's number?" she asked.

"Your mother had it somewhere I'm sure."

"You have been a real help, Winston. What's in it for you?"

He looked out the window.

"You turn off up here, at the next right."

The dirt road led them down to a large grove of cypress trees and to a lake just beyond. There was a frozen and darkly-rusted oil pumping station surrounded by chain link and a little shed beside it. A second one stood across the lake and was pumping away.

"It's about ten acres, I think," Winston said. "The rabbit hunting down here is great."

They got out.

"She struck oil?"

"Not exactly." He laughed but it cracked in the middle like he wasn't used to making that kind of sound. "The oil is over there, across the property line. She got taken to court for this too. She lost this one."

"It would be a pretty place without the pump. You could put a trailer out here to use as a summer cottage. If you liked that sort of thing," Daydee said.

"I don't think I'd want to watch that pump station over there from my front porch," Winston said. "I loved your mother most of my life. We were married to other people and had other lives. There were in between times. The last few years she needed my help. She couldn't get around much."

"Back when I was still here?"

Winston nodded.

"My father knew about you."

"What?"

"He called you the dismal donkey in the swamp. The one that loved my mother."

"You were little when he disappeared."

"Not that little."

Winston rubbed his face with both hands.

"I've got an errand to run. You can drop me back to my car if you want."

"I can take you. You want lunch after?"

"Ok."

He directed her back into town. Her driving was improving and she had given up on the speeding. They pulled up in front of a convalescent home. All brick and phony shutters. She followed inside without being invited. A nurse greeted him by name. They went to a lounge area where several of the patients in wheelchairs were parked in front of a television. One guy was wearing a football helmet. Winston pulled over a couple of chairs to a frail elderly woman with white hair.

"Deidre, this is my wife. Martha."

The woman didn't respond or look at either of them. He sat down beside her.

"I'm going to find a restroom, be right back," Daydee said. She took her time and tried to get some of the tangles out of her hair. The scene was the same when she returned. He stood.

"She's been here a long, long time. They are about to have lunch. You want to stay? The food isn't anything special but it's free."

"Sure."

He wheeled her into the cafeteria and set her up at a table near the window and they went and got trays. He opened everything for her and she ate slowly, absentmindedly. Little lunchmeat sandwiches and orange slices and pudding. Iced tea. Outside the sky was becoming overcast. Thick clouds were moving in over the trees. Rain. It gave her goosebumps. No one went out on the lawn here. No one stood in the rain.

"She still eats. The problem comes when she forgets how to do that," he said. "We have lunch almost every day. I'm not sure who she thinks I am."

"You're a good husband."

He laughed that cracked laugh again.

"We'll go see Edward next?" he asked.

"Sure."

\* \* \*

They drove downtown and parked in front of an old limestone bank building. His office was upstairs through a side entrance. It all looked too well-to-do. The suite office had double smoked glass doors with his name engraved in the glass. No partners. The reception area inside was walnut with law books and potted plants and a large oriental rug. And a very stern looking secretary. Winston seemed awfully apologetic about calling on someone he knew. He gave her their names and sat on the couch. If he had had a hat in hand, he would have fidgeted with it. Daydee wondered why the receptionist acted like she didn't know him. There was a Currier & Ives print of a steeplechase on the wall. The secretary disappeared and then came out to tell them that Mr. Stills could see them now. She held the door for them.

Mr. Stills didn't get up. He was behind a very large desk, with his suitcoat on. His square jaw looked familiar. He was as handsome as he was in high school, but he seemed pudgy around the edges, like he didn't move around enough. Definitely the stuffed shirt look. The frown was permanent, she decided. He motioned them to the chair in front of him.

"You don't mind. I have a legal responsibility," he said. "Can I see some identification?"

She took out her Louisiana Driver's License and handed it over.

"It expires in a week," he said. He gave it back.

"You plan to be in town a while?"

"Looks like," she said.

He handed her a document. It was two pages stapled together. It looked like it was her mother's will.

"You can read through it and call me if you have any questions. It all has to go through probate court. You get everything. There's a trust your great uncle set up that goes to you as well, but I don't have those documents. It was for his farm and the house in town. I know your mother sold the house and deposited the money into the trust account about five years ago."

"How much was that?"

"I don't really know. She had an accountant, he would be able to tell you."

Edward Stills had an awkward way of rubbing his nose often. One finger and then later with a finger and thumb. She found herself imagining him with a full white handkerchief, blowing it regularly.

"My aunt's farm?"

"That was quick deeded to me for legal fees."

"You have a copy of that?" she asked. She was feeling lied to.

"Your mother has copies. I lost money, that farm is almost useless. Too much K fertilizer."

"I told her the story," Winston volunteered.

"I'm sorry," Edward suddenly said to her. "I lost my father in an accident a few years ago. I know what it must be like to suddenly find out."

"Well," Winston interrupted. "Thanks for your time."

He started to get up.

"You think she did it?" Daydee asked the lawyer, ignoring Winston.

He leaned away from them and put his hands behind his head. Then the nose rubbing again.

"Your mother brought me something that if admitted as evidence would have sent her away for life. I told her to get rid of it. I do not recall what it was."

"She didn't kill anybody," Winston said.

"Your father probably had it coming," Edward said.

"He was just crazy," she heard herself say. It was time to go.

"The first thing is to file everything with the probate court. My rate is $35.00 an hour, but I can defer payment until final resolution."

If he were a john, she would have turned him down.

"I'm not sure I'm selling anything," Daydee said.

"Most liquidate and leave."

"I might just stay." She didn't like the little girl voice coming out of her mouth. She stood up.

"It's a little town. It's not easy to fit in here."

"Everybody has been real friendly until now."

She walked out with the will in hand. She took his card from the receptionist's desk. Winston was not following her. He seemed to be in a whispering, hissing discussion with the lawyer. She was getting pissed now. She went out and downstairs. She sat in the truck for a moment before starting it. Winston came rushing out. She waited for him to climb in.

"Sorry," he said.

"So, you want to tell me what's going on?" she asked.

"I… I was trying to convince him to give you a break. He's been angry about everything lately."

"I think I need another lawyer."

"I can help you find one if you want."

"I think there's a lot you are not telling me."

"I can't talk about it," he stammered.

"I hope you are not trying to screw me," Daydee said. "I've been straight with you!"

Sort of.

"Where is my uncle's house?"

"I can show you where it used to be," he said.

"Fine!"

Winston gave her directions and she soon pulled up in front of a modern one story office building. A big front entrance and a sign declaring 'The Paris Clinic & Medical Offices'. More new brick with larger windows. The house that had stood there had been an old money mansion. Six or seven bedrooms upstairs, a big grand staircase, a parlor with a huge fancy fireplace and chandelier. A huge front porch with stone columns. When she had run away, her great-uncle was still living there, in two of the rooms: the dining room and the kitchen. The rest of the house was empty. Your footsteps would echo. To a child it was a little scary. What had happened to the family that had lived there once? Her great-grandmother and great uncle were once brother and sister in this big house when it had furniture and people coming and going. Daydee's mother had talked about fixing it up when Uncle Alec passed away. Instead she sold it off, even though it wasn't hers to sell. She probably needed the money for her latest scheme. Daydee hadn't been inside too often, but just enough for it to leave an impression. There had been dreams of a secret room there piled high with gold. There was a little doll's chair that sat empty on her uncle's window sill in the dining room. She wasn't allowed to touch it. He wanted to keep it as a place for the doll to sit and rest if the doll should ever return? The two of them, her great-grandmother and her great uncle, never visited each other, never spoke about the other. They were in their late eighties when she took off. Alec spent most of his days on his tractor out in his fields. Her great-grandmother was bedridden, mostly blind and deaf. On good days, Daydee's spinster aunt would help her great-grandmother out to a chair in the living room of the farm house that belonged to that lawyer now.

Daydee had thought of this house on the bus up from New Orleans. It was a ghost now, like all of her family. And the ghost of Uncle Alec's doll that never came home.

"When your uncle died," Winston said, "your great-grandmother sent your aunt over to tear apart the house for hidden treasure. Your mother told me that Eunice took a crowbar to the tiles in the big fireplace and pretty much destroyed it."

"They were all crazy. Cracked."

"Your mother was practical."

"She kept her habit to the very end?"

"What do you mean?" Winston asked.

Daydee looked at him.

"Yes," he finally said.

"There's a hole in daddy's arm, where all the money goes," she said. "It's from a song. So, the accountant?"

\* \* \*

He directed her to the office. It was in a mall, next to a drugstore. It really felt like a real estate office. There were a couple of cubicles with low walls. Some plastic plants in pots. He was a slender man with very blonde hair. He was the only one in the office. And Daydee knew him.

"Mat," she said.

"I'm happy you remember me."

"Mat took me to one of your football games once," she told Winston.

"And ran into you on Royal Street in The French Quarter," Mat said.

The birthmark on her collarbone had given her away. It was the size and now the faded shade of a penny. His wedding ring was still on his finger.

"You never mentioned you cooked my mother's books."

"That's not fair. I don't cook books. And she wasn't a client back then."

He offered them seats. She was hoping that was the end of the conversation about New Orleans.

"I have been gathering all the reports and tax filings, but haven't quite printed everything yet. I'll have it ready by tomorrow."

"What's it look like?" she asked.

"Your mother was incorporated. She has operated at a loss the last five years. She was losing about ten thousand a year. I suggested she file for bankruptcy, but she wouldn't do it. Sorry to be the bearer of bad news."

"So she was making money some other way?"

"Nothing that she told me about. Everyone in town knows I'm honest."

Daydee looked at Winston.

"I can talk to you later," Winston said.

"That would be best for me too," Mat said.

"Ok. What time do I come back tomorrow?"

"The office will be closed. I take one day to make house calls. There a lot of clients that want me to come see them. You staying at her apartment?"

"Yes."

"I'll bring everything over – about two?"

She nodded. Daydee got up. The quicker she got out of here, the less chance New Orleans would come up again.

"It was real good to see you again," Mat said.

"It was. See you tomorrow."

All of her johns were happy campers.

In the truck, Daydee was suddenly tired. Why was she trusting this old man? She had spent the day with him and he was guiding her around like he was a tugboat and she was an ocean liner. Her John was the only man she would ever spend an afternoon with these last few years. There was no one in New Orleans that she would have let herself hang out with like this. This was a good way to get screwed over.

"So your lawyer buddy run a background check on me?" she asked.

"If he did, he didn't tell me."

"Where was her money coming from?"

"Probably dealing drugs. I didn't ask. Once a month, she would take a trip out of town. I never asked where."

"I'll take you back to your car. I'm done in for today."

They rode back to the cemetery in silence. He climbed out, but asked about tomorrow before shutting his door. She really wanted to gun the engine and send him scrambling, but checked herself.

"I'll call you. I may need to sleep in."

After he closed the door, she did gun it and skidded gravel behind her. He was left in the dust. He probably thought she was crazy.

# Chapter three

The telephone rang in the morning, waking her up. She was hesitant to answer. She figured it was Winston. It continued to ring. She should have brought her answering machine with her. She finally picked it up when she was sure it wasn't going to stop any time soon. Little towns. They needed to let it ring, so you would have time to come in from your clothesline. Thankfully, it wasn't the old man. It was a customer from the cemetery. A son wanting to make arrangements for his father. She arranged for him to meet her at the cemetery office in about an hour.

There wouldn't be time for a shower. She dressed and put her mane into a ponytail, something she never did, this was a young girl or a mom look. She guessed she was too old for the girl look. Bare minimum makeup. She would go for the worn out tired look. The skirt was too short, but at least it was black. Just sit behind the desk. Making a piece of toast, she carried it out to the truck. She squinted into the glare. Getting used to the daylight was going to take some effort.

She had to drive back downtown to get her bearings. Winston's car was in front of the café. At least he wasn't a stalker. Food and a map would be good things to bring home. She beat the son to the cemetery. She looked up their last name and found three different folders. There was little that made sense. There were a couple of receipts with different names and no information about where the plots were. If this was what all the files looked like, she was in deep shit. A car pulled up outside. She got up to greet them. The son was a tall string-bean of a farmer with a shaggy beard, about her own age. He had brought his aunt, a wizened skinny tiny lady with a patch over one eye under her glasses. And an odd colored pink jumpsuit. She had them sit.

"I've got to be honest with you both," Daydee said. "I'm trying to figure this all out. Tell me what you're expecting and I'll try my best."

They looked at each other.

"Well," the aunt said. "The funeral is Saturday. Goshen's Funeral Home is holding the service, so you can call them for the details. We are having an honor guard from the VFW come do a three-gun salute. He was in the South Pacific, you know."

The son handed her receipts from his shirt pocket.

"My mother had purchased the marker along with two vaults and the plot. Our family is here."

"Your mother was the most confused and distracted woman I ever saw. Everybody knows they have to bring receipts or she would make them pay a second time," the aunt said.

Daydee wrote down the details from the papers and handed them back. This wasn't going to be too bad. A grave opening and closing and the installation of the vault, all things that Jack could do for her. And ordering a marker.

"Can you show me where the plot is?" she asked the son.

He shook his head.

"I never come out here."

"I'll show you!" the aunt said.

They stood and the man offered his arm to the old lady and out they went. It was a slow journey over to the family plots. Daydee walked beside them.

"I try to come out at least once a month. My mommy and daddy are here. I bring decorations for every holiday," the aunt was telling her. "But it's getting harder to get around these days. Jack is wonderful! He will take care of anything you ask him to do."

"I'm glad."

"I'm so sorry about your mother. Did she suffer?"

Daydee didn't have an answer. Winston hadn't said a word.

"I'm sure she did. She's in a better place now."

"Betty's Florist is who I always use. You should get to know her. She's a wonderful person."

The old lady showed her the plots and Daydee stuck her pencil into the ground where she decided the corner of the grave was supposed to be. Excusing herself, she returned to the office. She didn't want to spend the slow walk back talking to them. This was nothing her own family ever did. She had only been in a cemetery once as a child when her grandparents died together. This really seemed a very odd business for her mother to get into. Her mother hadn't cared about the dead.

Now she was planted out there with them. The guy and his aunt got into their car and left. It was very quiet out here with no one around. And when you thought about all the dead people surrounding you in the ground, it got a little spooky. All these people, pickled and put in caskets and the caskets put in vaults. Did they all still look like they had at the funeral home? Out here, everyone was sure when the judgement day came, Jesus would come and wake them up. You were expected to put your best foot forward. Daydee shook her head.

She found Jack's number in the Rolodex and called. His wife answered. Daydee started to hang up and then stopped herself. This wasn't a john's wife. She explained who she was to the woman and asked to get called back. Daydee imagined her as a cute little blonde, Barbie to go with Ken. Ken with a bite out of his earlobe.

If there were vaults, they would be in the shed, wouldn't they? She didn't recall seeing anything, but she walked down to look again. It had to be something big enough to hold a casket. There was nothing there that could be a vault. She turned to go back and spotted a man standing in some high weeds way down the slope, way beyond the end of the cemetery grounds. He could have been a mile away. There was nothing out here to block the view except for the occasional tree. He seemed to be watching her. She waved and he disappeared. There was a grove of trees down there. This land reminded her to be lonely.

The phone was ringing when she got back. It was Jack. She told him the news and he agreed to come the next evening and open the grave. He asked her to stake it out so he wouldn't mess up. As soon as she figured that out herself, she told herself.

"I need a burial vault. Are they in storage somewhere?"

"There aren't any. Your mother got Winston to drive to Terre Haute for the last one. She bought them from the marker company. I can place it once you got it, but I won't be able to go get it. I'm working a construction site with the backhoe for the next several days."

"Ok…"

"The number should be there somewhere. Maybe you could sweet talk Winston into going. Remind me to tell you about your mother trying to make her own vaults."

"Funny," she said. "See you."

She found the card for the company in Terre Haute and called and ordered one. Then she taped the card into the Rolodex. She could probably get them to load it into her truck, getting it out here would be the problem. She really didn't want to call Winston. Something just wasn't right there.

She needed to stake the grave. She ransacked the office looking for a map of the cemetery. Nothing anywhere. The files were a mess. A few had notes written on napkins from the restaurant where she had breakfast yesterday. Going over the records again, she drew herself a map of where the relatives were and noted their plot numbers. The new guy was supposed to be next to them, so she assumed the plots were numbered in order. But in which direction was the question. She spent another half hour enlarging her map and going out to check how things matched up. She finally reached a conclusion about where the damn plot was to be and in which direction it was positioned.

She imagined Jesus waking up the wrong dead person because the maps were wrong. Maybe that was why her mother ran this place, the devil made her do it. She found stakes and a mallet in the shed and went out to lay it out. The work was hot and when she returned she was sweaty and her hands dirty and she had torn her hose. She removed them in the office, realizing there was no privacy to be had here without putting curtains in. But no one was about.

She had to get back to meet with the accountant that afternoon, so the drive to Terre Haute was out for today. She'd need a check to carry with her, to pay for it. She could wrangle something out of Mat, but she wasn't sure she wanted too. He had paid her for special stuff in New Orleans. These guys never forget.

She had forgotten him until yesterday. There were just too many of them with too many special things they liked. His only edge was that he had taken her to a football game when she was fifteen and then reintroduced himself to her outside an antique shop on Royal Street. If he was showing up at 2:00, she certainly didn't want him to see her mess — even though she certainly was feeling like one right now.

She needed lamps. She had the address, in her purse, to the house where her great-grandmother and great-aunt had lived. And supposed keys. Maybe there were things there she could take. It would be cheaper than buying replacements. She locked up the office and found her way to the house. Directions from a grandma and her grandson out for a walk got her there.

\* \* \*

The house was in a neighborhood of large yards without a fence anywhere. There were no sidewalks or streetlights. Hers was the one with the overgrown yard. The house was odd. It was really two houses stuck together. One half was a low farmhouse with a wide porch and the other half was a two story older Victorian thing with gables. The wooden sidings were two different widths. The roof was half faded green shingle, half brown. There was a huge old black oak tree in the front yard. It was taller than the house. It looked like a gnarled old man about a thousand years old. She finished her hot dog lunch she had picked up on the way and went to the front door. None of the keys worked. There was not too much to see from the dirty windows. It was dark inside. She went around back and tried the other doors she found. There was a window that looked like it might open. Everything else had been painted shut. It slid up easily. She found a garbage can to lay on its side for a boost up. Short tight skirts were not made for burglaries or break-ins, but she managed. The floor inside was just bare wood and dirty. She was afraid she might discover some squatter, so she took her shoes off to tiptoe quietly. The downstairs was empty. No furniture or anything. There were a couple of dirty glasses and a plate on the counter by the sink. There was a door that probably lead to the garage, but it had a big padlock on a special latch. She had no padlock keys on her ring. The living room was bare except for a blanket on the floor in a corner. And in front of it on a newspaper, a little heroin set-up with candle and spoon. An ashtray filled with cigarette butts. Everything was so dusty, it night have been here untouched for years. The newspaper had a headline in Spanish. Where would you get a Spanish newspaper in Paris? The upstairs was just as empty. The bathroom was filthy. She came back down.

"Hello, in there," a man called from the open window.

She froze.

"This is the sheriff, if you don't answer, I get to start shooting at you."

"I'm Deidre McIntire," she called. "I'm the owner."

He stuck his head in the window. The guy was thick, thick arms, big ham hands on the window sill. Big round head with hardly any hair left. A bald bear, a rather big bald bear.

"There you are," he said. "Kind of an odd way to get in your mother's house, isn't it?"

"None of the keys worked."

"You find anything interesting in there?"

"Nothing at all. I'll come out."

"You could just unlock the front door from inside and walk out."

"Then I couldn't lock it up again if I did get out that way. I'll come back through the window, if you will help."

"Yes, ma'am."

Playing a little Marilyn Monroe with cops had always worked. She didn't really know if she was giving a good imitation or not, but whatever came across had prevented her from getting roughed up. At eighteen, the cops in New Orleans were more than ready to manhandle her. She slipped on her shoes and put out her hand as daintily as she could muster. Halfway out the window he was more than happy to grab her waist. She was afraid he was just going to fly her down, but he waited. A gentleman. She held his hand a little longer, to brush her skirt and pretend to regain her balance. This guy would make anyone feel tiny. The big belly was off-putting.

"I sure do appreciate the help. I'll get a locksmith to come and redo the locks."

She saw his teenage boy reaction. At least he wasn't touching himself.

"How long are you going to be with us?" he said.

"As long as it takes, I guess," she purred.

She liked doing Marilyn, as long as they got it. The young cops now didn't know the movies. She offered her hand.

"What's your name?"

"Sheriff Rob Turner, ma'am."

"Sheriff Rob, it's nice to meet you," she said. "Oh, I should close the window."

"Allow me, ma'am."

"Thank you so much. Maybe we'll see each other again."

"I'd enjoy that, ma'am."

She went to her truck and waved at him as she left. She hoped she wouldn't see him again, but was pretty sure he would call her to ask her out. That would be a new experience. The belly would be hard to look at.

John had a small one a few years ago, but had lost it when he had to give up sugar and carbs. It went with middle age for most men. She wondered what he looked like now, after six months in prison. Some guys improve somehow. Some dissolve. She hoped he hadn't shaved off his graying curly hair. Or got tattoos. He was hard to figure. Smart, but a real drunk. He paid her to keep him company, there was very little sex. They had fun. He read books and could recite things. He'd get silly soused and stand in his kitchen and direct Brahms on the record player. He called them Matt Dillon and Miss Lilly. She would try to correct him, to Miss Kitty, but he wouldn't listen and repeat 'Miss Lilly Langtry!' He had black fingers that were as gentle as a baby's touch. He was a printer; the stains were permanent after twenty years. She would have to write him a letter.

She had to get back and organize the apartment.
\* \* \*

She ended up just gathering up everything and piling it on her mother's bed and closing the bedroom door. She made a rum and coke to relax herself for what she knew was coming. The pile of papers remained on the kitchen table. She'd get around to them. The television was stupid. A couple of channels from Terre Haute and one real fuzzy one from Indianapolis. How to cook something, the farm report and another murder in Indianapolis. It was a relief to turn it off when Mat knocked.

His tie was gone, but the top button of his shirt was still buttoned. They sat on the couch and he laid out the papers on the coffee table. He eyed her drink and she offered him one, but he took just a can of soda, saying he had other appointments that afternoon.

He laid it all out for her. Her mother had created a corporation that held all the assets. He showed her the farm revenue, and the apartment building figures as well as the cemetery's. And the tax filings for the last five years. The spreadsheet he brought showed the $10,000 deficit for each year. He wasn't condescending. He didn't seem to think her questions were stupid. And she didn't feel like she had to butter him up or flirt with him. They were finished, it seemed.

"I really appreciate your help," she told him.

He pulled a checkbook out of his briefcase and handed it to her.

"I talked to the bank and they have added your name to the cemetery account. I let Edward know so he could inform the probate court. We need to keep the cemetery operating for the community. You just have to go to the bank to finish the paperwork."

"You can just call the bank and get them to do things?"

"Everyone knows me."

"So, what do I owe you?" She waved the checkbook. "You accept tips?"

"Well, I have something to ask you," he said.

"You liked girly things? I kind of remember."

"Yeah."

"Mat, you aren't a bad-looking person, dressed up or not. I might even go for you if things were different." It was never about the money with the johns. "But you are married here, this isn't a fling in a faraway place. I came up here to change my lifestyle. Change my career, you know."

He started to cry.

"Mat. Come on," she said softly.

"I'm sorry," he said. "I wish I hadn't heard you were coming home."

She brought him a tissue box from the kitchen.

"How about that drink?" she asked. He nodded.

She went back to fix it.

"I could come do your books here. You wouldn't have to touch me."

With these guys there was always a woman somewhere that had given them approval when they were little. It was all about the approval.

"This would cover you for this consultation?" she asked.

He nodded.

"Wipe your eyes, honey. I'll be right back."

This was easy. She knew the routine. She went in the bedroom and checked the bottom drawer of her mother's bureau. Her mother had always kept lingerie for special occasions. Winston would have needed a little extra, at eighty. It was there. She sniffed to make sure it didn't smell weird. That would freak him out. She brought the outfit out to the coffee table.

"You have to take all your clothes off."

He complied. He draped his trousers and shirt carefully on the back of the couch. The tidy whities came off last. Why any grown man would wear them was beyond her, but a lot of them did. The erection was there.

"Turn around," she told him.

She helped him into the bra and panties and the baby doll nightie they came with. There was even a flimsy cover-up that didn't really. She took his hand and led him into the bathroom and told him to sit on the toilet. Painting him up with big eyes, foundation and blush and lipstick, it came back to her now. They had gone out walking in the French Quarter. He could actually pass as a girl if dressed and made up right. That's what he remembered. They had been lightly stoned too. Cinderella at the ball.

"This will never do," she told him. She made him stand and face himself in the mirror. She took his penis in hand from behind him. He went off like a boy into the sink. Less fuss, less muss. She cleaned him off and arranged him back into his panties. He was getting hard again. She pinched him.

"Ow."

"I'm the boss. You come back out and sit and talk to me like a girl and we'll have another drink. And you have to cross your legs like a girl too."

He came with her and sipped his drink.

"I remember now what we did in the Quarter," she said. "It was fun."

"It was."

"You have done it again," she said.

"There's places in Terre Haute and Indianapolis, and conferences, but I'd get all gussied up and then end up sitting in my hotel room all night, afraid to go out the door."

"You could have found somebody to help."

"I suppose."

"The wife?"

He shook his head.

"It's a box," he said. "I'm in a box."

"It's a small town. I'm afraid if I help you out again, people will decide we're having an affair and then it would get real messy."

"I know."

"Is there something I don't understand about my mother's stuff? Winston seems hell bent on helping me, but it smells like he has some kind of plot going on with the lawyer and Jack. I need to drive over to Terre Haute for a burial vault, but Winston is the last one I want to ask for help from. Was she involved with them doing something illegal?"

"Probably. They have been close since high school. They sit together if they show up at the diner at the same time. Your mother and the sheriff might have joined any of the three of them. I go over there for lunch. It's a good place to drum up business."

"Shit. I'm sure I'll find out soon enough what they were up to."

"I could help you tomorrow."

"In drag?"

"I could meet you out on the highway."

"You have passable clothes? Something that doesn't look like a drag queen bought it?"

"I think so."

"I figured I could get the company guys to load it for me. It's getting it off over here at the cemetery. You think the two of us can do it? Jack won't be out there. He's working at some construction job in town."

"I can help you."

"This will have to be the only time." She knew it probably wasn't going to be. But he was passable, if he didn't open his mouth.

"There's a bridge about two miles east of town," he said. "Right after is a road house that's been closed for years. I can meet you behind the building."

They agreed to meet at eight in the morning. He took his clothes into the bathroom to get cleaned up and go on to his next appointment. She hoped he would just go home. He smelled of rum and baby powder when he left.

When would she learn, she wondered.

# Chapter four

She awoke in the morning with a start, certain she had overslept. She hadn't. The sun wasn't even up yet. Going back to the couch didn't work, so she made coffee. Denying herself the cigarette she wanted, she showered and spent the next dark morning hour sorting through her mother's clothes. All she decided to keep was the old lady shoes and a couple of flannel shirts. There was a dress that she thought Mat might like – they liked to dress like their mothers – and put that aside as well. She wore one of the shirts and was going to bring the other one along so they could be the Bobbsey Twins today. God only knew what he would show up wearing. Then she realized she might want the scarves her mother had. She dumped everything else in the center of the bedspread and then tied the corners to make a big bundle. It was heavy, but she managed to drag it out of the apartment to her truck, and get it up into the back. When she started inside again, she saw it.

Someone had painted 'Whore' in big red letters across the door of her apartment. About a foot high. She ran to see if the paint was still wet. It was dry. They must have done it early last night. She touched the W and felt the tears welling up. Why? God damn them! She wiped her eyes quickly. Fuck them! Who would have done this? The frigging lawyer? Winston? It could even be a couple of redneck teenagers that had seen her around town. One of the tenants here that she hadn't even met? No one knew who she was except Mat and he wasn't a crazy person. It had to be a sicko who had just thought of the worst word they could come up with. This was scary. She had known johns with that look in their eyes. You could see they wanted to hurt you.

Everyone around would get a good look at it today. She didn't have time to paint it over, even if she had the right paint. She grabbed her purse and locked up.

The streets were getting lighter, but there wasn't a sunrise yet. Nobody out at all. She found the closed and dark Goodwill store and just backed up to the front entrance and pushed her bundle off the back of the truck and then drove away.

The sun was rising when she pulled in behind the closed road house just past the bridge. Mat was there, hiding in his car. She coaxed him out. He wasn't in too bad a shape. Tight jeans, with his privates tucked away. The boobs were normal looking and the make-up was ok. He had been practicing for years probably. The top was a little frilly. She handed him the flannel shirt and tied a scarf over his bad wig. They did seem like sisters or something. That was good – more credibility.

"Unroll the jean cuffs, that went away about 1955," she told him. He obliged her. "Ready?"

They climbed into her pickup. It was still really early. She wondered if stopping for breakfast down the road would work. He was trembling a little.

She told him about the graffiti.

"Who would do something like that?" he asked.

She shrugged.

"I've never said anything about you to anyone, ever."

"It's probably the football guys."

Neither of them could think of anything to say.

"Your mother was a real witch," Mat said.

"Thanks," Daydee glanced at him, smiling. "I was beginning to think I might be the only one who thought that. Winston was madly in love with her."

"Years ago, I thought there was something wrong. My old man hated my guts. I thought you were like me."

"You don't know the half of it," Daydee said. "I was whipped for everything. Crying, not crying. Messing my diaper. Not doing the dishes good enough. Having periods. At thirteen, I took the yard stick away from her and broke it. Then she started slapping me if she could get to me."

She shook her head.

"I was quick on my feet." Daydee continued. "And she was sick from the heroin most of the time. I didn't get hit much after that. But that didn't stop her from bad mouthing me."

"Sorry," he said. "I knew it. My old man beat the shit out of me – to make me a man, he said."

"I liked you. How come we didn't go out again?"

"You didn't go home with me the one time we did. It was the big playoff game and we won. Everyone went out to the pasture to celebrate. When I had to go, you wouldn't come back with me."

"I don't remember. Sorry."

"You were out of my league," he said.

"You guys," she said. She looked over at him. "Sorry, I forgot. You're Marcie today. You like that name?"

He nodded.

"Don't touch your face," she reminded him. "You want to try stopping for breakfast? I'll order for you."

They stopped after another half hour at a place just off the highway. It was uneventful. No one batted an eye. He came back out to the pickup ecstatic.

"That was so much fun!"

They were coming into Terre Haute.

"You going to settle in Paris?" he asked her.

"I don't know."

"It must have been fun in New Orleans."

"There was always music and drinks to be had. And friends if you wanted them. The sunrises in the French Quarter were always worth staying up for. The city at night was a great whore queen. You had to pay and pay."

"Wow, what a thing to say. Is that from a book or something?"

She ignored him. They found the memorial company in Terre Haute and pulled into the lot. She had handed him an emery board before getting out.

"This wards off men. Just file your nails while I go pay. And don't flirt, young lady!"

She wrote a check and two guys brought the vault out to load into her truck. It was just a fiberglass bathtub with a fancy top. She wondered what the mark-up had been.

Mat gave one of the guys a little wave as they pulled out.

Driving back, Daydee had to stop for gas and bought them both a beer. She turned the radio up.

"Sometimes, I just go off and cry by myself where no one can see me." Mat said as if he had been practicing it. "You ever get that way?"

"I haven't cried in twenty years."

They left it there, not saying much the rest of the way.

She drove on to the cemetery because Mat was going to help her get the vault off the truck. They came to the office and spotted Winston's car by the shed. He walked out in sight of them. Daydee quickly turned around and drove straight out the gate.

"Shit! Do you think he saw me?" Mat moaned.

"He saw the truck. I'll take you back to your car."

"Shit!"

He slumped down in the seat to hide as much as he could.

"Don't worry," Daydee told him. "I'll just tell him you were a girlfriend that I had to take to catch the Greyhound. We had forgotten the time. Come by the cemetery later to see if I got the thing out of the truck."

"I think he saw me."

"Just don't obsess about it. There's not much to do about it. It didn't happen. You weren't in the truck. My girlfriend was."

She let him out behind the closed roadhouse and he ran for his car. Daydee went back to the cemetery. Winston was still there, waiting for her.

She stopped beside him and talked to him without getting out.

"Hi. Sorry, I had to get my girlfriend to the bus. We had forgotten the time. What's up?"

"Well, I heard about the funeral and figured you might need some help. I talked to Jack and he said you were going to need a vault. Looks like you got one."

"Irene lives over there. She helped and rode back with me to catch up."

"She looks familiar. She from Paris originally?"

"I think she might be the accountant's cousin. I'm not sure. You must have been out here a long time, waiting."

"I just got here, really. You had that look on your face like you had seen a ghost. I figured it wasn't me. The vault was bouncing around in back. You were going to need help unloading it."

"It's a bit late to hang around out here that long," Daydee said.

"I have friends out here. I've been visiting."

"Well, hop in. I'd love some help."

They drove over to the grave site. The two of them pulled the vault off the back so one end was on the ground. They were straining. Daydee just pulled the truck forward so it fell off. They could pick up the lid between them and put it on the box. Jack would do the rest getting it into the hole when he dug it. Daydee figured he could just push it in with the backhoe. Winston was worn out. He leaned against the tailgate and slowly caught his breath.

Daydee jumped up and sat beside him. There was that farmer again, way down the slope, a tiny figure moving through the trees.

"I've met with the accountant. He's a real nice guy. Very helpful," she said.

"He's good. Your mother liked him. She was hard to please. A little odd sometimes, but reliable."

"He's got a family he said," Daydee mentioned.

"A little daughter he dotes on," Winston said.

They looked at each other.

"Deidre, I was wondering if you'd like to come with me to Jack's service on Sunday."

"Oh, I don't know."

"As a favor to me?"

"You know everybody in town. Surely there's somebody else to take along. Or just go by yourself."

"I'm afraid."

"Of what?"

"People might laugh. Or I could get sick or have an accident. I'm afraid God won't want me there."

How was she supposed to respond to that?

"Maybe you could go talk to a minister. You can't tell Jack this?"

"No!"

"Winston, I'm probably not the best person to talk to about this. I'm not sure I believe in God."

"You're the only one I can talk to about it."

"This is crazy. I don't think I can help you at all."

"I've done some horrible things in my life. Things that would put me in prison if anyone knew." He wiped a tear from his cheek. "I'm going straight to hell when I die!"

She had told Jack in front of Winston that she might go to church. Oh.

"I haven't been in a church in twenty-five years," Winston told her.

"It's not my favorite place in the world. If you promise not to have a heart attack, I suppose I could go."

"Thank you."

He clasped her hands with both of his and patted them.

"Thanks for the help today," she said.

\* \* \*

Daydee had been watching the other apartments for the few days that she had been there and had never seen anyone come or go. The parking was in the rear of the building and she just hadn't gotten an opportunity to go back there. Were they all leaving through back entrances? She waited until nine in the morning and went to knock on the doors. The big ring with the pass keys were in her mother's refrigerator in a coffee can. There hadn't been any money in the can. That made her smile.

No one answered at the first door. She waited and then let herself in. The apartment was empty. No furniture, no appliances. Not bothering to knock, she just let herself in the next one. It too was empty. As were all the rest, except the last one. There was a couch and end tables and a bed in that one. Everything was so dusty that it was clear no one lived there. And there were no lamps to take. She walked around to the parking. No cars. What kind of crazy person would have an apartment building and not rent them?

Taking a look at her mother's receipt book again, she realized that all the dated entries ended a year ago. She needed help. How could she make the mortgage without rent coming in? She recalled seeing a realtor's office down by the café. They might be willing to help or would know someone who would. She locked up. The "Whore" on the door needed to go. It didn't seem as important, now that she knew there was no one around to see it. She'd get paint and made a mental note to herself about the color. She had a gift for that: matching. But there wasn't a high demand for it in her line of work. Maybe a little town like Paris could use an interior decorator.

She found the realtor's office and parked. The office was cheery and bright with plants and nice furniture. There were pictures of houses for sale. The woman behind the only desk looked very professional. She stood when Daydee came in and shook her hand. She was tall, maybe four inches above her, but she was wearing heels. She was slender and wearing one of those women's business suits with the pencil skirt. The boyish haircut was kind of cute. She had intelligent eyes. And an English accent. Really odd for this place. Her name was Sarah.

Daydee explained her problem. Sarah was familiar with the building.

"You're in probate now?" she asked.

Daydee nodded.

"And you're the executor?"

"Yes."

"You sound like a southern belle. Where have you been hanging out?"

"New Orleans. Does everyone in town know my business?"

"Pretty much. It's a little town. Edward is my ex-husband. You should let him know what you are doing so he can notify the probate court. They will have to approve any sale if it's still in probate."

"I don't understand why she had no tenants."

"You mother was pretty wacko. The police were over there a bit, even though she was buddy buddy with Sheriff Turner."

"I met him. He seems ok."

"Really?" Sarah asked. "Let me see about getting you people to move in. Would you be willing to give away a free month's rent? We could still ask for first and last, that would get you some quick bucks. Just start the clock a month later for them."

"Ok," Daydee said, "I need to sign something?"

"Nah, I want 5% on the first two months' rent on each new tenant and you come to me for the sale."

"It sounds fair enough." Daydee wasn't sure how to make nice with this woman. "Edward is always grumpy and rude?"

"I don't talk to him much. We got divorced seven years ago. Our son is grown and gone. I'm doing business here. I like everybody," she said. "I have to run out to show a house. When can I start sending you tenants?"

"Monday? I have some cleaning and some painting to do," Daydee suggested.

Sarah stood, so Daydee did too. It was odd, looking up at this women. They were about the same age, she guessed. Sarah grinned like a Cheshire cat. It gave her goose bumps. This was a little scary. The other woman grabbed her purse and came around the desk. Daydee turned toward the door and Sarah's arm was around her waist, escorting her out. Then the arm was gone. Sarah was locking the office. Daydee escaped to her truck. Sarah waved.

Daydee had never felt like this. Was this what it felt like?

\* \* \*

Daydee went to the Goodwill. She needed conservative clothes to run a cemetery and she needed lamps. She had been going for years in New Orleans. It was cheap if you had no money. And even if you did, the things changed from day to day, so it could be a treasure hunt if you found something really remarkable. The thrift stores in New Orleans attracted all sorts of weird people. It was a wonderful place if you didn't want to feel self-conscious about the things you might be looking for. The drag queens were there all the time. The homeless folks would wander in and sit on the couches for hours. The crazies would wander about talking to bric-a-brac. She found old records she liked. The Kingston Trio. She found blouses that were timeless and odd and could only really be worn by someone like her. She gave up on tight after her twenties. The rich guys had taste, they wanted a suggestion of curve that couldn't really be hidden but suggested she was trying anyway. Taste. They were older and wanted the feel they got at home, that it was for their eyes only. That had been her gift, understanding men. Women had never been that easy for her. Most were stupid. The girls she knew on the street early on were so many lost lambs. She'd smile and nod, but they were never anyone to trust or like. She would get asked to help with a wedding that came up now and then. A girl would get an offer and she'd take it. That had been the only time she would be in a church. Or if someone died. It was all big Catholic weirdness. Going to church with Winston here was going to be weirdness beyond weirdness. She needed a church dress as well. She had gotten marriage and mistress proposals. She never took them. Then you end up over the hill with nothing. Well, that worked out, didn't it? Discarded people, discarded clothes, discarded little bric-a-brac that once meant something to someone, that was it, wasn't it? You pretended that none of this belonged to dead people.

Or maybe late at night, you did pretend that it had belonged to someone that cherished it and someone that cherished you and it became an imaginary heirloom. Sort of like an imaginary friend. There was a little clay pipe made by an Indian, that might have been really old. She had bought it as a knickknack and later she found out it was something made by the Miami tribe here in Illinois. It became something Uncle Alec could have smoked tobacco in. The housekeeper broke the little owl ears off and she was upset for days. There was an old children's book *The Happy Prince and Other Tales* by Oscar Wilde with a boy/girl prince on a pedestal on the cover that could have come from the old family house here when her great-grandmother and Uncle Alec sold everything off.

You pretended that it didn't matter that there was no one in the world for you, even as a friend. There were the needy people that wanted you to do something for them, for free or for payment. There were people in the world that wanted to take you home as a prize and put you on a shelf. And there was nothing else. John. And John. He needed another name. The experience of thrift stores always made her a little sad at the end of the day, unless it was forgotten with a great find. Like that brooch, that was in with all the costume jewelry that didn't belong because of the real stones. No one wore brooches anymore, but the diamonds were real diamonds and no one noticed until she got there. It was very odd. She felt like she was going to be arrested as she walked out. Sometimes you did find something.

She started looking for a dress to wear to Jack's church and one for funerals. She couldn't recall which church he ran, but she was assuming it was middle class, middle of the road kind of thing. He looked like that. Everything she owned was too short and too tight. It didn't seem the right place for Winston to find Jesus. He needed one of those Pentecostal tent things down by the river. Meetings where they dunk you in the water. The revival ladies wouldn't care about the way she dressed, she'd fit right in. There was a very thin line between the hooker and the born again, between the alcoholic and fire and brimstone. All the dresses she looked at had to be pulled out and checked for size. Nothing was sorted here. Some of her mother's clothing, which she had dropped off earlier, was already hanging here for sale. She skipped those. She had never liked dressing dumpy and the fact that she had gained a few pounds and was being forced into dumpy by circumstances was making this into a gloomy afternoon. She tried on several and finally decided on a flapper style dress that was pretty plain. Having curves in the right places livened anything up. It did look a little retro, but it was the right kind of blue for her complexion and to her knees and didn't demonstrate anything up above. There was a navy suit that would fit the bill for funerals. The first one was coming up. She wasn't sure it was expected of her to be there, so she thought she would just hang out in the office until it was over. Just in case there was something that still needed to be done.

There was a blue flannel shirt on the men's rack that caught her eye. She went to look. It was soft and untouched. It didn't look like a soul had ever worn it. It was obviously expensive. It was too soft, some kind of special cotton or something. Harvested from baby cotton plants? Were there designer flannel shirts? It was a warm color of blue and big enough to get lost in. The few high rollers she had as customers in her prime would ask her to hang around after. She would wear their shirt. If they were real nice guys and she didn't mind staying over, she'd order up room service for breakfast and fuss over serving them. All in their shirt. It was odd. It was only what she did on the job. They thought it was sexy. At home, she had silky negligees to lounge around in – her inner baby doll working. The only thing missing from this shirt was the scent of aftershave or someone's odor she appreciated. What had John used? It was probably Old Spice or something dumb like that. You could always add the scent yourself, but that was a little nuts. The shirt was hers. She could see herself sleeping in it. And with the sleeves rolled up, maybe raking leaves. She had property now. She could rake leaves if she wanted.

She looked through the costume jewelry in the glass case for something conservative and demur. It was all old lady stuff, large and gaudy and cheap looking. Daydee had jewelry. Some of it valuable. The brooch she had found at a place like this with all real stones she had reset in earrings and a necklace and a ring. All of it too high powered to wear to church in a little town. There were other things that the men had given her. You held on to them because there was some elegance to them and if you were really hard up, you could always sell them. Like bonds in a safety deposit box. It suddenly occurred to her that she hadn't seen her mother's jewelry box. That wasn't like her not to still have that old little girl white padded box. All that stuff her mother had never let her touch. She wondered what it would look like now. It was probably hidden somewhere in the apartment. Or crazy Winston had taken it for safekeeping. She'd look around when she went home. The lamps were easy. Bland and matching. If they all worked she was set up. The price was so good that she splurged on a set of cow salt and pepper shakers. They even helped take everything out to her car. You couldn't get that in New Orleans unless you were related to the clerk.

# Chapter five

She sat in the lawyer's reception area for a half hour before he would see her. He really was the grumpiest person she had known in years.

"You will need to make an appointment in advance in the future. I cannot interrupt my day like this."

She sat down uninvited.

"Well, what can I do for you?"

She told him about the necessity of putting the apartment building up for sale and how her real estate agent had explained how a sale in probate might work.

"So, who is the agent?" he asked.

When she told him, he turned away from her to look out the window. What was there to look at? It was a quiet little town's Main Street. A car went by. A woman came out of the hardware store.

"She is my ex-wife."

"She told me that you were on the Board of Directors for the bank that held the mortgage."

"Did she tell you I was a crook and a bastard as well?"

"Well, now that you mention it..." was what she wanted to say. But lying seemed a better option. "She didn't say anything like that. She didn't mention to me that you two were ever married."

He turned back to her.

"You know she is homosexual?"

"I didn't ask her."

"Well, just watch out." He wasn't really looking at her. There was something on the bookshelf beside her. His son's photo.

"The bank," he was saying, "makes its loan decisions separately from board actions. I can't help you there. I will make a motion for the probate court to agree to a date for the sale foreclosure. You will have to find a buyer."

"Your son?"

He nodded.

"Good looking guy."

"They grow up and fly away. He loves his mother."

"Grandkids?"

He rubbed his nose.

"I don't know." Edward finally looked at her. "Perhaps you could find out for me. I could put in a good word with the loan officer."

"Sure," she said.

Boy, she thought. She got up. He didn't. That was something she really missed from the south. There wasn't a man in New Orleans that wouldn't stand for you when you stood. He was growing on her, but she was still going to look around for a lawyer less grumpy.

\* \* \*

Daydee found her mother's jewelry box under the bed. As if that was a secret place that no burglar would think of checking. Like the coffee can in the refrigerator. She sat on the edge of the bare mattress to open it. The jewelry box was one made for a child, padded with a little ballerina that popped up and turned to the melody that played, if it was wound up. She didn't wind it up. Her mother had guarded it her whole life. Daydee hadn't been allowed to touch it. Even as a teenager. She wondered why she had hung on to the original box that she must have gotten as a child. She laid out the jewelry. There was nothing really there. A couple of slight chains of plated gold. A few rings and the pair of earrings that her mother had told her once were too valuable for a child to try on. They weren't even for pierced ears, but with those horrible clips that pinched your ear lobes. It was all junk.

Daydee had a large emerald that a client had given her. She tried to imagine her mother's face being shown something like that. She probably wouldn't believe it was real.

The emerald was for a week at the guy's house in Tallahassee. He was a nice guy. Going home with him was easy. She thought she knew exactly what to expect. Big house. Lots of evidence of a woman's touch. He was really into guns and had a shooting range in the basement. Besides the sex, all they did was shoot at targets. She had never used a gun before. He told her she was a natural. It did seem really easy. When it was time to go back to New Orleans, he gave her the ring. Said it had been his wife's. On the way to the airport, he told her that his wife had shot herself one morning without a note or anything.

She never wore it. It was valuable but the gift giving was such an off-handed gesture. Much the same as all the presents she was given here as a child. Things picked up from the drugstore at the last minute. Her whole life. God. Her mother had taken the jewelry from her aunt and great-grandmother's belongings when they had died. There was a brooch she recalled seeing her aunt wear. Even the older stuff was all costume stuff.

There was a story a girl had told her long ago. She had been one of Ringer's other girls. Daydee's first and only pimp when she had arrived in The Quarter. They were all stoned one night. The girl's mother would trust her with her jewelry as long it was returned the next morning. The story had been about how the girl had screwed it up. All about regret and lost trust and falling from grace. All the story meant to Daydee was a wish on her part to be able to fall from grace with something. There was absolutely nothing to screw up here.

Giving her mother's jewelry to the Goodwill would be for the best. She might keep a few of the older women's things as keepsakes. There were a pair of good church-going earrings that were her great-grandmother's. There was a simple small cross on a chain. The Spanish girls all wore them. Maybe she would keep that, but not wear it. It would probably burn her flesh if she put it on. It was for a young girl anyway. Like her great-grandmother at twelve in that big rich girl's house.

Why didn't she hate her aunt and great-grandmother? They weren't mean to her. When her mother parked her at their house on the farm, both women just ignored her most of the time, except to make her lunch. They were both just old and preoccupied. And not really very smart. What was there to hate?

\* \* \*

Daydee overslept on the morning of the funeral. She threw on slacks and her new flannel shirt. It was cool and overcast for a summer morning. A thunder storm seemed to be on its way. The service was already underway when she arrived at the office. It was too late for any last-minute corrections. She hoped everything was set up properly for them. Jack wasn't to be seen. The vault wasn't where she had left it, so she assumed it was in the ground. There was the little railing around the grave and the casket had been lowered. The aunt and the man's son were standing beside the widow. The minister moaned on and on. There was a four-man veteran rifle salute team in old uniforms. Nobody else. The widow looked upset. She kept her distance, so she wouldn't interrupt anything. She didn't want to listen to the guy anyway. They were always so morose or angry. She was hoping Jack would be better than that. She was taking Winston to church tomorrow. The salute team raised their rifle and fired into the air.

It occurred to her that there might have been times when Jack opened the grave, changed into a suit, performed the ceremony and then changed back to close the grave. That was probably the case at her mother's funeral. Had someone paid him for it? She reminded herself to ask. These guys here were all so noble about stuff like that. She hoped he was coming back shortly to close this one.

Everyone wandered away to leave the widow alone at the casket.

What had happened with her father's death? Had Jack just brought the casket out and buried it without a service. Nobody cared about him. He was just a crazy guy who was a lot of bother.

The widow joined her son and then walked over to where Daydee was standing. When she reached her, Daydee offered her hand, but it was ignored.

"We are all so sorry for your loss."

"And who are you?" The woman's jaw was set.

"I represent the cemetery, ma'am."

"You're the runaway."

"Not much of one anymore," Daydee said.

"This is the way you dress for a service?"

"I'm sorry, I was just here to make sure everything went smoothly. I didn't want to intrude."

"Since when does anybody need an invitation to a funeral?"

"I don't know, ma'am. It was a lovely service."

"Thank you," she said as coldly as she could muster. She walked back to where the limo was waiting.

What fun, Daydee told herself.

\* \* \*

They were late for the church service. Winston had appeared at her front door, sweaty in his black suit and tie. He looked morose. His hands were trembling. The suit was tight and showed its age. They drove to the church slowly, as if he was going to a funeral that he was going to hate. He asked if he looked all right three times. He was shaking all over as they climbed the steps to the front door. It was a regular looking white clapboard Midwest church with a steeple and columns. It was Presbyterian, not that she knew any differences between them. She had thought that the Presbyterians and the Methodists were upper class and the Baptists and Pentecostals were farmers and stupid, but she knew that was probably wrong. It was just the way it was in this little town. Most of the congregation were already seated in the pews. Jack was up in front in his minister suit. He was so good looking. Blonde with some gray, and a square jaw. The women probably came just to look at him. A few heads turned when they came down the aisle, but then more and more people were looking back at them. They were looking at her, she knew. But all their faces made Winston quake even more. He pushed them into the first available pew and sat down.

Jack looked directly at her and smiled. The nick in his ear was odd. It was something you could have fixed she thought. Daydee spotted Sarah, her skinny English realtor, and nodded. A wave would be too much, especially in front of the whole congregation. Jack started the introduction to his sermon. They were asked to bow their heads and pray. Winston put his face down over his two hands like a child would do. Daydee had never really prayed in her life. Well, maybe once. She watched the others. Everyone else had their heads bowed, no one noticed her. Jack had his eyes closed.

The prayer ended and he started his sermon. His was an instruction in God's grace or something like that. She was getting a little sick. The sweaty sweet smell of Winston's aftershave, and an overbearing perfume from behind her soon were overwhelming. The church was stuffy and she could also smell the Liquid Gold they used to polish the wooden pews. Nausea swept over her like a wave. She had to get out of there. She got up carefully.

Winston looked at her, stricken. Patting his hand, she started back toward the entrance, holding the gagging at bay. There had to be a restroom. She rushed in, found a stall and lost her breakfast. It still continued after there wasn't anything left. She dry-heaved for a bit, before she could stop. This was shit. She hadn't even been drinking last night. She didn't think she could go back out there any time soon. There was a little window that she managed to open. The air helped. She went to the old spotted mirror to see if she could fix anything. Her lipstick was gone, but she wasn't sure if she could reapply it. Her hand was shaking now. The door opened and Sarah and another lady came in. Daydee wet a paper towel to dab at her face.

"Are you all right?" the other lady asked.

Daydee nodded.

"You have it bad," the woman said.

Daydee looked at Sarah.

"This is Jack's wife," Sarah said. "This is Diane. She runs a lot of the church things, helps the shut-ins, the young mothers…"

"I was just using the restroom," Daydee told them.

"The restroom echoes out into the main hall. We don't know why. The church is old. We should put a sign on the door or something."

Diane impressed Daydee as a nervous chicken sort. Her short curly bob of blonde hair added to her slightly frenzied look.

"So the entire service heard me?" Daydee asked Sarah.

"If you need any help at all, just ask," Diane said. "My morning sickness was horrible each and every time. I swore the last time was it for good."

Daydee went out. Sarah and Diane followed her. Sarah gave her a shrug of her shoulders before returning to her seat. Diane seemed to want to escort Daydee back, but Daydee shook her head at her. Diane patted her arm. Heads were turning. Winston looked and then got up and came back. He was white.

"Can we get out of here?" Daydee asked him.

He nodded and they left the church.

They were in front of her building in no time. Winston scratched his head.

"Maybe I should come by to help you cover up that graffiti."

"I'll take care of it," she said.

"I mean it, I can help," he stammered. "So, who is the father?"

She got out of the car.

"Wait, would you go with me again?" he asked. "There's another church nearby we could try out."

"Let me think about it." She was going to be sick again, so she went in.

\* \* \*

Why wouldn't you know? She looked at herself in the bathroom mirror. The shower had felt good, there didn't seem to be any more nausea right now. Her period wasn't always on time. Pigging out usually made her grow thick. She was too old. She felt her belly, but it didn't feel any different. Her nipples were tender and swollen. The gift that keeps on giving. It had to have been that last night before they arrested him. He was nervous and excited, ready to bounce off the walls. She hadn't been able to get anything out of him about what was going on. No drinking really, which was unusual for him. And he wanted to jump on her bones. That was what the allowance was for, wasn't it? He did ask her if she wanted to go to Rio. She had told him sure. They made it to Rio, she guessed.

She would have to write him.

She could get rid of it. At sixteen, there had been no hesitation. That was right after she got to New Orleans and she had no idea who the father was. One of the boys in Paris. She couldn't even remember a possible father then.

This was hers. To keep or not to keep. John could know or didn't have to know. There should be some money coming out of all of this, though it didn't look too promising right now. The cemetery could be a livelihood. Live here the rest of her life? It could be a good place for a child. Like all of those other kids here that she went to school with. She could wait tables again.

It was hers. It was growing sweetly, warm and blind, tucked away, inside.

\* \* \*

The next morning, she ate breakfast and threw it up and sipped water from a glass for a bit. She showered and started off to find paint to cover the graffiti and a very large box of soda crackers. That was supposed to help, wasn't it? There was an envelope on the porch in front of her door. No name or address and it wasn't sealed. Inside was a typed letter to her, unsigned.

*I don't know what to say. You frustrate the hell out of me, like a machine that keeps breaking down. I am not brilliant, far from it. But I do pride myself on having some intelligence. Yet I am used to people thinking I am a moron. I think it is my voice that causes that impression. My own brother thought I was a moron and he was infinitely smarter than me for forty years. I have, however, spent 30+ years as a trouble shooter. I can take a machine which does not work, figure out what is wrong with it, and usually fix it. Sometimes I have to call an expert to help fix it (technician, computer programmer, mechanic, etc.) I listen to you and watch you and feel you have problems. The few times I have spoken to you, I feel like I am beating my head against a brick wall.*

*You may think that what you are doing is acceptable here. I disagree.*

*You dress and act like a prostitute. Plain and simple. It just doesn't fly here.*

*I understand that you don't like criticism. I'm not fond of it myself. But some criticism is constructive if we are only smart enough to put our egos aside and learn from the criticism. I have worked hard over my life to keep my ego in check. I have not always been successful, but I have tried.*

*I wish you good luck, but I thought you should hear the truth.*

There wasn't a signature. She smiled in spite of the scariness of it. Yep, you called that one, whoever you are. Was this because of the graffiti or a love note to go with it? It sounded like it was someone she had talked to at least. That narrowed the field. Crazy.

She put it in her purse. And put on her sunglasses to ward off the day. The goosebumps followed her to the truck. They were all thinking about her. Everyone in town. She went downtown and noticed that the diner was almost empty with no cars in the lot. Too late for breakfast and too early for lunch. They would have soup and crackers. She could hold that down. And she realized that she missed being alone. This was perfect.

She heard Winston's voice as she parked.

"I won't do it, goddam it!"

He was behind the building. She went to the corner to take a peek. He was with Edward and Jack. They were all puffing away with cigarettes in hand.

"You don't have any choice," Edward responded.

"I quit! You two can go hang yourselves!"

Edward grabbed him by the shirt collar.

"You shut up and listen. I have been more than generous in taking care of your wife's tab. You owe me."

Winston pushed away Edward's hand.

"You are a son of a bitch."

"Listen," Jack interrupted. "Both of you. We are smart guys. We can figure out a way to get her to leave. Think about what we can use."

Winston had that look of someone holding his tongue.

"Out with it," Jack told him.

"Let me think about it," Winston said.

"Well, I can probably get the bank to foreclose the mortgage on that apartment building. It's really long overdue," Edward said.

"Great. I've got to go. We'll talk again in the morning," Jack said. He was heading straight for her.

Daydee climbed back into the cab of her truck and hid as he passed. He was so worked up he didn't even notice it parked there. Edward came a minute later, walking toward his office. She got out and rounded the corner to Winston. He dropped his cigarette when he saw her.

"What the hell was that?" she demanded.

"You need to leave Paris."

He ran for his car and sped away. She considered her upset stomach and decided to try the soup and crackers. Going in, she spent the next half hour trying to eat, but mostly staring out the window wondering about what she was in for. She decided to buy ammunition and shoot them all if she had to.

\* \* \*

She came back with the paint and began to cover the letters across her door. The smell of the paint was horrible and she had to go in to the bathroom again. She stuffed Kleenex in her nose before coming out. Her aunt used to do that because dusting made her sneeze she said. It helped. She sanded before she started and sanded each coat so the letters wouldn't show under the new paint. This was making her angry. This was one of them. What couldn't she see? Oil under that property out at the lake that they wanted for themselves? Something in the locked garage at her aunt's house? Or something hidden out at the cemetery? Winston was the worst. He had taken advantage of her. The son-of-a-bitch. He had gotten to her, made her feel sorry for him.

Sarah pulled up behind her pickup. There was a couple with her. Daydee quickly opened the door so the lettering wasn't in view and scooted the ladder in front of the side where there were still traces. Sarah brought them over. She obviously thought Daydee was a sight. She was swallowing her grin with her introduction. They were a young couple. She hoped they were old enough to sign a lease.

"I'll get the keys," Daydee went in.

"I can take them," Sarah said. "You are busy."

Daydee handed her the keys when she came back. Sarah pointed at her own cheek.

"You have streaks, dear. Kinda cute actually."

How did this woman manage to make her feel so self-conscious? She went in to clean her face, she didn't want to be cute. Daydee was almost through with the second coat. It might need a third. Sarah came back without the couple.

"They signed," she said. "They are trying to make up their minds about which one they want. They are measuring both."

"I really appreciate your help," Daydee told her. That was what you were supposed to say, wasn't it? Daydee had never gone to another woman for help in her life.

"You'll get my invoice."

"I heard your ex say he was going to get the bank to foreclose on me."

"You sure? He's real close to his chest with his plans. He never tells anyone anything."

Daydee told her about the parking lot conversation, leaving out the tail end conversation with Winston.

"Any idea why they would want me gone?"

"I don't know. Let me think about it."

"When I went to meet with Edward about the apartments, he asked me to find out if he has any grandkids."

"Really?" Sarah asked. "He doesn't want to talk to our son. He's sure he will get yelled at, which is probably true. When you talk to him again, you can tell him no grandkids – no wife."

"Is there a way out of foreclosure?"

"Well, you could get another lawyer. Write Edward a letter to fire him and send a copy to the bank president as well and then go visit the bank with your new lawyer. I can give you a couple of names. And everybody's names at the bank. That way, you wouldn't have to talk to Edward again."

"Ok." This was what you did with men who wanted to take charge. You let them think they are in charge. She guessed it was the same.

"I'll see if I can corner some of the bank people. You wave money at them, they wave back."

"Your ex is not going to be pissed by you interfering?"

"He leaves me alone. He knows if something happens to me, our son will kill him."

"I thought I had a crazy family."

"You did," Sarah said. "They taught you to stick Kleenex in your nose?"

"Aunt Eunice."

\* \* \*

She finished covering the graffiti the next morning. There was no trace left to see. She even showed another tenant an apartment and signed a lease in between coats. She called the lawyer Sarah had suggested and made an appointment for them to go meet with the loan officer at the bank. She finally sat down at her kitchen to write the fire Edward letter. Since it was going to the bank and the probate judge as well she wanted it to be correct and not demonstrate how dumb she might be. This was hard. She had never finished high school. There were probably rules for writing business letters, but she didn't know what they might be. Finding a letter from one of her mother's credit card companies, she thought she could use it as a model, but that turned out to be hopeless. Except for how to do the heading.

She worked up a hand-written copy, finally just writing what she had to say as if she were telling him face to face. She'd change some of the 'you's to Mr. Stills. There was a typewriter at the cemetery office. She hoped it still worked. What could you do to make a typewriter not work? She had never learned to type and knew she might be out there all night. And she had to make three copies.

She thought of asking Sarah for help, but she didn't want to feel any more obliged to her. Nor did she want to look stupid in front of her. She thought of Mat. She called his office, but the phone just rang and rang. No answering machine, no nothing. She thought she might call his home. Did she have that number? But she thought better of it. His wife was a john's wife.

Why hadn't she taken night classes? Had she really thought her looks would last forever? You passed on that filthy rich guy because he looked like a fat chicken. And he had been a professor as well. There was no accounting for taste. Her John was proof of that. She finally ended up with a couple of paragraphs that worked. Grabbing her keys, she headed for the cemetery.

It was dinner time and there was not a soul out. She parked at the office and noticing the mound of earth on the new grave, she reminded herself that she had to order the marker. Did she have the right information for it? The typewriter was electric at least and she discovered it would back space and erase her error. What a wonderful thing. There wasn't any carbon paper, so she would have to find a place to copy it in the morning. Her spelling had never been great and now trying to hunt and peck for the letters while trying to remember how to spell the word was challenging. There was a dictionary in the drawer. She took it out to double check herself.

It was nearing dusk by the time she finished. The cemetery had no outside lighting except for a porch light over the door to the office, so now the windows that had provided such a great view were now mirrors, reflecting her at work. The dark glass didn't show age or wrinkles. Nice, she told herself, as she stretched when she finally got out of the chair. Not bad for an old broad. She sat down again and pulled out a blank piece of paper and a pen. Since she was writing letters…

*Dear John,*

*This return address is where you can reach me if you want to write. I hope you are surviving. I'm permanently here until further notice. My mother died and I'm dealing with her things and property. It looks like it may be doable here. I miss hanging out with you. Sorry I didn't visit, I was trying to make a go of it with very little money and just couldn't spare the car fare. Write if you want and tell me how it is. It must be real rough. You were a lot tougher than you let on, so I figure you'll make your way. I'm real sorry for you.*

*John, I'm pregnant and it's yours. I've decided to keep it if I can. I've not even been to a doctor yet, so I'm being real dumb. But I thought cause I'm so old that maybe it would just miscarriage or something. But it's growing now and I'm sick in the mornings, so I'm going to a doctor pretty soon. I don't expect anything from you. The situation here looks good, so I should have a living. I'll tell you more as I know it. If you don't want to write me, I'll understand.*

*It wasn't going to last forever down there. I know that now. I've never done anything but make a living and sit on easy street. This may be a last chance and I just have to take it. I may be too old to see it through. I want it to be a girl. I'd like to love it the way I wished I had been loved.*

*The town here is a little frightening. I've created quite a stir showing up and looking like I look. Everyone acts like I'm some kind of ghost that has come back from the dead. And it's all about the boobs and the bod, I suppose after years of strutting, it's only right that that's all they see. Maybe it's all I see.*

*God, I'd like to have a drink with you and have you make me see the silliness of it all. I hope you are all right,*

*Love…*

She started to erase the 'Love' when a car door slammed outside. She jumped. An engine gunned and tires skidded out the gravel drive. What the hell was that? She hadn't heard anyone drive up. She went to the closet to see if there was anything she could use to protect herself with. There was an old rake. And a shotgun. She grabbed it. She didn't even know how to see if it was loaded.

She turned the lights off inside and out and stood in the dark by the door. There were no other sounds. She went right outside, but it was pitch black, the moon wasn't up yet. She turned the porch light back on. No sign of the car. She went down to look around the corner back at the entrance to the cemetery. There were tail lights far away. What was that about? She turned toward the truck. On the side was the red 'whore'. God damn them! There was a hose at the side of the office. She propped the shotgun by the front steps and turned on the water. The paint was still wet and a lot of it ran off under the spray of water. She found a rag and dish soap in the supply closet and came back to scrub it. She broke two nails cleaning it off, but it looked like she got it all. She was as wet and soapy as the truck. Shit! She sucked her broken nail and she checked the other side of the truck. And she had been so careful on the typewriter too. There wasn't anything written anywhere else.

"And it wasn't over there, it was over here," someone said behind her.

She turned. It was an old man, in rags and as dirty as sin, sitting on the front step of the office with the shotgun in his hands. He seemed to be looking at it rather than at her.

"Hello?" she said.

"It wasn't much to lookee see," he said to himself.

"That's my gun," Daydee said to him.

He cocked his head as if listening for something. He placed the gun gently on the stoop and stood up. It was an effort to get to his feet and he looked very old and rickety. He wouldn't look at her.

"Here is over there," he said and shambled across the drive and walked on toward the back of the cemetery.

Thank God he put the gun down. New Orleans was filled with crazy homeless people. This guy seemed just like all of what she was used to.

"Did you see who tagged my truck?" she yelled after him.

He turned, but not all the way. He was talking to the mound of earth on the new grave.

"Just a lookee see, little Dede, just a lookee see. No harms, no hits, no errors."

He disappeared into the darkness. She went to the shotgun and managed to get it open. There were two shells in it, but they were probably real old. How long had it been sitting in the closet? She took them out with the idea of going to buy new ones. She would need to know what to get. She took it back inside and put it back where she had found it. Slipping the shells into her purse, she gathered up her papers. She would figure out how to mail John's letter later. There was a flashlight in the desk. It needed new batteries, but it worked. She brought it with her when she locked up.

She started the engine and then turned it off. The old man had called her little Dede. She got out and started across the cemetery on foot, following the direction he had gone in. This was real stupid, she told herself. She found him about fifty yards beyond the back boundary of the grounds. There was a grove of trees and bushes that were never mowed and the weeds were high. He was sitting on the ground next to a shopping cart full of crap – cardboard and plastic bags filled with God knew what. He had an old ratty blanket on the ground and another one wrapped around his shoulders. The flashlight was barely working. He looked down, shielding his eyes. Like a dog waiting to be run over. He smelled like roofing tar. She put the light on his face and he looked away and hid under his hand.

"Just a lookee see, for God's sake!"

She didn't know what to say. She was afraid to be right or wrong. She was afraid to say it.

"Daddy?"

"Oh nooo. No god here, no over there, no god here. Oh noo."

She watched him. Hid under the blanket and she moved the light from his face. She needed to get away and think this over. The light would die and she would be stumbling her way out of here.

"I'll come back," she said and turned to get away.

She wasn't sure at all. If this was her father, then who was buried in the ground with a marker? She was afraid he might follow her. But there was no sign of him as she reached the truck. She needed to go home. What if the asshole went back to the apartment to tag her there again?

# Chapter six

The broken nails from that night would have normally sent her off in search of a fantastic manicurist to get them replaced, but when she got home, she trimmed them all back to the same length, took off the polish and filed them into shape herself.

It was another hot summer day. Daydee had gone to the bank with the new lawyer and the meeting had gone ok. The new guy was very persuasive about the apartment building and the loan guy seemed ready to grant an extension on the mortgage payment that was due. Hooray for small towns.

She had just gotten back to the apartment. Diane, Jack's wife, appeared at her door. She was the ditzy skinny blonde that had come after her in the bathroom at the church. Her hair needed a brush which made Daydee think she was trying for the tousled look.

"Hi!" Diane seemed ready to hug her for some reason. It turned into a half hug. "Would you like to go for coffee?"

Daydee could sense an agenda. Was it concern for her or concern for appearances? Like in the bathroom.

"I'm pooped, I just got back. How about some coffee or ice tea here?"

"Ice tea sounds a lot better," Diane said.

Daydee picked up the living room a bit. She was still sleeping on the couch and the blankets were still there. She cleared the coffee table as well and offered her a seat.

"I'm not the best housekeeper these days. There's a lot going on. I was over at the bank this morning about the estate."

"Oh, are there problems?"

"Not really, but all the legal stuff means you have to write letters and have meetings. At least, that's what they tell me."

She went for the tea. There were dishes in the sink, but she had clean glasses and the tea was already made in a pitcher in the fridge.

"So how is your morning sickness?"

"Not fun," Daydee replied sitting with her on the couch. "You would think it would make you lose weight, but it doesn't. That's not the purpose, I suppose."

"Soda crackers and chamomile tea work the best."

"I have the crackers."

"You just have to ignore Mrs. Burton. She's the prim and proper sort. She thinks she's an expert. Everyone ignores what she says."

This was the woman that had just buried her husband at the cemetery.

"Did she say something to you? I was out there to make sure it was all going well. I didn't know I was supposed to be in attendance."

"If you're not sure about someone, give me a call. I'll give you the low down."

"I'll remember that," Daydee said. And she would provide the low down on me as well, she was sure.

"I hate being nosey, but I was wondering if there was a hubby around. We like to make everybody feel welcome.

I could get him invited to football parties or some such thing."

These kinds of people were incredibly stupid. Didn't she realize how transparent and evil she was right now? She would smile and act ditzy and it was all ok. God, how she hated women.

"Well, if you promise not to tell a soul. It's hurtful." Daydee told her intentionally. It would be very easy this way, the entire town would know the story in a week and she wouldn't have to remember it to retell it. Maybe even Mrs. Burton would say to herself: the poor dear.

"He's in prison in Louisiana. He had never broken the law in his life, but the stress about the baby coming and how we were going to live was too much. I hadn't gotten the call about my mother yet. He was a printer. His printing company went belly up. He and a buddy tried to rob a bookie in the French Quarter. He had just come home when the police showed up to arrest him. They took him out in handcuffs. I was so mad, I threw my wedding ring at him and it bounced somewhere and I never found it again. We were in this cheap place living off my money from waiting tables. There were cracks in the floor boards. I guess it fell into one of the cracks."

Was that too thick, Daydee wondered.

"You poor thing." Diane patted her hand. "Is this your first?"

Daydee nodded.

"I'm here to help. Anything you need at all." Diane smiled. "Would you mind if a bunch of us throw you a baby shower? We've not had any new moms in four months. It will give you a chance to meet some of the ladies around town and maybe a couple that have toddlers."

Daydee was surprised. This was supposed to be about snooping her out, wasn't it? What was she going to say to a group of women?

"I don't know."

"I'll do it all, you just show up. Everybody loves new babies on the way."

"There will be silly games and stuff like that?" Daydee asked. She was suddenly that little girl that was never invited to birthday parties. Her mother had been white trash. She couldn't recall being in another family's home here.

"It will help you with the things you need for the baby. And expert advice!"

It was the expert advice part that worried her. What if this group decided she wasn't fit to be a mother? She really didn't know how to live up to anybody else's expectations of her. It wasn't anything she wanted to do anyway. Nobody here had ever been kind to her until she reached puberty. Who gives a fuck? This was new. These hormones, she guessed. She could almost feel her heart melt.

"All right," Daydee agreed.

As she walked the woman out, Daydee mentioned the tagging, without telling her what the word was. Diane acted indignant.

About an hour later, the sheriff rolled up in front of her door. Diane had called him.

Daydee at first thought he was here to make a move on her, but when she found out he was here about the tagging, she invited him in. He wouldn't sit. Taking out a pad, he took notes about when it happened and how.

"Can't say when we had this kind of problem, ma'am. A few years ago, right after the high school graduation there was some graffiti on the water tower. Try to get the license number on the car if it happens again. What did it say?"

Daydee didn't want to tell him.

"Whore."

He scratched his head with his giant hand.

"Ma'am, I'm really sorry. We must have somebody very disturbed. I'll ask the night patrol to swing by here.

That might help to scare them off. Sometimes, those teenagers out on the farms get crazy notions in their heads. I hope you don't judge the town on the basis of one crazy person."

Why didn't she want to show him the letter? She suddenly understood that the letter was from a second person. She didn't want to let him know that two people were calling her a whore. It was all too close to the truth.

"Thanks, I won't."

He offered his hand and she shook it and he held on a little too long.

"Jack said you came to church. You like it?"

"It was all right, except for the echo."

He laughed.

"Don't know if there's ever been a McIntire in a church here before. I go to the Baptist Church over on Wilson. If you'd like to visit some Sunday, I'd come to escort you."

This was probably the strangest request for a date she had ever gotten.

"Thanks, Sheriff. I'll keep that invitation for a couple of weeks if I could. I feel kind of overwhelmed right now."

"Rob."

"Sure, Rob. Thank you."

He departed. She knew he wasn't going to forget the two-week put off. Andy of Mayberry was still alive, she thought, and waved from the door.

\* \* \*

She went back to look for the crazy man early in the morning on the next day. She was dressed for action, expecting God knew what. Tennis shoes she'd picked up for the occasion, jeans and the flannel shirt she was falling in love with. No jewelry, with her hair back in a bandana. The crazy homeless people she knew in The French Quarter could go off now and then. The magic bead lady had a violent screaming fit outside a shop only a couple of months before she left. She didn't want to have anything that he could grab at. She hoped she wouldn't find him, that he had moved on. Then she could pretend that she had been mistaken. That it hadn't really been him, but just her overactive imagination. She parked in front of the office and walked down. She didn't want to scare him away and if he was still there, she didn't want him expecting her.

The day was overcast, with thick wooly clouds. Another summer thunder storm. The grass was high and wet. Had it rained in the night? She came back to the spot before the trees where she had found him two nights before. There was a flattened space in the grass where he had been sitting, but no sign of anything. Except an empty potato chip bag. She picked it up and folded it to slip it into her hip pocket. It would just blow up on the cemetery grounds.

A trail led away in the grass. She followed. It was wide and wandered down across a meadow and toward a fence and another grove of trees. The fence was barbed wire and had been trampled down with one of the fence posts uprooted and laying across the wire to hold it down. The shopping cart was sitting on the other side, filled with bags and junk. She didn't see him. He might have gone off to town for something to eat. He might not be back for hours. She wouldn't wait.

"Sos, youse come exploring," a voice said.

"Where are you?"

"That's for you to know."

He was sitting on a tree branch above her. It was dark up there under the leaves. She couldn't see his face.

"You hungry?"

"You have posse possum?"

"Not me. You want lunch? You want to come down and have lunch with me?"

This was not planned well.

"You can have it right there," he told her.

"I have to go get it. You'll be here when I get back?"

"No."

"You like McDonald's?"
"He had a cow?"
"And hamburgers."
"No."
"You used to like strawberry shakes."
"No."

She headed back up to the cemetery, trying to recall where she had seen a McDonald's. There had to be one. This was stupid. He was obviously nuts. She was kidding herself. Her father was in the ground. She drove to the main highway. There had to be one out near the Wal-Mart. Finding it, she drove through and sat the bags in the passenger seat. It didn't smell bad. She couldn't remember the last time she had eaten this stuff. There was so much cheap food in the Quarter better than this. She wished she was sitting in Ruby Red's right now, with her heels in the peanut shells on the floor. With a real hamburger that you would cut in half to take the second half home for later.

He was sitting on the front steps of the office when she got back. He wasn't that crazy. And it was her father. The face she recalled was there, almost buried in old age and wrinkles. God. He was looking past the truck somewhere. He watched the sky as she got out. If she looked away, she felt his gaze on her.

"He was such a porcupine that he was porcupining all the time and they had to give a haircut. Snip. Snip. Snip."

When she approached him with the bag, he leapt up. She stopped, sat it down on the sidewalk and backed away. He grabbed it and took it back to the steps. Sitting back down, he pulled out the food and began stuffing it into his mouth. The lid was off the shake and he gulped it, some of it dribbling down his chin. Daydee sat down cross-legged on the concrete and took out her hamburger.

"So," she asked. "How have you been?"
He nodded his head to a tree off to the right of them.
"I was in New Orleans all these years."
Nodding, like he was autistic.

"Mama died. That was the reason I came back."

He was licking the inside of his paper cup. His nose was in his bag looking for more. She got up and approached him, offering her French fries. It was like trying to get close to a squirrel or a bird. His hand was out, but his face was screwed away like she was causing him pain. His smell was terrible. He accepted the fries and she retreated and sat down again.

"You're crazy, aren't you?"

"They snipped and snipped and his pants fell down."

"Do you know how long you have been living down there?"

"When hell freezes over!"

"I don't suppose I could talk you into a bath and a warm bed."

"Deedee knows. Lots and lots. It came out of her bear!"

He jumped up and ran back down the hill towards his hideout.

\* \* \*

She would go out every day at lunch time with bags from McDonald's, bringing him two lunches so that she wouldn't feel guilty about not bringing him dinner as well. She didn't want to be out here at night with a crazy old man while there was still some mystery tagger out and about. Her father never came back up to the office again which required her to go to him. For a few days she didn't see him at all. The bags were left on his grocery cart and the next day they were gone. She'd carry out trash if she spotted it. It was random. He had made an odd little bush decorated with drink lids and straws. She left that alone. Then he would be sitting there on the ground waiting for her. He wouldn't look at her, but greet the bags like they were long lost friends. She could feel him looking at her when her eyes were diverted, but try as she might she could never catch his direct gaze. Occasionally he would make a mention of Deedee, in the midst of his odd talk.

She wanted to believe he understood who she was. His tears on the first day with lunch had told her so. Most of what he said made hardly any sense. There were troubling mentions of people snipping him or poisoning him. And he would pop about. He would suddenly leap up and then settle in another spot. Over and over. She never went too close, he would move off. She told him things about her life. Nothing made an impression on him.

She would ramble on about New Orleans. How she had grown to love the city and all of its excesses. She left out the part about how she made money. She talked about Saturday afternoon strolls through the humid run-down neighborhoods. The old black men were forever gentle and kind. The food. The rain that came for just a half hour every summer afternoon just after lunch. Mardi Gras. The church bells, the streetcars and the music. The way everyone talked so slowly and patiently. The alcohol that could make an evening glow like a real romance. The snails on the sidewalk after a heavy rain. The big porches and the windows you could walk through. How leather would turn green if you left it in a drawer too long. The hurricanes that always seem to miss the city. The antiques you could find everywhere. The odd little places you could live that were sheltered by moss-covered trees. And you could be a lady twenty-four hours a day no matter what you did for a living because it was the south. The old white men with their moustaches and white hair and suits the color of ice cream. And their canes. They might even call you missy, if they were sweet on you. How she learned to love being attractive because it meant daily little gifts, a door held, a twinkle of an old man's eye. The nervousness of a sweet teenage boy. An old woman's smile and pat on the hand. It was the south after all and it had been created solely for her to erase all the pain and loneliness and loathing she had been taught as a child. She was confessing, but she doubted he heard any of it. He was too far gone, he had been long ago.

What would she do with him? She could have him committed somewhere, but then he would hate her. She kept thinking about somehow coaxing him into her truck and taking him home and giving him a bath. That once inside he might be more relaxed and less crazed and get lazy about being schizophrenic. It was a long shot, but if he was willing, she'd give it a try. Fat chance. What would winter bring? Was he going to be huddled out here in the snow? He probably would be, he had survived twenty years without her. She would go to a thrift store and bring him back better clothes at least. The owner of this pasture is eventually going to realize someone was living out here. Then the sheriff would be called. She wouldn't be able to fix that scenario. It just couldn't go on forever this way.

\* \* \*

The day of the shower arrived. The women seemed to be overjoyed at putting this on. On two separate occasions, women had come over to introduce themselves at the grocery and had told her how they were looking forward to the shower. The red-haired one seemed really ecstatic. She was new to town as well and this was her first invitation to anything. Diane came early with a couple of trays of hors d'oeuvres. Daydee had just had the heaves about an hour before and had lost all of her breakfast. Somehow the bacon and cream cheese aroma wasn't too bothersome. Diane helped tidy up the place and arrange chairs in the living room. She had even brought a bag of cardboard baby shower decorations, which she taped up on the walls and across the front window. Everything was pastel yellow, pink and blue. All really silly. They reminded her of babies that came straight out of those Dick and Jane readers she knew from first grade, except that there were no babies in those. But if there had been babies, this was what they would look like. Some foreign world that she was told about as a child, but never really saw. Another woman came with a cake and baby shower paper plates. Sarah brought a couple bottles of Champagne. Daydee didn't know everyone, but it soon became apparent they were all from Jack's church. Hanna, the stringy-haired boy-lady that she had met on the bus coming into town, came with a big smile and a pie she had baked.

"The clock is out at the cemetery office," she blurted out. She had forgotten it completely.

"Really?"

"Come and get it anytime. I can meet you if you want."

"That would be great. Tomorrow morning?"

"Sure."

Hanna was one of those persons you knew would be a great friend, even though she didn't talk and you were sure she was probably as quiet and as crazy as hell.

Another woman came with her three-month-old baby. Daydee watched her like a hawk. There were things to learn here. The woman barely was there. She seemed totally wrapped around the child, a little boy, and would look up and smile from time to time. She would steal time for cake and drinks and to watch, but she was perpetually rocking, cooing and then breastfeeding and burping and maintaining a quiet repose as the child slept. This was exactly what she thought it would be. She had to get ready and arrange her life.

There were ten women there. The red-haired lady came and Daydee was introduced. Her present looked like the biggest one. They had all brought presents for her. She was lost at sea, paddling to keep her head above the waves.

"So how did it go with the bank?" Sarah asked her.

"They gave me a three-month grace period. No payments, nothing." Daydee looked at her. She wanted to kiss her. "I didn't think banks acted that way."

"John said he hadn't seen Edward that angry in a long time," said a friend of Sarah's whose husband was apparently on the board. "He walked out of the meeting and slammed the door after him."

"Thank your husband for me," Daydee said. "Thanks, everyone. For everything."

Sarah opened the Champagne. Diane passed out pieces of yarn to everyone.

"Okay, the idea is to tie a knot at the right length to fit around Deidre's tummy. Deidre, you can do it too, but you aren't allowed to win."

They were all holding up their pieces of yarn, eyeing her waist. She had gotten larger in the last two weeks, but she had just been telling herself that she was getting fat and it was too early to show. But she really was showing and they were happy about it. She had to stand so each woman could try her length of yarn around her waist. Her own was much too short. There were two that were very close, so they had to re-measure both to decide the winner. It was Hanna, the sharecropper's wife. She won a box of chocolates. This prompted stories about when they started to show. One woman claimed she didn't until the last three months. And that she hadn't realized she was pregnant until then. Daydee wished for that – no morning sickness. Somehow the conversation got on to how odd people would just come up and touch your belly. As if it was good luck or something. They all seemed to agree that they didn't like it, but that it was expected and so a few resigned themselves to it. Daydee didn't think she had ever seen anyone do that. Maybe it was a Midwest thing. But then she wasn't around any pregnant women in the French Quarter. She didn't think she wanted that to happen. She would swat hands.

The next game was a 'who's got the needle' with a diaper pin. Daydee had to leave the room and when she returned, all the women had their hands together like they were praying. Daydee's job was to go from one to the next and ask them by name if they had the safety pin. They were supposed to answer her by replying with her name and telling her yes or no. Daydee was supposed to find the pin by reading their faces. The use of each other's names was to add some sort of psychological lever to it, but it just seemed stupid. Daydee had to ask their names again as she went around the room. She was embarrassed by her lack of recall. The ladies seemed to take it in stride. The Champagne was being sipped freely and the group was getting tipsy. There were a couple women who tried to act as if they were lying when they said they didn't have it. The rolling of their eyes and the giggling was just silly. She knew before she got to Sarah that she was the one that had the pin between her hands. She tried not to let on that the game was too easy. They were having fun trying to tell her the truth. When she made her guess some of the women were indignant about her guess being correct. There was collusion! Daydee was certain that some of them would never know the right answer to this game.

The silliness got worse. They then tried holding a cucumber between their knees and passing it to the next person without dropping it. The women were turning red and laughing hysterically. The only one capable of doing it successfully was Diane, the minister's wife. The women collapsed in their chairs, exhausted and flushed. Daydee hadn't ever rubbed up against so many women in her whole life. She was ready to call it a day now. Over cakes and more drinks, they began to get sentimental and each had their own stories to tell about childbirth and raising children and the early times before the children entered school. She was feeling her age. They had all had their children in the twenties and thirties. By the time she could trade stories like these she would be fifty. They were all younger than she was right now. She wondered if she'd be able to play the cucumber game at fifty. Luckily, the game was easily fumbled. You couldn't fumble the real thing. It turned out this was as risqué as they got.

Then came the opening of the presents. There was an abundance of things. Clothes and a diaper bag and a bathing tub and bottles and diapers and more clothes. Diane made a list of who gave what. Daydee whispered to her to write 'red hair' next to Nancy's gift. She knew she would never remember all of their names. She was overwhelmed by their generosity. She tried to ooh and ah like she thought was expected of her, but started choking up. She tried saying thank you to one women she didn't know at all, but nothing would come out of her mouth. Her hand on her heart. Tears began. This incited hugs from all of them. She wasn't sure she would come out of this. Sarah's eyes were the only reality check in the whole room. There had been a time in her life – most of it actually – when she would have had to get up and leave and not come back. She had hated and mistrusted women that much. How dare anybody give her anything? Only the johns were allowed because that was a transaction, her business. A friend was someone who might give you an aspirin from her purse after a long night. Or distract a barfly for a minute so you could escape. That was it. You didn't ask for anything. They didn't either. There was no one.

Except for an old drunk printer with ink-stained fingers who made you laugh harder than you could ever remember laughing and paid you even though he hardly ever got it up.

They wanted to know if it was going to be a boy or a girl. And she was embarrassed. She hadn't even been to the doctor yet. She lied and said she didn't want to know.

Finally, it began to end. Several of the women had to leave. The lady with the baby had just disappeared at some point. A handful stayed to help clean up. One of the ladies who had introduced herself at the grocery was helping her do the dishes. What was her name?

"I heard all about your husband and I'm so sorry. I hope it works out. My little brother had to spend time in Stateville and it was horrible, but they let him out early. When is your husband eligible for parole?"

Daydee looked at Diane who was taking down her decorations. She hadn't wasted any time at all.

"In about a year I think."

So, they all probably had the low down. Well, that had been the plan.

Sarah smiled at her.

\* \* \*

A letter came. She couldn't quite remember mailing the one she wrote, but she must have. Her memory seemed to be going. Or she was just perpetually distracted. She brought the mail back to the bedroom where she had spent the morning organizing her shower gifts on her mother's striped mattress. It looked like she had everything she could ever need. But she wanted to start a list. The lady with the new baby could tell her if she had a complete list, or at least what she was missing. She was trying to remember her name from the gift list, but wasn't having any luck. She would have to ask Sarah or Diane.

She left the project and came out to the sofa to read John's letter:

*Daydee,*

*Wow. That's quite some news to get here. I'm 'grandpa' to a lot of these punks. Well, if you want to have it and keep it, great! I'd love to come and see it when I get out. If it's as gorgeous or as handsome as you, it'll be something to see. I'll help with money. It shouldn't be too hard to get another job on the outside.*

*Keep me posted. Sorry I'm going to miss seeing you pregnant. I always thought that made women as sexy as they ever would be, the thought of you that way is an instant turn on. I hope you don't mind a freebie in my dreams here.*

*Well, I've gone cold turkey. The shit you can buy here or earn by doing crap, will make you blind, rob you of all sense and probably seriously injure you if you use. So I sweated and sweated and stank for a month and I no longer shake now.*

*They have a 12-step program here so I joined for help. It's a whole lot of crock mostly, but they are other guys like me. I suppose I got to come and get down in front of you on one knee and apologize for all my abuses at one point. Make amends and mend fences. I never harmed you at all, did I?*

*That's 12 step for you, a bunch of drunks that are still so fucking self-centered, that they think they were actually important to somebody and were capable of hurting people. I was never very good at being important to people.*

*I got a job as a kind of librarian here. It beats being a cook or making license plates or doing laundry. It's fun. I had forgotten that I used to like to read books. Can you imagine me with a book in my hand? I pass them out and collect them and get guys things they want. I'm reading Travis Magee right now, a detective that lives on a houseboat in Florida. It seems like paradise compared to this.*

*Got a bunkmate who is a serious lifer. We don't talk much, but he likes a good silly joke now and then, so we're friends.*

*Write more, tell me about what is going on. You making friends there? You making a living? God, I wish I could help.*

*John*

She would have to write back. John sober could be a good thing. Or a bad one if he has a temper now.

# Chapter seven

She brought her father's lunch out to the cemetery and found Jack's truck parked by the shed. He was hammering on something behind the building. Was there trouble with the mower? He was sitting beside the cemetery's back hoe, hammering away at the bolts that looked like they held the shovel bucket on the end of the arm. This wasn't anything they had discussed. And she knew it wasn't right.

"Hey!" she yelled.

He jumped and then stood to face her. Caught in the act. Whatever the act was.

"What are you doing?" she asked.

"Well, I thought I could borrow this bucket for my backhoe. It's the right size for grave opening."

"You weren't going to ask me?"

"It's not like you know how to operate it," Jack said.

"It's my fucking back hoe!" she yelled. "How can it be used if it has no shovel?"

"It doesn't matter. The bolts are rusted permanent."

"It looks like you were trying to break it."

"Calm down. I wasn't trying to break it. I should have asked you." He frowned. "I was just trying to make my job a little easier."

"I heard your discussion behind the diner with Winston and Edward the other day. None of you saw me."

"What did you think you heard?"

"You know what bullshit that question is?" Daydee wanted to grab the hammer away from him and beat him with it.

"I guess I'm out of line." He was looking away now. Down the hill. "You should probably find somebody else to take care of the grounds. I can stay until you find a replacement."

"You should clear out." Daydee put her hand out for the hammer. He gave it to her. "If I ask Diane about the conversation, is she going to tell me?"

"Leave her out of it. She doesn't know anything about it. What you heard didn't happen."

"We'll see," she said.

"I'm sorry, Deidre."

"For what?"

He started for his truck. Opening the driver's door, he looked back at her.

"You..."

"You what?" she yelled.

He climbed in and drove away like he was some kind of zombie. Shit! This was how ministers acted? What was she going to do now? She could cut the grass herself if she had to. How hard would it be to ride a mower around? The backhoe was the problem. She would have to find another backhoe expert, someone who could teach her how to use it.

Her father's lunch was still in her truck! She walked it out to his spot, but he wasn't around. She left it on his shopping cart. Her share, the three orders of fries that she had ordered for herself, smelled wonderful and she managed to eat them all before she had got to the office. This was bad. A sack full of salty fries – not even with any ketchup.

There had to be a manual for the backhoe someplace. She found it in a bottom drawer and she sat at the desk and went over it. It told you what all the parts were and what the levers did, but nothing about the sequence to run through so you didn't destroy something. She took the book and went out to the hoe. The key was in the ignition. It was coming with her when she was done checking it out. She didn't have friends among the men here. Her tagger might just decide to drive it away.

The women she knew from the baby shower didn't seem to have a clue about Winston and his goddamn aging football team. They wouldn't have thrown her the shower, if they were trying to get rid of her. God, was it all of the rest of the team of guys that played for him? Someone probably had a yearbook from the school for that year, but she didn't know for sure what year they had won state. She could see who the rest of them were if she could find the right one. That was scary, there were at least twenty guys on that team. Then she realized that her ladies would know which guys were on that team and still around. There was nothing like a guy to brag and tell the story twenty years afterward. Was it the year she ran away?

The book said to let the machine warm up. She turned it on and gave it gas. It purred. Now would be a good time for a cigarette, but she was quitting for the baby's sake. Or at least was trying to. She lit one. It was the first of the day. It was easier not to smoke in the mornings because she was so sick. She rubbed it out on the side of her tennis shoe and stuck the butt in her shirt pocket. That was another reason to quit. It was getting hard to bend over like that. She's couldn't just flick it out on the grounds. She was afraid to start playing with the levers here, she would probably wreck the lawn, so she drove it down the lane to the back of the property. She rolled off into a patch of undeveloped ground. A hole back there wouldn't hurt anything.

She played with the two big levers and figured out how to lift the bucket and stretch it out in front. When she started it down the entire cab leaned forward dangerously. She stopped. The sweat was dripping from her forehead. Jesus Christ! Now what! She studied the book, hoping the whole thing didn't pitch forward before she figured it out. The stabilizers! She worked the little levers and the stabilizer legs went down and straightened the cab up again. Trying again with the bucket, she made a motion like she was going to scrape a hole out of the ground, but she missed the ground, so it was a whole lot of motion for nothing. She spent another hour playing with it and trying to make it work. She'd have to come out every day to practice. There would be another grave opening eventually.

By the time she got it to work correctly and she was scooping dirt out and laying it beside the trench, she was exhausted and wet with sweat. She took a break and climbed down to stretch her legs. Her back and arms were aching. This was hard work. She reached for another cigarette, but talked herself out of it and put it back in her pocket. There was something in the dirt she had dug up. She held her arm up against the sun to see better. It was a human skeleton. The skull and ribs and backbone were all uncovered. Another scoop and she might have broken it apart. A few yards away in the trench was another skull. She lit her cigarette now. What was her mother doing? Emptying out the plots and selling them a second time? Murdering people? Was this what Winston and his boys were afraid that she'd find? She walked back to the office and called the sheriff.

\* \* \*

He showed up alone. He seemed so nonchalant that she wondered if he considered this a social call. His uniform was well worn today, wrinkled and stained with dots of coffee. There was no trace of a woman about him. His fringe of hair did look freshly clipped. But the barber hadn't noticed the sheriff's nose hair. Maybe it wasn't spoken of in polite barber company. If they were old, it was a sure sign there was no wife around.

"You are looking rather becoming today, ma'am."

She almost laughed.

"Thank you, I guess."

"You have that glow. It's a lovely thing."

"You have a marvelous imagination."

"What were you doing?"

"I'll show you. I was practicing operating my backhoe."

They walked down to where she had left it parked.

"Where's Jack?"

"He no longer works for me."

"What happened?"

"Maybe you can ask him. It looked like he was trying to rip me off."

"That's hard to believe, ma'am. I thought you were going to his church. His wife gave you a baby shower or something, didn't she?"

"You know there are folks around here that want me gone."

"I don't. Any more trouble with your tagger?"

She shook her head. God, did she not want his favors.

"You shouldn't be doing this in your condition."

"Is there somebody that can teach me how to use the backhoe correctly?"

"Well, Jack. And that sharecropper of yours. Hell, I can see him."

"Sean?"

"Yeah, that's him. He and Jack are who people call."

He stepped into the open trench for a closer look at the skeleton. It looked like it was as hard for him to bend over with that belly. She knew what that was like now.

"You need a heavy equipment license to drive the backhoe out on a public street. Just so you know. Most people load it on a flatbed to transport it." He scratched his bald head. "Well, I'm afraid I've got to ask you not to touch it. We need to take a good look at all of this. I'll have the forensic guy out tomorrow. We need to rope off the whole area and probably do some digging ourselves. You don't have a funeral coming up, do you?"

"No."

"You know anything to do with your mother's businesses that you are not telling me about?"

"No. We hadn't talked in twenty years. She only knew where I was because I sent her a Christmas card for the first time last year. She wrote me a letter saying hi. That was it."

"You involved in anything here you want to tell me about?"

"What?"

"You seem all right to me. Maybe I'm prejudiced. But we will need to come make a statement and we might want to ask some questions. You can bring a lawyer with you if you want."

"Ok."

"Nothing you want to say about anything?"

She shook her head. What was this?

"Nothing about that accountant of yours?"

"Mat?"

"He's left town. With a bunch of gossip behind him."

"What kind of gossip?"

"I'll leave that to you women. It doesn't appear that any laws were broken."

"He was married. What did his wife have to say?"

"I've not talked to her yet. If I do, it becomes an official inquiry. I just thought I'd give you first chance, if you wanted to tell me anything."

"I don't know anything."

He nodded at her.

"I trust you not to touch any of this?" he asked.

"Of course," she said. She thought of her father out in the thicket. What if they found him tomorrow? "I'm going to walk around a little more for exercise. You can call me at home, if you need me."

He nodded and went back up to his patrol car. In the city, that police tape would be out immediately. Maybe he didn't want to draw attention to the site. When the sheriff drove out the front gate, Daydee went back down to look for her father. She needed to figure out some way to keep him out of sight. And Mat! She hoped it wasn't about what she knew it was about.

There was still no trace of her father. The lunch she had left earlier was still untouched. She pushed the cart down into the trees and pulled some fallen branches over in front of it. It was getting harder and harder to do anything now. She was out of breath and flushed. God, did she need a shower. She hadn't any idea it would be like this. Where is the comfort in this? Why would a woman want this? She brought his lunch with her as she walked further to find him.

Her mother never talked about having her.

There are those women who just pop them out one after another. Her neighbor across the hall on Louisiana Avenue. Pretty girl. Three boys in Mississippi with their father. As soon as her divorce was final, she immediately got married again and had another one. All boys. How she loved those boys. And she seemed overjoyed with the last pregnancy.

We'll get through this, she told her belly.

What was she going to do with him if she did find him? She doubted she could make him understand the danger about the cops appearing tomorrow. It occurred to her to make a trail of fries back to her truck. She knew she might get him there, but she wasn't going to be able to get him to climb in. If they found him, they would hassle him and arrest him. Then he would be out in the alley the next morning with nothing. They all had their fucking routines. She could remember coming out in the morning, dirty and smelly and without bus fare home. Only a notice to appear. What kind of person would pick that for a livelihood? If you were young and cute, you could panhandle bus fare, but what if you are seventy and crazy? He probably wouldn't even know where he wanted to go. She had seen a couple of little buses around town, but those were probably church buses.

She sat down on a log. This was pointless. It was turning into the biggest frigging mess. Now the cemetery was going to be investigated. And the sheriff would book her for whoring even though it was a little make believe tea party. And she still hadn't gone to the doctor. It might not even be a baby. She knew what a molar pregnancy was. She knew the worst. She began to cry. She thought she could do this. She thought she could handle anything. So why was she sitting here, lost? She drew her knees in and rocked herself. She was trembling.

"Deedee making babies," he said from behind her. "Hard, hard."

She jumped and then laughed without looking back at him.

"You're damn right!"

He patted her head. She was afraid to turn, afraid she might spook him.

"Did you see the sheriff?" she asked.

"Sheriff invibable. He saw ghosts and not ghosts. Lot of nots. Not and nots. He don't like."

"So you stay away?"

"I stay home. Warm."

"Sure," she said smiling. She dried her eyes with her knuckles. "It's too bad you are crazy."

"Deedee stay home."

"Sure."

He withdrew his hand. She already missed it. She stood and turned. He wasn't running off. She offered her arms. He stepped up to hug ever so gently as if she was made of brittle twigs which might snap if squeezed. Then he backed away. She picked up the bag and handed it him.

"Thank you," she said. God!

He nodded his head as he walked away, and started stuffing French fries in his mouth like a hungry little kid.

\* \* \*

The sheriff's four people were out there all day. They were already there when she came. They removed five bodies, or at least there were five body bags with something in them. Daydee stayed in the office and didn't go over to watch. She could see some of it from the window. The Chief of the Paris Police showed up in his police car, but didn't come over to see her. The chief was a small guy, with muscles and a goatee. When he looked over at the office window, she pretended to be busy. She didn't want to look like she was interested in the proceedings. She was innocent. This was a good excuse to start going through her mother's papers. The desk just had advertisements and catalogs. She could buy caskets it seemed, but immediately realized the funeral homes were doing that. The undertakers weren't going to allow their customers to supply their own caskets. She tackled the customer files next. It was all a mess. There were no standard forms completed. Some of the files had contracts. Other had café napkins with unreadable notes on them. Were these supposed to be receipts? After a few hours, she was exhausted. She had thought that the cops might want to talk to her some more, but it was clear she wasn't needed. She locked up and drove by to tell them that she was leaving for the day. She got a nod.

She had hesitated until now. Driving to Mat's office, she parked and got out. The office was dark. The 'Closed' sign was up. There was a sheet of paper taped to the window that said to contact Samuel Craig, CPA, if there was an urgent matter. She took out her checkbook and wrote the name and number down. She might need it. Craig might be willing to tell her what happened.

Sarah's office was open. Daydee parked around the corner, in case anybody spotted the pickup. She already knew the worst. She just needed the details. What she would have to deal with. Sarah's face said it all.

"Don't worry, I won't bite," Daydee said. "I guess I've ruined lives, or something. The sheriff came out to see me at the cemetery about something else and hinted around some gossip."

"I don't like repeating stories that I don't know are true or not."

"You tell me and I'll tell you if it's true."

"Your accountant was driving around with you dressed up like a drag queen?"

"It's true."

"Well, there you go. His wife is crazed. He has left town."

"Shit."

"Why would you do that?" Sarah asked.

"It's a long story. Mat spotted me in New Orleans when he attended a conference there. We had dated as teenagers."

"Have a seat," Sarah said.

"You not concerned about somebody seeing me in here?"

"Naw." She drew a couple of shot glasses out of her desk drawer along with a bottle of whisky. Daydee nodded to the offer.

"I guess I've blown it for trying to fit here," Daydee told her.

"A few of those ladies at the shower won't be coming to see the baby. And Jack's wife isn't going to give you the time of day, but that's because you fired Jack." Sarah took a second shot. "This may be none of my business, but I get the idea that this wasn't for love."

"Strictly business," Daydee told her. "But I really liked the guy."

"I'm a friend. You out all your friends?"

"God, no. He wanted to do it. I was just being helpful."

"I could use some help," Sarah said.

Daydee looked at her.

"I've never done it," she told her.

"Well, think it over," Sarah said. "I'm not really interested in a business relationship. We already have that going."

"You do push a couple of buttons."

"That's probably the best lie I've heard in a long time," Sarah said. "My friends who don't belong to Jack's church aren't going to give a fuck what you have done with whom. This is a little tiny town. Something is always happening. God only knows what goes on with these old bachelor farmers late at night."

"I should probably go," Daydee said, getting up.

She wanted to hug her, but the motion wasn't quite fulfilled. It was a polite pretend hug. They were both embarrassed. And now she was blushing. These hormones!

"Thanks," Daydee told her and escaped.

\* \* \*

Winston was just leaving the diner when Daydee drove by. She wasn't looking for him, but there he was. Turning into the alley, she circled back to meet him in the parking lot behind the restaurant. A toothpick was in his mouth. No one else in the lot. She cut him off and jumped out of the truck.

"You goddamn son-of-a-bitch!" she screamed and shoved him.

He fell on the pavement. He was shielding his head with his arms.

"Don't hurt me," he pleaded.

"He didn't do a damn thing to you!"

"It wasn't about him. I think I'm bleeding."

"You were my friend!"

She was sorry now. His elbow was bleeding. He was just a little old man sitting on the pavement. Just another john that had screwed her. He had tears in his eyes.

"Deidra, forgive me."

She recoiled.

"What the hell does that mean?"

"I need help to get up."

"You got down there on your own just fine, you motherfucker." She got back into her pickup. "You say a word to anyone and I'll put you in the hospital!"

"Deidra, I'll tell you the truth."

She waited.

"The truth about what?"

"Help me up."

"Screw you."

She wanted to kick herself as she drove away. You could have found out. You could have killed him if you stayed. She wanted to scream.

# Chapter eight

She sat down at the kitchen table that evening to write back to John:

*John, Honey,*
*Being preggo is a whole other thing. You have no idea of the hormones that are dripping on my brain. Probably good that you are not around. I just knocked down an old man today and made his elbow bleed. It's a long story and he deserved it, but I feel bad just the same. I've always been capable of hurting people. It was my lovely upbringing. I want you to know who I am, what I can do if I have to. If you are coming up after you get out, I want you to know what you are getting into. My first pimp – 'Ringer':*
*He was ok at first. That was what they did, right? Sweet talk, gentle stuff and sweets and flowers and hugs in public. I was 16. Right off the bus. I think I knew it was a game. It was too hard out there on the street by yourself. You got beat up. I went along, but the whole thing was to get you back out there, but under his control. When I got scared at some of the requests, his thumb came down. And criticism. All of us knew criticism, we grew up with it. That was why we were there. It was something you knew and understood. You would never be good enough. I wasn't good enough at the sex. I needed to make more money, I was eating too much. I didn't know*

*how to dress. This was some kind of attention, better than no attention. I was with him almost two years with a couple of other girls in his stable.*

*As time went on, his drug habit grew. He couldn't say Deidre after seven o'clock at night, so I became Daydee. One of the other girls got restless. He beat the shit out of her. He'd time it so I and the third girl would never see it, but we knew it was going on. She never said a word, but she would wince when he would touch her. I was waiting to see what would happen. Nothing. She started shooting and did what he said.*

*So when it came time for me to go, I knew what I had to do to get out. I knew Ringer was disappearing when he was supposed to be out taking care of us. He had started going back to the apartment for a beer and a toke once we were all off with a john. So I decided to meet him at home. All I had to do was grab some wanna-be john by the arm and walk him around the corner and lose him by telling him I had lice. So I beat Ringer back and was standing behind the door with a baseball bat. I butchered him. I left him on the floor with a broken arm and probably a broken ankle. His nose was bloodied and he was black and blue. I told him if he came near me again, I would kill him. And I left. He had never even bruised me, but I knew he would if things dragged out.*

*I worked the other end of the quarter. I didn't see him for almost another year. Then one night there he was down the street. He saw me and turned and disappeared. I was fucking lucky. Another guy would have probably killed me.*

*I'm my mother's daughter after all, I guess. Write me back. Tell me horrible stories. But if you don't, I'll understand.*

*Daydee*

The bodies made the newspaper. It turned out it was the State Police that had been there for the investigation. They had dug a half acre around the trench. There were five bodies in all. All male, all in their thirties. There was no identification found with them. The forensic people decided the men had been buried there about fifteen years ago. One of them had gold fillings, but no dental records could be turned up. A reporter from the paper came out to interview her at the cemetery office. He was young and serious at first, but had an odd kind of mock seriousness as the interview went on. She just ignored it. Daydee swore that she had done a record check of the last ten years and there were absolutely no irregularities. That sounded official, didn't it? She wanted to reassure her customers that there was nothing questionable about the cemetery. The grounds were only two thirds sold, with about one hundred available plots left. There would be no need to relocate anyone's remains. Daydee speculated that the bodies found might be illegal farmworkers. No one cared about them. She had spotted a few around out on the farms. When the interview was printed, she was happy with it. She must have won him over because she sounded reasonable and calm and professional.

The sheriff came back for an interview as well. He asked twenty questions about the cemetery, asked to see her records going back fifteen years. She had found a logbook that was started about twelve years ago, but she knew from cross-referencing it with the files, it was all incorrect. It really looked like it was a fake record that her mother had created to cook her financial records. She handed it over to him as if was the Holy Bible and entreated him to guard it well. She knew she would get it back without a word. No one in their right mind would want to examine cemetery records.

He asked her to go to church with him. She accepted. It would be good public relations to be seen hanging out with him. He lit up like a Christmas tree. He would pick her up.

Was there any news about Mat? The sheriff hadn't heard anything. The office was still closed. No one knew anything. He asked her what she thought of the whole affair. It was clear that he didn't care. He wasn't going to blow his date over some weird gossip he didn't want to believe anyway. Daydee told him that what she had heard was incredibly absurd and didn't know how it had gotten started. Whoever made it up was sick. He went away a happy man.

After he left, she began to feel really lonesome. She had no friends except maybe Sarah and that was a case of the hots anyway. God. She had no expectations coming here, other than getting some money. Life wasn't going to be any different. But suddenly it was. So she shouldn't have played with Mat. It had seemed so harmless. If they were all like him, it would have been easy street. It was the rest of them that she was hoping to get free of. The ones that would hold you down and jam you like a pork loin. Or the slobbering little boys that needed you to do it all for them and then they would lie there latched on your nipple like they were starving. Or the studs that would just go on and on like it was a measure of their manhood and their stupid belief that all women wanted marathons. And you would be sore for days. The old men that took forever to get off. And the Romeos that thought they should romance you, bring you flowers and a gentle touch and music and candles and wanted you to come.

Hookers don't come. She had wanted that sign up in every hotel room. She wanted it framed and hanging above the bed. "Hookers don't come, Assholes!" But they were all men, almost all with no sense of a reality check in their lives, that's why they were paying money. They were stupid. Quick was always the best. You looked for their buttons. Quick was always best. Sometimes it was only one little word.

The reality was she was getting too old. They didn't want her anymore. Except here.

\* \* \*

A letter came back almost immediately. He must have read hers and sat down and wrote back a minute after reading it:

*Daydee,*

*You are the toughest and the sweetest woman I know. We lived in the biggest easy of them all, New Orleans. More damaged goods per square inch than anywhere else in the world. We all washed up down there as pieces carried by that river from every flooded house and garbage dump from the Midwest to the gulf. I saw a news story once about a flooded cemetery where the caskets were floating down river for miles.*

*I killed my brother. We had this tree in the back yard that had this bark that furled and curled off the trunk in these thin paper-like pieces that I swear looked like parchment. I wanted to make a treasure map out of a piece. The best ones were way up in the tree. He was a better climber than me, so I talked him into climbing up and getting a piece. I was twelve, he was nine. He would do anything I asked him to. He fell and I wasn't quick enough to get under him. He died instantly. His body was all twisted and broken. And I was afraid he was still alive and in horrible pain. But he wasn't. I ran to get my mother. But there was nothing anyone could do.*

*If I could take it all back, I would. If I could go back and think and tell him don't do it, it isn't safe, I would. If there was a God in the heaven, I'd pray to make it right. But there is nothing I can do to change it. I can't even forgive myself for being young and stupid. There's other stuff too. Don't worry. I think I love you. I've only said that to one other person in my life. I won't be surprised or horrified. Tell me everything you want to tell me.*

*I ain't going anywhere.*
*John*

Daydee decided to bite the bullet and drive out to Hanna and Sean's house the next day. She had brought the clock that had belonged to Hanna's family home from the cemetery office to make it a legit visit. She was nervous about calling ahead, afraid they would make some excuse. So she looked up their address in the phone book and looked at the map of Edgar County she had bought at the drugstore until she finally found them out off of Lower Terre Haute Road. She didn't need anyone's help.

The farm looked small, but was planted with the same crops that he had planted on her Uncle's farm, soy and corn. Sean's truck was out front. Daydee carried the clock up to the front screen. Hanna must have been sitting right inside.

"Hello," came her voice from behind the dark screen.

"Hi," Daydee said. "I brought the clock. It was out at the cemetery office."

"I see." The screen opened. "Why don't you come in?"

She stepped in and handed the clock to Hanna.

"I didn't touch it. I hope it's in working order."

"You take your chances. How much do we owe you?"

"Nothing. I wanted to thank you for the baby shower. It was a blast."

"Yeah, well."

"I hope…"

"Deidre," Hanna cut her off. "I don't listen to gossip. You've been all right by me. I don't care about anyone else's husband. There been stuff going on around here for years. But I'm fond of mine."

"Sean doesn't like me."

"I know, but you could probably change a man's mind if you wanted."

Daydee could hear his feet in the kitchen.

"I don't much like him either," she whispered.

Hanna smiled.

"I came to ask him something too."

"Sean!" Hanna called.

He came out, wiping his hands on a dishtowel.

What's up?"

"The sheriff said you know how to run a backhoe."

"Yes. I've been reading about your bodies."

"How much would you charge me for lessons?"

"Twenty an hour."

"You are hired. Can you come the cemetery at three tomorrow? Hanna can come too, if she wants." He nodded. "Would you be available for grave openings too?"

"Sure. Same price. But I think a woman might have problems with using it."

"I'll keep that in mind. Thanks. See you tomorrow?"

He nodded and she let herself out.

\* \* \*

What would you see if you watched her lesson with Sean? Across the way, down the hill, sitting on a blanket you might watch the two of them in the cab. He, the one with the white beard, was angry. She would move a lever and the arm out front would move slightly. He would huff and puff next to her. Show her again. She was sweating, tense, and anxious. She was woman, mother. She was little girl. He was little gnome of a man, a white-haired midget. He was bad, bad papa. No love there, only tense anger, tense acceptance. Even mad men understood hate and love, kindness and cruelty. Like a dog. Dogs understand the same things. And they can't even talk. Better. No confusion, no levels, no fog to get through. Put your head up and hope somebody pat you, stroke you. He needed to pet her. He was ready to run up the hill, pull the little creature by the beard out and beat him until he was dead. But she had asked him to stay away. She was kin, daughter. You remembered. We all remember, even in the dreams we live in. She would be ten, trying to pull him in from the front yard. Don't know why, but it was important to her. Crying. He would do it yet. Make it right, once, like he was supposed to. She was smart, so smart. He wandered, couldn't seem to find his way out. They had come all of them and dug and dug and carried away things and he hid because she had asked. He didn't know. The whole thing and he didn't know. They were so far away. He dreamed and walked in these dreams like a lost soul and he didn't know how to reach back and be with them like he was once so long ago. What were they? Why didn't they see what he saw, or talk to those he talked to? He couldn't understand any of it, but he saw a little. Her. How long had he waited to find her again? It was years and years and there was no hope. No hope, no hope and still he hoped. There had to be. Please. And there she was. One more minute and he would kill the little white beard. She came out and smoked. She saw him. She waved. Ok.

\* \* \*

Sean climbed down from the cab when she lit up.

"You shouldn't be smoking if you're pregnant."

Daydee just shook her head. She was ready to send him away, right now.

"I understand you don't like criticism. I don't like it myself," he said.

She looked at him. "You wrote that letter," she told him.

He looked away and then decided what to say.

"Yes."

"So, was the graffiti easier than writing?" She blew smoke at him.

"What graffiti?"

"You didn't paint my front door and my truck?"

"No. I wouldn't do anything like that."

"The sheriff knows about the graffiti. How about I give him that letter and tell him who sent it?"

"You can do what you like. All I did was write you a letter because I wanted to help you."

"Like you are trying to help me now?" she asked.

"Yes."

"You know, I've been helped enough for one day. You can go. I'll send you a check for your time."

"There are still things you should know about the backhoe."

"Well, don't write me a letter."

Going to the cab, she took the keys out and walked away from him back to the office. She pretended to be busy at the desk, until he came up and got into his truck and left.

\* \* \*

Mowing the grass in the morning was hot and sweaty work, even though she was just riding the mower around and around the grounds. She had bought a large straw sun bonnet at the drugstore and tied a big multi-colored scarf on it as a hat band. She laughed at herself in the mirror. Daydee at eighty, mowing the grass. God, what a thought. She found a pair of gloves in the equipment shed. The birds were singing in the trees down by her father's hiding place when she had started. By ten, she was soaked with sweat and ready to call it a day. She parked the mower and walked back to the office. She had just laid her gloves on the desk and found the last soda, when Winston stopped out front. He got out hesitantly and walked to the office, looking old and frail. He was limping. He knocked on the screen.

"Hello?" he asked.

"What do you want, Winston?"

"I came to talk to you."

"About what?"

"Can I come in?"

"All right," she told him. She sat down on the corner of the desk and stretched her aching back. He stumbled over the threshold.

"So talk," she said.

"Do you mind?" he asked, motioning at the chair.

"Sit."

The sunlight was streaming across the desktop and chair. He squinted and then backed the chair out of the glare. His bald head was dewy.

"I came to tell you the truth," he said.

"Ok."

He glanced up at her.

"We're trying to get you to leave town because we're afraid you've come back for revenge."

"Revenge for what?" she asked.

"You know."

"I'd like you to tell me."

"I'm sorry for my part in it and I'd take it all back if I could. I was the adult."

"Winston, I don't know what you are talking about."

"I need to apologize, whether you want to accept it or not."

She stared at him.

"All of this is about something I don't even remember?"

He looked up in disbelief. She took her sunglasses off.

"So tell me what you did to me."

"The rape?" he asked softly.

She had been pregnant when she got off the bus in New Orleans. She got rid of it immediately. It was easy to do there. Her last year of school here had been a string of blackouts because of the drinking and the dope. She had just figured the pregnancy was the result of one of those blackouts. Just one of the boys. She was always sore the day after. She was much more careful in New Orleans. There was no more overdoing it. New Orleans wasn't a little town. No one had to face you at school or on the street the next day. There would be no one to drive her home and tuck her in. She had always awakened in her own bed here in Paris.

"So tell me about it," she said.

"The boys were having a party in the pasture above the football field. They had just won the Homecoming game. I was putting away gear and locking up. It was real late and everyone was gone. There were a couple of cars still in the pasture and a bonfire." His voice was a whisper. "I knew it was Edward and Jack up there. I went up to shoo them home."

The best players had to be looked after. They could get into drunken accidents.

"The car radio was blaring. Edward had all of your clothes off and was on top of you when I pulled up. My headlights caught him."

"All three of you?" she asked.

"Edward was pissed at me. He told me that if I didn't cover for him, he would quit the team. He and Jack were the reason we were going to win state that year. He had whisky and marijuana."

"So Jack was next?"

"Edward said you did this all the time. You were singing along with the radio, stoned out of your mind. He said you wouldn't even remember. You were so gorgeous."

"Did I smile at you when you stuck it in?" Daydee asked him.

Winston didn't look up from the floor. He shook his head.

"And then Jack?"

"You had had enough I think," Winston said. "That piece missing from Jack's earlobe? You bit him real good. His scream shook you loose."

Daydee suddenly realized that this was the night she had gone to the game with Mat. And there was something else, something that she had thought was just a barely recalled nightmare. She remembered vaguely Jack's screaming and her teeth holding on to something for dear life. She had thought it was just a dream. There hadn't been any other trace of that night. A little sore the next day, but she had been a little sore before.

"I put a blanket on you and carried you to my car and took you home. Your mother thought I had rescued you. I never talked about it with anybody."

Daydee didn't really know what to say. In the measure of things, what were three more penises she couldn't remember? There were a lot of penises she didn't want to remember.

"Then you were gone. You mother was sure you ran away. You took some money and some of your things. She didn't seem too interested in finding you. So we all pretended it didn't happen."

She looked out at the grass and the markers.

"So why confess?"

"I'm afraid."

"Of me?"

"I'm going to hell. I've been a drunk most of my life. I've been sober about 500 days now. I want to make amends. When you showed up, it stirred up the hornet nest. I've never seen Edward so crazy. He and Jack are sure you are here for revenge."

"So who tagged my apartment and my truck?"

"I'm not sure. It wasn't me. Probably Edward or somebody working for him."

"So the idea is to rape me some more?" she asked.

"I can make it up to you. I can tell you what they are planning."

"Winston, you've been watching too much television. This isn't a fucking soap opera. I can just call the sheriff and tell him what's going on."

"You can't do that."

"Why not?" she asked.

"He's involved."

"With what?"

"Edward got him elected."

And she had a date with him. Shit.

"Winston, go away," she said. She was tired. "I'll have to let you know about the forgiveness part."

He stood and left with his hands deep in his pockets. He looked back at the office before getting into his car. Twenty-five years, she wondered, did she even remember how it felt when she left?

\* \* \*

So they were off to church. The sheriff, Rob, appeared right on the dot, in a clean suit and tie, his strands of hair neatly trimmed. She looked good she thought: conservative. It was going to be a whole new group of people. A different church. Going with the sheriff was a respectable entrance into another group of God-fearing Paris folk. She had never heard anyone call themselves Parisians here. She wondered why? It had always been 'from Paris' or 'from Edgar County'. She asked the sheriff that as they were driving over. He laughed.

"Probably too highfaluting," he said.

They parked and entered the church. There was not one hello to the sheriff. Daydee had noticed the red-haired lady from the grocery and the baby shower and she shot her a little wave, but the woman acted like she hadn't noticed. Ok. The mom with the new-born, also from the baby shower, was up in the front row, but Daydee didn't have the courage now to greet her. She was preoccupied anyway.

They sat halfway up, near the aisle. The sheriff was very solicitous. He found her the correct hymn book and showed her where the songs were when they came up. These people all stood to sing. The sheriff liked this part of it. He had a deep resonant voice, though he didn't always hit the notes. The congregation all heard him. Daydee didn't know any of the hymns. They had never gone to church. She vaguely recalled her father playing piano, but that might have been a dream. She looked at her date.

Could this guy help her out when the shit hit the fan with her father? He seemed a good enough sort. Good manners anyway. It was really like going out with a dancing bear. She would have to work on her attitude toward his looks if this was going to go on. But he even moved around like a bear.

The sermon went on too long. Something about the prodigal son's return. She had a nagging suspicion it was supposed to refer to her, but she just couldn't believe she was important enough to be talked about even in a bible story. None of the people here seemed the least bit aware of her. Or they were doing a really good job of pretending they didn't know her. The little social coffee reception after was the same. The minister spoke to the sheriff and welcomed her to the service and that was it. No one else had a word to say. There was one nod and a half smile as they were leaving.

They went to brunch at the other restaurant where everyone went on week mornings with family. They had to wait for a table. She asked questions about his work, about family and his divorce. He enjoyed the attention. There was another couple of nods as they were leaving. It had been all right. He had even asked her questions about New Orleans. He liked the parts about the fancy food. He might even ask her out again, dreaming about some fancy dishes that she had made him think she could make.

He walked her to her door. And did ask for a dinner and a movie date. She agreed and pecked him on the cheek before going in. This was harmless enough.

# Chapter nine

She stayed up late thinking about what she should do. Winston had her believing that he was telling her the truth. What would happen when they found out he was crossing them? The television was on, but she wasn't really following it or listening. She finally turned the sound off. She wished John were here and they could both just get drunk and shine it all on. The baby she got rid of in New Orleans probably belonged to one of them. It was early with her pimp, Ringer, and he hadn't started sending her out to the sidewalk yet. He paid for it. That was a secret revenge in itself, wasn't it? No, probably not. Revenge is supposed to feel like revenge. She really didn't want revenge for what happened so long ago anyway. Who cared? She wanted revenge for what they had done to her in last few months. Maybe 'Rapist' in big red letters on a couple cars? Or across the entrance to Edward's office? But that would just lead to more graffiti on her stuff. A quick and deadly physical attack wouldn't turn out well. She'd probably go to jail. There had to be something else to do.

It didn't occur to her what she could try until early in the morning. She got gussied up, as her mother used to say. And went calling. Down to the café to have breakfast with the guys. The entire restaurant looked up at her when she came in the front door. The three of them were at their usual table. Edward seemed to be turning red. She sat down with them.

"So, what's up gentlemen?" she asked.

Winston stood and left, going out the front door. He hadn't said a word or looked at her. He had carried his napkin with him, tucked into his collar. Jack smiled at the air around her.

"So how are you doing these days?" he asked. "I see you had a little trouble at the cemetery?"

The waitress was hovering nearby. Daydee waved her over and ordered an omelet.

"I'm hungry all the time. And sick and throwing up all at the same time. According to what time of the day it is."

Edward was eating slowly and deliberately.

"So, either of you heard from Mat? He seems to have disappeared?"

"I think he's gone to look for himself," Jack said with that smile.

"That's too bad. I just bought the cutest little nightie. Either of you want to come over and try it on? It would match your eyes perfectly, Jack."

"I'm not that kind of sicko."

"No? You like them to lie real still with their eyes closed? Like they are dead? You like them dead, Jack?"

"I don't think this is a great conversation. What's the point?" Jack asked.

"There is no point," Edward said. "No one will believe what she has to say. They all know what she is."

"How about a child?" Daydee asked him. "How old do you think he would be now? Who do you think he looks like?"

"What?" Edward asked.

"It might be real easy to prove who his daddy is. Maybe he'd want to know."

"I don't believe you," Edward said.

"Well, come on over and try on that nightie, and I might show you pictures. I understand you've been single a while."

"What do you want, Deidre?" he asked.

"I'm here and I'm not going away. If you push, maybe I'll push back. I am my mother's daughter. And I could have the bouncing baby boy come to visit. Wonder if the town would notice the resemblance?"

Jack got up.

"Wish you all the best, Deidre," Jack told her.

"So, you know whose it is?"

"I leave myself in God's hands."

"You already been forgiven?"

He walked out.

"I seem to be driving men away."

"So what if there is a kid, what of it?" Edward asked. "He's grown now. Maybe you're a pregnant grandma."

She eyed him.

"Could be. How's your son doing?"

"Ok."

"Sarah says there's no wife and no kids yet."

"So you did find out for me?" he asked.

"I guess I did. I don't know why particularly. You guys aren't helping me out at all."

"I've been seriously embarrassed in front of the bank board. Maybe we are even."

"Not until I have pictures of you in the nightie."

He laughed. All the heads in the restaurant turned. It wasn't exactly a natural laugh. He needed practice.

"You aren't so bad as I thought. Maybe you're not the problem," Edward said.

"Maybe next time you're out driving around at night with your little spray can, you might think about a woman frightened in the dark with a loaded shotgun in her hands."

"Now there's a scary thought," he said. "I got to go. I'm buying breakfast. That ok?"

"It's a free country."

He got up.

"So who does he look like?"

"You know," she said.

He handed a twenty to the waitress and left. The entire restaurant was watching her. It felt heavy. She ate slowly and then finished as if she had all the time in the world. Rob came in.

"Hey, handsome!" she called.

His grin was the escape key. But she had to dabble some more, while he ate. At least the gossips in here would know she wasn't going anywhere.

\* \* \*

Sarah just appeared one afternoon at the screen door at the cemetery office. Daydee was sitting on the floor, surrounded by stacks of files, her back against the desk. An overflowing wastebasket was next to her.

"Come in," Daydee hollered.

"You don't believe in working at a desk like other people. There's one right there."

"It's more comfortable down here. The filing is a disaster. It's not so serious here. I'm a little girl again playing paper dolls. Great for your perspective. My back is really sore."

The windows were all open and the room was cool. Outside it was at least a hundred degrees.

"You're cute," Sarah told her.

"There's soda in the fridge."

Sarah got one and sat at her desk.

"Good news."

"What?" Daydee asked.

"You don't already know? I got a letter this morning. Yours is probably waiting for you at home."

"What?"

"There's an offer on the apartment building. A real good one."

"How good?"

"165."

"Take it!"

"You really don't know anything about it?"

"No, why should I?"

"It came from a holding company from Springfield. It's really from Edward."

"What?"

"I heard you had breakfast with him and made him laugh."

"I told him I had a nightie for him in his color – to match his eyes."

"That was it?"

"You guys don't talk at all?" Daydee asked her. "I told him about your son."

"He avoids me."

"He was the one tagging me."

"What?"

"He spray-painted my door at the apartment and my truck."

"He can be dangerous. And he's buying the property because he wants something else."

"I know."

"What?" Sarah asked.

"Winston came clean, I think. He told me why Edward was freaked out about me being here." Daydee couldn't help grinning. "Apparently they, the three of them, Edward, Jack and Winston gang raped me in one of my teenage black outs. They thought I was out for revenge. I didn't even remember it."

Daydee looked at her. She didn't want to repeat the lie about her aborted baby. Something was going on. Sarah looked confused, then a little horrified.

"It's you!" Sarah said. "All those years. I was being asked to role play you?"

Daydee understood what she had just found out. They just looked at each other. Sarah made a little shudder.

"God," Sarah said. "The vision of that is fucking disgusting. Winston?"

Daydee laughed. "It's good I don't remember."

"Edward is dangerous," Sarah said. "There are things that I kind of know, but never wanted to know. He's mean. He will injure you."

"I can really take care of myself. I came back here after twenty years only to find that these guys are all still sixteen and all they want to do is put a hand up my blouse."

"Makes you feel like you're welcome," Sarah said. "You should really leave him alone."

\* \* \*

It was moving day. Sean was coming with a friend to load up the heavy stuff and bring it over to the old house that Daydee decided she would try to live in. She had been over there most of the week before, cleaning. A locksmith had been hired to change all the locks. He had removed the padlock from both garage doors for her as well. There was a lot of stuff in boxes in there and a lot of other things, maybe even an old piano. She decided to leave it be until she had moved in. It was all too much. She had replaced a couple of window latches all by herself, which she was proud of. The wood was really soft and if someone wanted to force it the screws would probably pull right out, but they looked new and she was hoping that would dissuade anybody from trying. The place had been filthy. She had brought a few things over, but today was the real day. She was slowly carrying boxes out to her pickup truck. The heavier ones were large and bulky as well, so she would have to stop several times and set them down to catch her breath on her way out. She should have pulled the truck up to the front door, but she hated to wreck the lawn with tire tracks. She was sitting atop a box, breathing heavily, when Winston pulled up. He got out and came running over.

"Let me help you!"

She wanted to scream at him to get the fuck away from her, but she was tired. She nodded and stood. He scooped up the box and took it the rest of the way. She went back to the house to get more. Why did she feel like she was waddling? Winston followed her inside.

"You really can't do all of this yourself," he said.

"Sean is coming with somebody for the furniture. If you want to help with the boxes that would be ok. I would appreciate it."

"Sure. I am a friend."

Daydee grimaced.

"It's all linen and dishes and cooking stuff and all the practical crap my mother had bought over the years. I'd just have to go out and buy it again."

"I have got all sorts that my wife collected. You get used to it being there."

She sat down on the arm of the couch.

"It's nice to know you don't have to immediately wash up after a meal. That there are more than a couple of dishes and a couple of glasses."

Winston looked at her.

"How did you live like that with a child?" he asked.

Oh. What she had told Edward.

"I was poor. And later I put him in a boarding school."

The trouble with lies was that you had to remember them.

"So all the boxes in the kitchen and bedroom go."

Winston went to work. He had a whole lot more energy than she did. She went for a box in the bedroom. She was hoping that with the bed moved that she might be able to sleep in it in a new location. She had purposely picked a room that she had no memory of her mother occupying. Then it wasn't her mother's bed. And Winston hadn't ever snored in it.

It had occurred to her this morning that with the sale, it meant that Sarah was promoting and renting apartments for her ex-husband. She wondered if they had worked that out, but Sarah hadn't been around of late. She'd leave it alone.

They loaded the truck and Sean arrived. She told them the old house was open if they got there before her.

"Winston, I need to run an errand. If you want to come help unload, I'll be over there in an hour."

"Okey dokey."

She had to go get her father's lunch and deliver it. She had almost forgotten. Then, as she drove off, she wondered why Winston hadn't noticed her father's presence out there. Hadn't anybody else noticed? Jack had been out there a lot.

\* \* \*

It had been a long day. Everything was moved and the furniture placed where she wanted and the bed back together. She paid Sean and his friend. Winston wouldn't take any money for helping. Stretching out on the couch after they all left, she looked at the boxes surrounding her. She hadn't thought to label them. She couldn't remember what was in each one. Finding the bed linen meant the first night in a real bed, so she would have to dig through them when she got up again. A black sedan pulled up out front. She knew who it was. She had been waiting for the other shoe to drop.

Edward walked very deliberately to her front door. His dark suit and shoes and the tie made him look like a stuffed lawyer. She got up and met him at the screen, but didn't invite him in.

"So, what business brings you here?" she asked.

"Mind if I come in?"

"I'm hardly ready for company, but ok. You are putting your reputation in jeopardy, you know."

She offered him the couch and pulled a kitchen chair over to let him sit by himself.

"You've got a lot of work to do around here," he said.

"Yep."

"I wanted to see if you were interested in selling the parcel of land out by the lake?"

"Why do you want it?" she asked. More money!

"The rabbit hunting and my land runs on two sides of it."

"I'll give it some thought," she said.

"I can offer a fair price."

She nodded, letting the conversation lapse. She still had an idea of the oil derrick removed and a little summer cottage sitting out there. But why not sell it, she wasn't going to stay.

"You planning to remodel here?" he asked.

"I thought I'd just start by painting."

"Your mother used the garage here for storage. I imagine you've turned up some interesting things."

"Like what?"

"I don't know. Antiques, that sort of thing."

"You have a claim to make on something in there?"

"No. not at all. Just being nosy," he said. "There might be some evidence or record about your father's death in there. You might want to hand it over to the sheriff."

Edward looked uncomfortable. Daydee realized he had to look up at her. She was sitting higher than he was. She smiled.

"Or you can come talk to me about it," Edward said. "I represented her when they were looking into his death. It might not be smart to hand it over to the authorities."

"That's an odd thing to say."

"Your mother was something. You were lucky with the wetbacks in the cemetery."

It didn't seem to be the time for her to ask questions about what he meant. He stood and waited as she pulled herself out of her chair.

"Are there pictures?" he asked.

Oh. Damn it!

"Somewhere in these boxes," she laughed.

"Next time," he said. "Would you like to come out with me for a bite to eat sometime?"

"I just couldn't tonight."

"Like Friday night?"

"Ok. Six?"

"Sure," he said. "You know if you need any help here, just holler."

She walked him to the door. He left looking happy. He had a date. She wasn't sure she was happy about it.

She went to look into the garage again. It looked overwhelming. But now she was sure there was something to find in here. Not tonight. She still had to find her bedclothes. She really wanted to sleep in a real bed tonight.

Digging through the boxes turned them up and she made up the bed. This was the room her great-grandmother lived in. She could barely get out of bed and was really deaf and nearly blind. There was nothing in here but the bed and the dresser she had brought along. The wallpaper was curling in the corners and color was faded by the years. Certainly no ghosts here. It was a thousand years ago that the woman died. Daydee had been ten. Great-grandma had been ninety-seven. Outlived her husband by thirty years. Her bones were sitting out there in the cemetery, probably nearly dust now. There was an envelope on the dresser.

Her name was typed on the front. It was the same typewriter, Sean's. Shit. She imagined him sitting up out there on their farm, typing through the night. Hanna already in bed long ago. The crickets outside the screen windows as he scribbled out what he wanted to say on a notepad – that was what she would do, you couldn't commit it to a typewriter until you were sure what you wanted to say – and then typing slowly and carefully.

This was unbearable. It was like being handed somebody's intestine. What should she do with it? Give to Hanna? No. Mail it back to him? No. She opened it. It was only one sheet. In the middle of the page was typed: "I apologize." She took it to the kitchen and dropped it into the only wastebasket she had. Rest in peace, kind letter.

* * *

She stumbled to the kitchen for coffee about ten the next morning. The summer sun was pouring in the front windows. Curtains. She had to dig around for the coffee maker. The overhead light in the kitchen blinked and went out. And light bulbs. Plugging in the television, she watched the Terra Haute traffic and weather before she dressed and started unpacking. At noon, she couldn't stand it any longer. She left the dishes half put away and went into the garage. Sunlight shone through the one dirty window. It was a ray of pure swirling dust. There were boxes of stuff everywhere. And old furniture and tires and tools. No caskets at least. No body bags. She opened the first box in front of her. It was old dusty moldy bibles. A real big one looked like it must be important. She pulled it out and realized it was the family bible. There were all the family records written down in here. Starting in 1857, it listed all the marriages, the births and deaths and ended with her birth in 1952. Some of the names were familiar. There were cousins and family that had moved away or were dead that she didn't know at all. Having a book that big, made you want to keep it and read parts of it like you were supposed to. Maybe someday.

She set it aside and opened another box. It was full of money. All neatly stacked with a rubber band around each stack. There were stacks of twenties, fifties and hundred dollar bills. She couldn't quite believe it. She carried it out to her kitchen table and got out a notepad to count it out. She stacked it out in front of her. The box had fifty thousand dollars in it. She held several of the bills up to the light. They looked real. She was silly with disbelief. This would help a lot, if this was all real. If they weren't stolen and somehow marked. She threw them back into the box and went out to look for more.

She found six more boxes with money in them. Slowly counting it out, as if the counting was going to make it really come true, she tallied up eight hundred thousand dollars. And there were other boxes in the garage that she couldn't get to. She just kept shaking her head.

Was this what Edward was interested in? Were they partners in some kind of illegal thing? Selling drugs? Why would you hide money in boxes in your garage if it was legal? This explained a lot. Her mother didn't need money, she could just come over and get whatever she needed. This was crazy. If you had this kind of money, wouldn't you live better? Buy yourself nice things?

Daydee guessed it might be considered part of the estate, if anyone knew about it. Why was she even thinking like this? When had she ever been law-biding? It would be subject to inheritance tax and federal tax. Better no one knew. She got out her empty suitcase and filled it and put it in her closet and piled some boxes in front of it and then closed the door and stacked more boxes before the door. The rest she put in garbage bags and squeezed it under her bed in the middle so it would take some getting to. And then pushed a couple of old blankets after it, so you would have to pull out a lot before you'd ever find the money.

The very last of it she stuck in the bottom drawers in her bathroom and put feminine stuff on top, like Kotex and make-up and a bag of rollers. Things the guys would avoid touching. While she was doing this, she was fantasizing about what she could do. With this kind of money, she could go anywhere, do anything. Go back to New Orleans. Open up a shop or something. Go to Paris, France! She was goddamn free!

# Chapter ten

She had a hard time falling asleep. All of this was too crazy. She must have dozed, because a loud crash woke her up. What was that? Glass was shattering on the floor outside her door. A window was being forced. She could hear grunts like somebody climbing in. What the hell? She was on her feet in a second. The shotgun was out at the cemetery. There was a broom and knives in the kitchen. A frying pan. She flicked all the lights on as she dashed for the kitchen.

"The police are on their way asshole!" she screamed.

She was grabbed from behind in the kitchen. The lights were off again and two guys had her by the arms. She kicked but couldn't connect.

"Shit, Mujer-Parada!" one of the guys ordered.

"I'm going to scream my head off, you sons of bitches!"

They stuffed a dishtowel in her mouth. The big one slugged her.

"Calm down and you won't get hurt."

They forced her down into a kitchen chair. There was now a pistol in her face.

"Don't move."

Her jaw ached big time. She hoped nothing was broken. There were others moving in the hallway. All the lights were off again. Five women came past the kitchen doorway and filed into the living room. The way they moved made them seem as frightened as she was. She reached up to remove the dishtowel. The gun waved at her.

"No se supone que no se debe a nadie aqui," the big guy said.

The other one shrugged.

"¿Y ahora que?"

"We spend the day, like planned. There's nowhere else to go."

He waved the pistol at her as a question.

She pulled the towel out of her mouth. Her jaw really hurt.

"I'll be quiet."

"Why are you here?" the big guy asked.

"I live here," she said.

"Since when?"

"About three days ago."

"You have to share it with us until this evening. When it gets dark again. You understand?"

Daydee nodded. It was beginning to get light outside the kitchen window.

"We rented this house. We should get a refund. Who told you could live here?"

"My mother owned it. She died."

"You can give us our money back then."

"I don't have any cash here. I can go to the bank."

"How about food? You know how to cook?"

She nodded.

"Rosa. Blanca, come help this women make something for us for breakfast."

Daydee needed to make friends with these women. They came in and without really talking, made a stew with everything she had. It wasn't really enough to feed six people, but they served up bread and butter and jam with it. Everyone seemed starved. Daydee went into an unpacked box to pass out blankets to everyone. The two women cleaned the dishes. The other two women in the group, a grandmotherly looking lady and a teenage girl both ate, but then sat on the floor in the corner of the living room close to one another.

The big guy looked at her.

"You have a bedroom?"

Daydee nodded. He waved the gun at her, so she led him into the bedroom.

"We are going to sleep now," he told her. "You tired?"

"You woke me up."

He laughed and sat down on the bed.

"We will leave after the sun goes down. Can you be friendly until then?"

Daydee knew she had to make a decision right now.

"I can be real friendly."

"You are not bad looking, even with a baby. How old are you?"

"Too old," she smiled at him. "You want to feel good?"

His eyes widened.

"Sure."

She went over and closed the door and came back to him. They all looked like little boys stealing cookies. She got down on her knees in front of him and carefully unbuckled his belt and unzipped his fly. He pulled down his jeans and underwear. He was hard. Taking it in her mouth, she began to work him.

"Jesus."

It had been a while since she'd had an uncircumcised cock in her mouth. It wasn't very big. His hand was gently on her hair. She looked up at him. They really liked that, the looking up, every one of them. He tried to smile.

She bit down on him as hard as she could muster and he screamed. He tried to get up. She grabbed the gun from his hand and bit until she could taste blood. He pounded her head with his fist. They both fell over sideways on the floor. Letting go, she jumped back. The other guy came through the door and she shot him in the leg and he fell. She scooted out of their way and pulled herself up by the doorknob and fired the gun at the floor between them.

"You fuckers move and I will shoot your fucking brains out! You understand?"

They were struggling, both in pain, but neither tried getting up.

"Ladies! I need your help!" she yelled.

Rosa looked in.

"Go to the kitchen and bring back a roll of tape that's on the counter. Understand? And bring back your friend."

The two she had cooked dinner with returned with the duct tape. They secured the second guy's hands behind his back and his ankles together. And she told them to tape over the spot on his leg where she shot him, hoping that would stop the blood flow. They did the big guy the same way. His penis wasn't looking good. She got a towel from the bathroom and tucked it around it. The guy seemed to be in shock. She needed to do something with him pretty quick.

She looked at the two women.

"What do we do with them?" she asked.

"They were taking us to work on a farm," Rosa said. "I need to work. Like the rest of us."

"Well, we'll figure something out." She shook her head. She motioned to the one she had shot. "Rosa, ask the guy to write down where they were taking you. The address. There's paper and a pencil out in the kitchen too. Or you write it down for him."

She came back in a second and the guy was cooperative. Daydee left them to go call the cops. A sleepy answering service girl answered. Small towns. She told the girl to find someone, not to just pass the message along. When she came back Rosa handed her the paper.

"Ok, come with me."

She took them to garage door and opened it.

"Get the other women and come in here and hide at the far end and sit on the floor and don't make a sound. I am your friend. You will get to where you need to go. You have to trust me."

Rosa smiled.

"I trust animal que come pene."

They ushered the other women into the garage and disappeared into the darkness. While she waited for the sheriff, she tried to give the two men some water, but only the one with the gunshot wound would take any. The one she had bit looked bad. He didn't respond and looked clammy.

The Paris Police Department called her back. Daydee told the guy an ambulance was needed immediately. Both the cops and ambulance came at the same time. Another car arrived. Rob's sheriff car.

Rob spent time with the two young Paris policemen the paramedic and the two coyotes, before he came out to talk to her. This was his case, he told her, his jurisdiction, but he was going to let the PPD officer interview her since he knew her personally. The young cop came with his notebook and they sat in the kitchen. She told it pretty much the way it happened, without mentioning the women. She showed them the broken window.

The paramedic loaded the coyotes into the ambulance and left with the second PPD officer.

"Sorry you had to go through this. Are you all right?" Rob asked.

She nodded.

"We have a lot of these people coming through here. The farmers want the illegals because they work for nothing."

"They both acted like they had been here before," she told him.

"That may be. We don't have much of a budget for graveyard staffing. Your mother might have told them how to avoid us."

"And the drug trafficking to Chicago?" Daydee looked at him. "My mother paid people to ignore things?"

"I thought we were friends, Deidra."

"We are. I'm just trying to figure out what I've gotten myself into."

"Bigger fish to fry?" he asked.

Damn this little town. Everyone knew everyone's business. Or had Edward told him to back off?

"No. I'll call you."

"Uh-huh."

Rob was not happy. She watched him out front with the young policeman, until they finally separated and drove away. Bringing her charges in from the garage, she made up beds for them in the living room and taped up a piece of cardboard over the broken window. She told Rosa that she would deliver them where they wanted to go the next day. And everyone tried to go to sleep, but Daydee didn't think any of them did. She lay awake thinking about John. She owed him a letter, but didn't know what to write about. He was further away than ever. She was having serious doubts about encouraging him. Their entire relationship had been based on drinking together. What could it possibly be with a child in the picture and both of them sober? What if he turned out to be the clingy kind? It had been years since she had actually slept all night in a bed with a man. It would be very strange. One of them had snored. Who was that? The boyfriend she had tried out — that college student that was slumming it. He had been cute and kind, but way out of her league. He had gone back to college.

She would have to write John and just tell him the truth.

It was getting warm. She turned to her other side. The day was bright outside. Her jaw still ached. Damn the son-of-a-bitch.

She needed to go to the doctor. She was afraid of going, of being told that there was a problem with her or that there was something seriously wrong with the baby. That had to change, she told herself. She could not know what was right if there were complications. She couldn't deliver the baby by herself. She would go tomorrow after she got rid of these women.

Sarah probably knew a good one.

And what about that? A roll in the hay with a woman you're attracted to? That was hot and so scary. A mother you never had? A wife? Women could be so mean to each other. She didn't really want to be made to cry by anyone ever again. John was the one person she knew in the whole world that would never make her cry. How did she know that?

\* \* \*

She awoke sweaty. It was hot in the bedroom. All the windows were closed. She must have slept a little bit.

The women were already up and had breakfast waiting for her. She sat with Rosa and figured out where the coyotes were supposed to take them. The women were piled into the back of the pickup and she gave them blankets to hide under. It would be hot, but she couldn't think of any other way. If they stayed below the sides of the truck bed, they wouldn't have to stay covered for the entire trip. She explained this to Rosa who told the others. They needed a van or something like that to get them up there. It was a farm near Champaign, about seventy miles north. She suddenly realized that the coyotes had to have a vehicle. She left them in the truck and went around the house to look, figuring they might have hidden it out back. Nothing. She came back to Rosa. They needed to get moving. She was afraid of neighbors driving by or the cops coming and getting suspicious.

"Rosa, how did you get here last night?"

"There was a van. They were supposed to come back and get us tonight."

"Stay put. I have to get something from the house and we'll get out of here."

She went back and brought out two of the boxes of money. That was all she could carry and she didn't want to waste more time trying to bring more. If she was robbed while she was gone, at least she would have saved part of it. One she put on the floorboards in the passenger side of the cab and the other just on the seat, because it wouldn't fit anywhere else. She locked up and took off.

A stop for gas was at a self-serve and there wasn't anyone around but the cashier at the window.

This was a disaster in the making. She was sure she would get pulled over at some place on the highway, probably in some small-town speed trap and they would find her truck bed filled with hiding illegals and two boxes of cash in her cab. Try to sweet talk your way out of that. Why was she so suddenly generous? She knew poverty. She knew about being a woman out in the world trying to survive in a very unsympathetic world. This was a sudden new way of looking at things. She owned land. She had money. If she didn't get busted, she was empowered. Her whole life was almost getting busted or getting busted. It no longer meant anything serious. Unless it was for what she was doing now. No more needing anybody's help. No more needing anybody to like her and give her things. She could be generous.

She turned the radio on and rolled the windows down. Her hair was going to be a disaster in the days to come. It was only seventy miles. All she needed was a beer in her crotch and a pack of cigarettes and life would be perfect. Maybe a little Dolly Parton on the radio. If she could sing, that's who she'd be. A hand reached into her window, startling her. She swerved. One of the women had reached around to hand her a bandana for her hair.

Grabbing the offering, she pulled off to get her breath. Jesus Christ! She smiled through the back window and put it on. She modeled it for the one that had handed it to her. The women nodded, smiling.

The drive went quickly. No speed traps. Nobody really out. She stopped on the highway near the entrance to the farm. There were some trees, for the women to run from the truck and hide behind. Daydee scooped some money from the box in the cab. She walked over and gave each woman five twenty dollar bills.

Their eyes were as wide as a doper's.

"I trust animal que come pene," Rosa said softly, smiling.

She hugged her and jumped in the truck.

Daydee spent a long time going home. Stopping in every little town on her way back, she found a bank, opened an account and rented a safe deposit box, and filled the box up with cash. This took most of the day and the boxes were empty by the time she reached Paris. There was her nest egg.

And she didn't get busted. And she had a very nice lunch in an odd restaurant, The Amishland Buffet, a giant red barn out in the middle of nowhere. The waitress had been very sweet. The idea of driving a half hour each way to be a waitress in a cheesy giant Midwest restaurant out in the middle of God's country seemed somehow a fate worse than death, but the girl was quite happy with her life.

\* \* \*

The house was untouched when she got home. The next morning, she started out again with the rest of the money and drove to Terre Haute. All in safety deposit boxes scattered from here to there. The money locked away made her happy. There wouldn't be any need to return to Paris if something happened. She stopped at a high-end department store in Terre Haute and bought a couple of nice maternity dresses as a present to herself.

The first of the trees by where she was parked were starting to change color. They were maples, she thought. Today it felt like someone was giving her a bouquet. What would the rest of the autumn look like? She wondered what the tree where her father lived would look like soon. Then she thought of the winters. Surely he wasn't out there last winter. It snowed here, sometimes heavily. She would have to get him out of there in the next month.

On the way home, she brought him a couple of meals. She even carried the bag with two dresses down with her. She was going to show him. But he wasn't around.

\* \* \*

At home, that evening, she tried to write John again, but it just wasn't coming out right.

There was a knock on the door. It was the Chief of Police, the little guy with the goatee who had been out to the cemetery that day. He wanted a word with her. He wouldn't sit. He seemed to be interested in who had taken the report when they came to take the coyotes away. She told him that it was one of his officers, with the sheriff's blessing.

"The sheriff wasn't in the room with you?"

"No, not that I remember."

"And you didn't know the Mexicans?"

"No. The sheriff seemed to think that it was something that my mother had arranged. That she was renting this house out as a stopover for illegal farm workers."

"There were only the two men?"

"Just the two."

"Did the sheriff know them or talk to them?"

"Not that I noticed."

"Is there anything else you know? Did the sheriff mention anything to you later on?"

"Nothing."

He went away. It occurred to her that the van that had brought the women to the house had not come back. Or it came back after she had left with them. She went back to trying to write the letter, but now she was worried about what she had done with the women. Had someone seen her drive off with them? She wadded the sheet of paper and tried again. After five wadded up pieces of paper she gave up.

\* \* \*

She put on the new maternity dress that she bought in Terre Haute. It suited her to a tee, she thought. It will scare the hell out of him. It made her look younger, sort of a Hindu hippie print. She worked on the hair and the make-up. She wanted him as turned on as she could get him. They drink too quickly then. They get confused. He was scary. She wanted him off guard.

Edward showed up at the door with flowers in hand. Lilies. He was quiet. Offered to help her put them in a vase. Even offered assistance in arranging them so they looked good in the center of the kitchen table. He immediately spotted the picture she had left out. It was one of her collected pictures from her imaginary life. It gave the johns something to talk about. It was a black and white instant print she had found in a thrift store in New Orleans. A woman in a big sun hat with a boy on her knee. It looked like the New Orleans Jazz Festival was going on behind her. You couldn't see the woman's face, but her boobs were as big as hers. And the boy looked blonde and about six or seven. The married ones with children liked it.

"The New Orleans Jazz Festival. He was six," Daydee told him. Why the hell was she doing this?

He put it back gently. They went out to his fancy black car. He held the door for her.

"You've had a little excitement at your house," he said.

"News gets around fast."

"Just for us in the know."

"The coyotes were the reason you hadn't broken in yourself?" she asked him.

"Didn't know when or how many. It's not clear how many. We looked the other way for our cut. You were lucky this time."

"I have to hand it to her. Hide the stash where the criminals and smugglers can guard it for you," she said.

Edward looked at her with genuine surprise.

"It was there?" he asked.

"The money has flown away to safe little nests out there in the trees."

"Some of it belonged to me."

"Finders keepers. So sue me."

"Deidre, I'm trying to be a friend here. Let's relax. The money isn't important to me now. You are welcome to it. Things change."

"You have been nice for a change."

"There may be more coming through," he said. "I can help."

"I am beyond relying on anyone for anything. I thought a big vicious dog and a good shotgun would work just fine. Maybe you could remind your buddy the sheriff that he's supposed to be out there catching the bad guys."

"He's not happy right now. Let's not talk about him."

They arrived at probably the only good restaurant in Paris. It appeared that the town couldn't really afford the country club thing, so this was the next best place available. A family-run restaurant that stayed open late and had good wine. He even motioned to the waiter to have her sample the wine before they served it. She could like this. There was a guy at the piano in the adjoining bar. The music and his voice drifted out to them.

"You know tongues will wag," she told him.

"So, tell me about your life," he said.

"You first."

He was pleased.

"I went to Indiana on a football scholarship, stayed to go to law school. And then came back here."

"You guys won all those games you were always playing?"

He laughed.

"We were hot stuff. Jack and I. Winston got offered an assistant coaching job at IU, but he didn't take it."

"That's it? You're a big-time lawyer in Paris for a lot of years?"

"I make money. Money is good. Most of the businessmen I know have done well by bending things a little so they work better. Atlas Shrugged… you ever read that book?"

"I think I've heard of it."

"You don't strike me as anyone who ever cried over spilt milk."

"You have no idea what a pregnancy does to your tear ducts."

"Well, I did it once. I'm sorry you are friends with my ex-wife. I'm sure she's telling you horrible things."

"Not yet."

There was a small moment of what to say or ask next.

"I'm running for state senator in the spring; to try it out, to see if I like it."

"All that limelight. To go to Washington?"

"The state senator job for the state assembly. In Springfield, not that glamorous."

Their dinners were served. The food was good, though a little Midwest bland. She hadn't eaten this well in a while. She smiled. But she was rich now. She could bring herself.

"What do you have planned?"

"The baby. Then I'm not sure, besides trying to be a good mom."

"The father doesn't want to be around?"

"He's in prison."

"I heard that from someone."

"Me and my big mouth," Daydee said.

"You don't want him around maybe."

"I really don't know."

"You have other family? To help, I mean. Your boy?"

Daydee shrugged at him. She knew all of this was loaded.

"You know you are still a gorgeous woman. You could have anything you want from anybody."

"That seems to be the party line in Paris, Illinois," she said.

"I didn't intend to feed you a line. Sorry. Talk about New Orleans."

She didn't want to tell him anything. So she started asking him questions. It was easy. Most men wanted to tell you all about themselves. Like they were the most important people in the world. He did seem surprisingly aware of every man, woman and child in his town. He got off on a story about the sheriff and how the man simply refused to ticket or arrest a little old lady that would drive into town every Saturday afternoon as drunk as a skunk. The sheriff wouldn't even stop her. He would wait for her in his patrol car and follow her around. She would run a couple of errands and then stop in a tavern. Then he would call one of her boys to come get her. This went on for years until her family finally took her car away.

"What is his cut?" she asked.

"Not much really. Just enough to buy a new fishing boat every few years and the latest TV."

She refused dessert. They came out for the car. He asked her to go dancing. He wasn't ready to take her home just yet. She asked for a rain check. He wanted to know what else they might do. There was a Tasty Freeze down the street.

"You can buy me an ice cream cone." He reached for his car keys. "Let's walk," she suggested.

They strolled down the gravel shoulder of the road and she let him take her hand. Just to see how it felt. He was very gentle, no sweaty palm stuff.

"Sarah?" she asked.

"That's a very long story. Nice woman, huh? She left me."

"You drive women away?"

"Only one. And she was driving, I wasn't." He smiled at her. "It was time, I guess. We barely spoke and our son was off in college. Now I get to ask about the father of the baby."

"John Seegum, a printer by trade. Very ink-stained hands."

"And…"

"I've never seen him sober. But he has written that he is now."

They reached the stand and he bought her a cone dipped in chocolate and a fudge bar for himself and they sat at a nearby picnic table. There were three teenage girls a few tables away.

"You must have had your choice of men."

"More than you could guess."

"Think we can do this again?" he asked. He touched her fingers.

"Ok. Maybe start with that dancing idea earlier. You really hated to see me when I appeared."

"I was embarrassed. Guilty. I have never forgotten you. What happened to your long red nails?"

"Just working my fingers to the bone these days."

She stood up. "Brain freeze."

They walked back to his car. He was sweetly quiet. He took her hand again and she let him. He held the door again. On the way back to her house, he slowed and nodded at a house behind some trees on her side. It was a huge house. It looked like it went on forever.

"Yours?"

He nodded.

"It's a rough life."

When they got to her place, he was out opening the door again. He offered a hand to help her out. At the front door there was his kiss. Gentle and passionate.

"I'll call you," he said and left.

# Chapter eleven

Sarah appeared at her door at 9:00am with one of those British scarves around her neck. It was overcast and cool, they were due for a thunder storm that day, but it seemed an odd fashion statement for autumn in Illinois. It wasn't a woolen scarf, more flimsy, like something you'd see in a movie about a flapper in the 20s. Maybe her being British made Daydee think it was a British scarf. It wasn't the Midwest or the South.

"Come on," she said.

"Where are you taking me?"

"You'll see. Come on. We've got an appointment."

"Ok, I'm coming."

Daydee grabbed her bag and keys and tried to figure out if there was anything she needed to think about. She guessed not, and came out. They got in the car.

"How have you been?" Daydee asked. "Nice scarf."

"Thanks. I'm very popular right now. A thousand questions about you. You need a press agent."

"Oh, I'm sorry. I should have told you something."

"You did. And I don't want to know. Ice cream at the Tastee Freeze is beyond my understanding."

"Sarah."

"I don't want to know. I'm on your side. I don't want to know."

They were parking in front of the medical building that had been built where the old house had once stood.

"Not a word. Come on."

Daydee followed her inside and into a doctor's waiting room. Sarah signed her in.

"Have a seat," she told her.

Daydee obeyed. This was very scary.

Sarah brought over a medical history questionnaire for her to fill out.

"If you don't remember, just make something up. If you don't want to tell them the truth, just lie."

Daydee was close to getting up and leaving.

"You were going to wait until your water broke, weren't you?"

"Well, maybe."

She started to work on the form. She was almost done when the guy from the newspaper office on Main Street came in with his much younger wife who was as far along as she was. He had let her leave her bag with him that first day. He remembered who she was. He was kind of good looking and kind and obviously really bright. She looked at Sarah. He was supposed to be single.

There were hellos. He was telling his wife who she was. He was saying how good it was to see old classmates from high school back in town. How he admired anybody that wanted to bring another human being into this world. How he was looking forward to chasing the little one around the playground. And maybe the two babies might have play dates, or something like that. She finished her form and was thinking, thank God for this silly man, and could she buy one just like him somewhere, she had money now. She looked at her friend, her only real friend and smiled.

They took her into the examining room. Sarah didn't come. She felt her heart freeze like ice as she waited. She knew in her soul of souls that it wouldn't be right. It would be all of the horrible things. Not even a baby. A mass of tissue that had no organs. A horrible misshapen thing that would not have a mind. Or something that would live six months and die. The doctor finally came in.

There was heart listening, lung listening. There were blood tests to take after. It went on. There were questions. Then there was an ultrasound. They showed pictures on the screen of a baby girl, after they asked whether she wanted to know, a heart beating. Everything apparently going fine.

She was going to cry. The doctor said everything was fine. He would let her know about the results of the tests. But everything looked good.

She did cry. The ultrasound nurse gave her tissues. The doctor patted her shoulder.

"I was afraid," was all she could get out.

\* \* \*

Sarah brought her back home. Big drops were falling on the street. The sky was growing darker. They ran for the front porch just before the rain broke loose. There was a flash somewhere and then thunder. They went in and Daydee made them tuna sandwiches and they carried them out to the porch to watch the storm.

"Not much to do today," Sarah said finally.

Daydee was worried about her father out there in the rain. He had a tarp, she thought.

"Nope. I need to run an errand later. Thanks for getting me to go."

"Sure."

Sarah produced a joint and lit it and passed it to her after she had a toke. Daydee didn't hesitate. They passed it between them until her head began to swim a bit. It seemed to just rain and rain. Sarah took her hand across the table. It was weird, but Daydee didn't pull away. Then Sarah was on her knees in front of her. Her eyes were so clear, and blue, bright blue. Sarah's hand was on her cheek.

And her lips were ready to kiss hers. Pretty red lips. Daydee closed her eyes. The kiss was nice. Loving and gentle. It made her tingle. Their tongues played, were friends. When they parted, Daydee started to giggle. Sarah was smiling, caressing her neck and shoulder. So gently. Making goosebumps. Sarah stood and took her hands and brought her up to kiss again. And opening the screen, she turned her and guided her inside ahead of her, her hands on her shoulders.

"Where are we going?" Daydee asked.

"To bed."

"Oh."

She didn't resist. When they got to the bedroom, Daydee let her undress her. So slow and so gentle. And kind. And kisses everywhere. On her shoulders. Her neck. Gentle fingers on her growing tummy and her rear. She stretched out on the bed for her and watched her undress. She was so skinny. Slender. A ballerina. Another flash and more thunder. And the rain and more rain. Sarah liked her boobs. Her hand was warm between her legs. It was happening so fast. She was so moist and she guided Sarah's fingers to her. God. Her friend, her friend. And she exploded.

She held her close. She felt so good close. So slender and smooth. It was her turn, Sarah guided her hand and Sarah sitting atop her, below her belly. One hand on Daydee's nipple. One hand on her own. And Daydee's hand helping her like it was her own.

It was so much a dream. A silly dream. Daydee wanted to make it nice for her friend. She rolled her over and scooted down to look at it and then to kiss it. And to play with it with her tongue. She was sweet, so sweet. Her hands on her hair. Her noises. Her gasping. And she stiffened and pushed her away and froze and moaned. In a moment, she was down with her, wiping off Daydee's face and kissing her and holding her. The holding was the best part. They were happy. Daydee giggled.

\*\*\*

They awoke much later that evening. The rain had stopped and it was cool. It was dark outside. The crickets were talking to the dripping water. Daydee brought her friend iced tea. Sarah's touch now tickled and she shivered. The grass had mostly worn off, but it still all felt like a fog. Sarah tucked her in with a sheet, kissed her and got up to get dressed.

"Maybe we can do this again sometime," Sarah said.

"Maybe."

"I can guarantee this is better than that big poker of Edward's."

"It's big?" Daydee asked.

"Please stay out of trouble," Sarah said.

"Yes, ma'am."

"I'm gone for a week. I'm taking the train across Canada. See you when I get back?" Sarah asked.

"Yes, ma'am."

Sarah bent over and kissed her passionately. Daydee wrapped herself in the sheet and walked her to the front door. Then she plopped on the couch and watched television. What a thing. A friend.

\*\*\*

She was out at the cemetery again. The bookkeeping and the records were a mess and it kept nagging her. She was sure someone would show up, claiming a grave and a hole to be dug that she couldn't find any record of. Then what do you do? What if you bury the body in the wrong plot? So she was going through each customer, and making notes and trying to create a master list on a big ledger she had bought. The new accountant she hired had raised the question of the perpetual care account. Apparently, Illinois required a portion of the plot sale to be set aside for a fund to ensure that the cemetery was kept in good shape. The interest from the fund was supposed to pay for upkeep. They figured out that the fund was maybe $50,000 short. About what her mother had lost each year for the last five years. The money she had stuck in the safety deposit boxes would easily cover it, but Daydee wanted that money for herself. Her mother was really crazy. Why would she steal money when she had money?

She would have never spent her time doing anything like this six months ago. But she was beginning to get comfortable here. There was no more graffiti. No more pissed off guys around. She had a silly notion about taking her daughter out for a ride on her lap in the backhoe. Role model practical skills better than the ones she used to know.

Winston pulled up in front of the office.

She wasn't very presentable. The flannel shirt and the preggo pants had become a uniform. She had taken to just wearing a bandana over her hair. And no make-up at all. Who was she going to see that was vaguely important? Edward wasn't the spontaneous sort. He would call to schedule a date if he wanted another one. The rest of the world didn't want to see her except for Sarah. The sheriff had disappeared.

He knocked on the screen.

"Winston, I'm sitting right here where you can see me. Come on in."

"Hello," he said. "I came out to visit, if you aren't too busy."

"Come on in and sit. I could use a break." She got up. "You like a cold drink?"

"Like what?"

She laughed.

"Well," she said in her deepest drawl, "we have Dr. Pepper. What you got?" She missed the south.

"That would be fine."

She got one for each of them and settled down behind the pile of papers on her desk.

"This is what folks drink in New Orleans," she told him.

"Not bad," he said. "Different. Deidre, I've decided I need to buy a family plot."

"Ok."

She wasn't prepared. This would be her first sale, if he decided to buy one. There was a brochure in the desk drawer. Handing it to him, she wondered if the pricing was current.

"This is what I have. I can show you the location choices. I've figured a few of them out."

She took him outside to look. He seemed to like the view from one location. He stood and eyed the horizon.

"My wife has cancer," he said.

"I'm so sorry."

They headed back toward the office. He paused by her parents' grave.

"You were the one that he told me to talk to."

"He?"

Winston rubbed his face with his hands.

"Deidre, Jesus told me to talk to you."

She was dumbfounded.

"Winston, I don't know Jesus."

"I know."

"Well, has he got plans about talking to me?"

"I don't know!"

She wished she had a hard drink right now.

"Ok, so what do you want me to know?"

"It's about your father."

Daydee nodded.

"Your father just showed up again. Out at the old farm. Your mother still owned it then. The sharecropper had spotted him. No one lived out there then. The house was surrounded by crop and the barn was about to collapse. It was leaning way over."

"Winston."

"The sheriff could have run across him and they would put him in a home. Your mother didn't want him around. She was afraid she'd be stuck paying for him if they put him away. She made a deal with Edward that we would get rid of him for her. We got Jack to come along so we could handle him. The plan was to go kidnap him and drive him to Chicago and drop him off somewhere that the cops would find him and have him committed up there where nobody knew who he was. We all remembered him as really crazy, so it was a plan that seemed possible. We had brought duct tape to tie him up.

"Well, he got away from us. It was so dark out there. No moon, no nothing. We chased him, but he was real erratic. We were running around in your mother's car with the headlights off on those trails around the crops to get the tractor in and out. I don't know how Edward got your mother's car. I didn't realize whose it was at the time. I don't know if she gave it to him or what.

"He popped out and we tried to avoid him and he turned and ran in front of the car. Edward ran him down. The body was pretty beat up. We were pretty shook up. It's the only time I ever saw Edward cry. I thought we should just take the body and drive till dawn and dump it far away where nobody could find it.

"Edward said your mother needed a dead body. So we left him. We ditched your mother's car out near the river and Edward made it look like it was hot-wired, like somebody had stolen it. And Edward went in alone to see the sheriff. He told him that he went out there to find him and he was already dead.

"They went to get the body and afterward they decided that you mother's car had killed him, so they brought charges against her. She got off because she had reported it stolen the day before."

"What happened to the barn fire story?" she asked.

"What?"

He didn't remember.

Daydee got up.

"Come with me," she told him.

She headed out and toward the back of the cemetery. Winston trotted after her, a bit out of breath.

"Where are we going?"

They passed where she had found the bodies and went down into the field. The shopping cart was there. The lunch she had left on it earlier was gone. They entered the grove of trees.

She shushed him when he started to ask again.

"Daddy?" she called.

He shuffled out of the shrubs. His head was cocked to one side.

"Bringing old caw-caws and young moo cows, we wearily await. A pack, a pack, a pack! He's a whosit!" He began gathering anything he could find, sticks, weeds and began throwing them at Winston. "Vile little twart! Vile, vile."

Winston backed away. Daydee got in front of him.

"You remember him?" she asked him.

"He ate your mother!"

"I'll take him away. You relax. I'll come with dinner in a little while."

"He ate my children!"

She shooed Winston out ahead of her.

"How long has he been here?" he whispered.

"I don't know. He appeared right after I arrived."

"Jesus Christ!"

"So who did you kill that night?"

"I don't know. Edward said it was your father. Jack and I didn't question him."

"Well, I want you to go. And if you don't tell anyone, I'd appreciate it. I want to protect him, until I can figure out what to do with him."

They went back to the office and Daydee sold him a plot.

\* \* \*

Edward appeared in jeans and a polo shirt, with a picnic basket. He had asked for an afternoon date, wouldn't explain why. He was clean and neat. He might have dressed casually, but he didn't look or act any less formal than he had before.

"So where are we going?" she asked.

"Someplace you will like, I hope."

She didn't like this 'trust me' stuff. It made her feel like a little girl being dragged somewhere. If he was paying her, she would have demanded to know where they were going. They drove out into the farm land. She didn't recognize anything until they turned on the driveway that led back to the old house. The mailbox at the gravel road was the same one that had stood there for thirty years, with the handwritten McIntyre in red letters on its side. It was her great-grandmother's, her great-aunt's farm. The one her mother had traded to Edward for her court case or whatever it was. Soybeans were planted up to sides of the old house. There was a lane that passed in front of the porch. Edward parked.

It was a little squeeze to get out the passenger side door even with him holding it. He wasn't ready to step on any of his crop.

"It looks like your soy is doing pretty good despite the K problem." She had mentioned it in passing to Sean a couple of months ago, so that he could explain it in detail to her.

"It was a hell of a lot of Epsom Salts the first year!" He stopped and eyed her and tried to smile. "Sorry. It just annoys me silly when things aren't correct. I thought you might like to see the house."

She nodded.

"There's a nice spot down by the creek for a picnic. We could even throw a line in if you want." The handkerchief came out to blow his nose. "The door isn't locked."

She went in. It was empty. And dusty. She wandered through the downstairs, the dining room, the parlor, the kitchen. There was no longer any glass in the window panes back there. Edward was waiting outside the front door as she came back and went upstairs. It was very quiet. She remembered it all, where the furniture sat, the old pictures on the walls. It was a quiet and lonely place back when her mother would park her out here. Her great-grandmother and great-aunt were old then. They mostly sat downstairs and watched television. Aunt Eunice would run an errand into town. Daydee remembered playing dress up in the extra bedroom upstairs. There were a lot of old clothes. Her great-grandmother had been a looker and a socialite type in the 1920s. She had kept all the clothes and the hats and the odd underthings and the shoes. And the two women were more than happy to ignore her for hours on end.

Eunice enjoyed making sly remarks about her mother's antique clothes. She had never ever dressed up in anything. She probably would have worn men's clothes if she thought she could get away with it. She never married. Daydee had a sudden appreciation for her difference. God, what it must have been like out here feeling trapped your entire life.

The house was still just a sad and lonely place. She went down. Edward was blowing his nose again.

"Sinuses?"

He laughed.

"Let's go have lunch," she said.

They drove on down the rutted road to where it turned and bordered a grassy mound and a shade tree by a creek. The water was low this time of year. Edward opened her door. Took a card table and two folding chairs from his trunk and set them up in the grass. She took a seat as he went back for the very traditional picnic basket. She was afraid of laughing if he tried to hold her folding chair for her. The only thing missing was the tablecloth. The lunch had been packed by a maid or a cook.

"Wow, did you do this yourself?" she asked.

"I had help."

They nibbled. It was apparent that she would have to start the small talk.

"So what happened with Sarah?" she asked.

That took him off guard.

"I don't know. We struggled to have a child. We worked hard to give him a good life. He went off to college and never came back. He was sick of us. He still talks to her. We decided to build a new house and she threw herself into that. She designed, planned and decorated and after two years when it was perfect, she packed and left me."

"I told you, no wife and no grandkids yet?"

Edward just looked at the ground.

"What was it like?" he asked.

"What?"

"New Orleans?"

What did she want to tell him?

"Well, I used to ride the streetcar out to the old zoo, before they closed it. I was there before they redid it all. They just had old steel cages and sick seals. I took long walks around Audubon Park and the universities. I would wander over to the Tulane library and look at random books like I was a student or something. No one ever questioned me."

"You didn't enroll?"

"I wasn't serious about it. And I didn't have any money. It was a fancy private school."

They sipped their wine.

"So, tell me about here. What have I missed?"

He laughed.

"There was football… There was an old store front pool hall on Main Street. It was run by an old man. It was open all day and late into the evening and that old man would just sit there day after day. The farmers might come in during the day on their way to the feed store or the hardware store for a game. The tables all had wicker baskets for pockets. And he had a real billiard table with no pockets at all. The summer before my senior year in high school I was in there every day. I smoked rum soaked cigars and had a whisky bottle in my car out back and would go have a shot every so often. That old man finally got off his stool and started to teach me how to really play."

And she asked him about the football.

It poured out. He played and they won the State Championship two years in a row. He and Jack went to Indiana on scholarships. The first couple of years were good and then there were other younger and more talented players. Jack stuck it out. Edward quit the team at the start of his Senior year at IU. He was no longer the star and was looking at sitting, watching others play. He stayed in Indiana and went to Law School and worked at a restaurant across the street from the building where he studied and took classes. The owners were big football fans.

And then he just ran down, like his battery ran out.

He finished his glass and poured another.

"So tell me about your son," he said.

Daydee was tired of this. There was no way to continue. And she was seriously interested in him.

"Edward, I've misled you."

"What?"

"What I said to you in the restaurant that morning wasn't true. I was trying to get you and your buddies to stop hassling me."

His jaw set somehow. He looked at his wine.

"Winston had just told me why you three were so paranoid. I was pissed. I was pregnant when I got off the bus in New Orleans, but I got rid of it. I actually have no memory of that night you guys did me."

"I see."

He stood suddenly and began throwing everything from the table into picnic basket. He poured their wine glasses into the grass and put them away. He began carrying everything back to the trunk. This was a little frightening. She stood because she was afraid he would yank the chair out from under her. After everything was packed away, he held the car door for her. She complied. He drove her home without speaking another word. She didn't say anything. When they pulled up in front of the house, she got out by herself as quickly as she could. And he was gone.

# Chapter twelve

She had started a letter to John. It was still on her kitchen table:

*John,*
*I'm so sorry I've not written. Things have been developing here at a very quick pace. I don't even know where to begin. It looks like the child and I will be covered for money for a long time to come, so you mustn't feel obligated to me or her (I think) for support in that way. I care for you and would think it better that you figured out where you belong and what you needed for a secure life, making enough money for you to live comfortably. There may be jobs for printers here, I don't know. But they do know you in New Orleans.*

*I've been lusted after my entire life. What if you found a person that had been in love with you for twenty years without any hope of being with you or even knowing for sure that you are alive? How would you treat that person? Would you shine them on? Tell them lies? There's someone here like that.*

*What if you suddenly felt attracted to another man after a whole lifetime of being straight? I'm very confused these days. These are two different people. I don't know what to do. I'm really sorry to burden you with this. You who can't be here and I'm sure I'm upsetting you a great deal.*

*I've never ever hung out with women. Suddenly I was one of the girls — for a very brief time — it was fun. I had never thought it possible. I think it has been ruined, but it could happen again somewhere else. Could you even stand me as one of the girls?*

*I have never cried so much in my life. Late at night. Over TV commercials. Over the strangest thing that could have ever happened. It's the pregnancy thing. I discovered my father, still alive, living the life of a crazy shopping cart seventy-year-old, out in the woods behind the cemetery...*

She wadded it and threw it in the trash.

\* \* \*

She was very jumpy the rest of the week. Edward could do anything. Tag her again. Come after her with some other thing. She occupied her time cleaning and fixing up the house and working on the cemetery books. Hardly saw a soul. She didn't stay out at the office after dark, and with the time change, it was getting dark at 5:30 now. Parking the pickup in the yard behind the house made it invisible at night.

So when she came home Thursday just before dark and found the odd-looking woman sitting in a car before her door, she was scared and almost didn't stop. She took a deep breath and pulled up behind. It could be a potential customer, or who knew what. She walked over to the driver's side. The window was down. The woman was smoking.

"Hi, can I help you?" Daydee asked her. There was not a soul around.

"You Deidra?"

"Yes."

The women got out. She had the dyke look going. Trousers with the key chain and work boots and the man shirt. Short hair.

"I'm Sarah's friend from Effingham. I want you to stop seeing her."

Daydee didn't want to get hit.

"Sure."

The woman scratched her head.

"You're bullshitting me?"

"No. Not at all. I'll stop. I'm having a baby. The whole thing is getting uncomfortable now. And the baby's father is showing up soon."

"Well, all right then. It was nice talking to you."

She climbed back into her car and left.

\* \* \*

Edward called her bright and early the next Monday morning. He wanted to meet for coffee and suggested the diner. She countered with the Tastee Freeze right after lunch. He hesitated, then agreed. She ran to bring her father lunch a little early. The brisk air worried her. She was going to have to get him inside for the winter somehow.

Edward was at the picnic table already, with coffee for her as well. He looked at her sheepishly.

"Coffee with cream, no sugar," he told her.

"Thanks." She took the lid off to let it cool. "So, what's up?"

"You don't exist in New Orleans."

"You tried to find me out?"

"You weren't there apparently. Where were you?"

"I was, but I had a different name. And a different life."

"How do I believe you about anything?"

"Like normal people do. 'So, what was that like?' would be a good question to use."

"Look, I don't like being lied to. It drives me crazy."

"So don't ask me any questions that will make me lie to you," she said.

"What the hell is that supposed to mean?"

Daydee smiled at him.

"Look, I kind of like you," she said. "I understand you want to hang out with me now."

He was looking away.

"A lie is just a polite way of saying it's none of your business," she said. "Think about it. Boundaries. It's supposed to make me more mysterious," she laughed. "More sexy."

"Do you have any diseases?" he asked.

"Hepatitis A. From a restaurant in the French Quarter. Pregnancy. Oh, and a doctor told me I had a Histoplasmosis scar tissue on my lung. That's supposed to be spores from chicken droppings, from guess where."

"I want you," he said.

"How about another dinner and some light dancing?"

They made another date.

\* \* \*

It was dinner and a little dancing. The dancing didn't last very long.

Edward escorted her to the car and they drove over to his house. There seemed to be an urgency to this for some reason she couldn't quite understand. Was he afraid she would change her mind? There was an automatic gate that opened from a remote in the car. There was a block long curving drive up to the front door. The lights were on. It was two stories, a good old fashioned wood frame mansion with real window panes and a huge front door with a real knocker.

He didn't say a word.

Inside was a foyer leading to a curving grand staircase. There were doorways and more doorways. He went from one to another and opened them for her to look around. A library. A billiard room. A dining room that could seat ten and a large kitchen. A living room that opened out on a deck with a pool. He preceded her without a word. The place was spotless.

"You have live-in help?"

He nodded.

"So how many bedrooms?"

"Six. Four bathrooms."

"You never wait your turn."

He smiled.

"When was the last time you saw the help?"

"This morning. Shall I introduce you?"

"That's all right."

After the tour, he brought her back to a room with the French doors that opened to the pool and they sat at stools at his wet bar and had another glass of wine. The silence was overwhelming. He took a little vial out and made a line of cocaine on the bar between them.

He offered her a little straw. She shook her head. He finished it off by himself.

"You don't do much entertaining."

"None at all. Sarah had friends. I have Jack and Winston."

"I'm not sure I'm supposed to have penetration," she said. "You know I'm pregnant?"

"There are other ways to have fun."

"You'll show me?" she asked.

"Surely." He looked at her. "What?"

She smiled, shaking her head.

They wandered up to his bedroom after a little bit and undressed and started to make love on the giant bed. She liked this. Everything was soft and slow and gentle. There was all the time in the world. He was arousing her, but she didn't seem to be able to get him working. She tried out different things but nothing was happening. He shined it on. He seemed to be all right with not getting aroused. She gave up and let him bring her to orgasm. Then after a little rest, she started in on him. Nothing at all. She had known men who got aroused and came without ever getting hard. She tried this strategy, but it just wasn't happening at all. After a long-extended try, he told her to relax. It didn't matter. They lay intertwined for a while and then he got up and brought back wine for them. She only sipped it, feeling guilty about the baby.

"Anything you want to tell me. This is make a wish night," she whispered.

"Anything?"

"Well, until I say stop, ok?"

He nodded. He got up and went to the dresser and brought back silk scarves.

"You say stop and we stop," he said.

"Ok."

He tied her wrists one by one to either side of the headboard. Then blindfolded her.

"Not inside, all right," she said.

"All right."

Then there it was against her mouth gently. She took him in this way. And it was over instantaneously. He was a teenage boy exploding.

He untied her and took off the blindfold and they lay together, with no urge to move or go. They slept. Sometime in the middle of the night she awoke to find him next to her, his head on his hand, just looking at her. She dozed again and didn't wake until the sun was in the curtains. He was gone.

This wasn't bad.

* * *

There was a letter from John:

*Dear Daydee,*

*I haven't heard from you for a while, so I thought I'd write to say hi. I'm glad things are looking up for you and you've made some new friends. Hope they can support you in your new lifestyle. I've made a few friends in here. We might go off and start a drug ring after I get out.*

*I'd watch out if I were you. Little town people were always the worse kind of people. They all have their own agenda and think like bigoted small minded people, which is why they stayed when the rest of us left.*

*Jesus walks those streets at night, looking for scared peoples' dreams to haunt.*

*You have always been willing to step into the middle of shit and let people beat you up. I love you, for what it's worth. Probably nothing. I'm sober now, hopefully for good. I could be a good man and a good husband. Black fingers and black soul thrown in for free. I could be a decent father. And you probably need somebody to cut the grass at that cemetery. Ask yourself if any of your new friends are willing to mow the grass. And that's a lot of grass.*

*Anyway, I'm trying for early release. Thought I'd head your direction come hell or high water. If for nothing more than to see the baby. It sounds like you will be busy. I'll try to be quick. Would like to know an offspring of mine is as beautiful as I could imagine.*

*I do love you damn it. And I could be good to you.*
*John.*

She would have to write him.

\* \* \*

She avoided Edward for the next two weeks. She would pick up the phone and wait for the other person to speak before she would answer. When it was him, she would hang up without a sound. He left messages. He was sitting out in front of her house in his car one afternoon when she returned from the cemetery and she turned before coming abreast of him and then drove around for an hour before trying to get home again. His car wasn't there when she came back again. When he appeared at the cemetery, she locked the office door and hid inside the file room. She stood out of sight with her hand over her mouth as he walked around outside and called her name. It was only after his car started that she peeked out. He drove around the grounds once before leaving.

This was unbearable. He had melted her reserve away. All she wanted, more than anything else was to let him tie her up again and do to her whatever he wanted. She couldn't stop thinking about it. It scared her to death. How could she give herself away like that? It smelled like destruction. And she wanted it with all her soul. But she didn't think she could do it again.

There had been a john in the French Quarter that was hotter than hell. Tall and blonde like a Viking and who had the sweetest smile. And rich. He didn't really need to pay for it, but he was kinky. He liked to bite and draw blood. She let him and she cried and reveled in the pain, and the marks took forever to go away. And it went on and on and she didn't know how to stop. She would dream about him at night and wait days on end for him to appear. And weep, and tell herself not to show up when he called. She was addicted to the pain. It was her fulfillment. It was the dark morass of everything she deserved to be punished for. She made up a scenario about how she would kill him and then kill herself with her little revolver in the hollowed-out book on top of the refrigerator. The gun she had never fired. There was still one mark on her neck that never went away. Then one day it was over. He disappeared. No word. No trace. He had just moved away or had died. She went to look for him and no one knew where he had gone or why.

With time, she slowly came back to her wits and recovered. But here it was all over again. She couldn't stop wanting what he had done and would do again.

\* \* \*

She saw Jack's wife out in front of the diner with her finger in Jack's face. Heated words. Not much for being an example for the community. Daydee hadn't really spoken to the woman since she had fired Jack. It was probably just as well. She knew that she had been dropped from her social circles. And eventually the woman would have to get back at her one way or another.

\* \* \*

Winston stopped by to tell her he couldn't pay the plot off for a couple of weeks. She told him ok. His quizzical look said it all. He wanted to take her to church again, but she put him off.

\* \* \*

Daydee was out riding the mower around the grounds, trying catch up on the grass getting high. It was a hot afternoon despite it being October and she had on just a t-shirt and jeans and a big straw sun bonnet that she had picked up from the thrift store. The t-shirt was soaked. Her face felt bruised from the grass and dust. The mowing seemed endless. A sedan entered the cemetery and drove over to the office. She rounded her circle to see who it might be. It looked like Jack's wife and a couple of women she didn't know. Diane waved and Daydee headed back over to the building. She stopped a few yards short so she wouldn't get grass and dust on the ladies. They were dressed like they had just come from church. It was Saturday, so it was something else. She climbed off and walked toward them, feeling like a waddling duck.

"You'll have to excuse me," she said. "If anyone has a teenager looking, I have work."

The women looked away.

"What can I do for you?"

"Well," Diane said, finally eyeing her. "Given the circumstances, we would like to relinquish our family plots here."

"Ok... Would you like to come into the office out of the sun?"

"No."

"Well ladies, I will have to research your accounts. I will need to write down your information."

"We'll wait while you go get a notepad," Diane said.

Daydee took off her gloves and went to the office. She brought back a steno pad and a pen and handed them to Jack's wife.

"Please write down everyone's name and address and phone and who they think bought the plot."

Diane looked put out that she had to be the secretary.

"Can't you write it down as we tell you?" another of the ladies asked.

"Afraid not."

Diane wrote and passed the pad on.

"I'll need any receipts you might have. And of course it's impossible to refund anything if there are graves occupied. And I've noticed that some of the contracts have a clause that does not allow for refunds at all. You all understand this?"

"We've found buyers for the plots," Diane said. "There will probably be others to approach you as well."

"What... oh never mind. I take it, the ladies auxiliary has decided that I'm not a good person."

"We didn't come here to discuss anything like that with you."

"You want your shower gift back as well?" Daydee asked her.

"I'm sorry," was all she got.

They handed the pad back to her and all climbed into the car and left. Daydee went inside. She sat down to rest. This meant she would be snubbed in the stores. She suddenly felt very lonely, something she hadn't felt in years. The sharecroppers were no one that she'd ever want to hang out with. Her father and Winston were off their rockers. Sarah was probably pissed at her.

She rubbed her stomach and somehow understood it was the hormones, but it still didn't matter. She'd have the baby to keep her company and to keep her busy. Lonesome was going away forever pretty soon.

\* \* \*

It was Saturday evening. Daydee was sitting on her front porch with a glass of ice tea. Almost dinner time but she had no inclination to go make something. The sun hadn't gone down yet. But the crickets had started serenading each other. She was exhausted. There had been a service at the cemetery. The first opening and closing. She had plenty of time to screw up the opening. The second morning found her on the phone to Sean. No one answered, so she went back to finish it up herself. The closing was the big-time work. You can't just leave a grave open for days. She would make it look better next week. The grass would have to be replanted.

Sarah pulled up at the curb.

"Have you eaten?" she yelled.

"No," Daydee hollered back. They were teenagers now, yelling like kids to each other?

"I just have the best chicken in town," Sarah said, getting out with bucket and bags in hand.

She plopped it all down on the little table. Pulling a bottle of rum from her purse, she showed the label off and added it to the meal.

"There's iced tea in the fridge," Daydee told her. "You mind bringing the pitcher out. I can't move. We are very tired."

Sarah returned with another glass and the glass pitcher. They ate and Sarah convinced her to have a touch of the rum in her tea.

"So," Sarah said, as they threw the remains into the empty paper bag. "I went to talk to Edward."

"God."

"So the bottom line is that I told him I would kill him if he touched you."

"Sarah, stop."

"How about I kill you if you touch him?"

"Please. I can't deal with this. He seems ok. People change. You did."

"Dee, you don't have to be with me. But there are other decent men around. The guy who owns the Beacon. How about him?"

"He's married, remember? He was at the doctor's office with his wife. I know what you want," Daydee told her. "I will try to be the best friend I can be."

"Oh fuck you."

"Your friend came to see me," Daydee said.

"What?"

"From Effingham."

"What?" Sarah said.

"She smelled me or something. She snooped."

"I'll talk to her."

"Have some more rum," Daydee told her. "Don't fight with her. You need to be the center of your universe, not me. I can't promise you anything. I know it doesn't feel good."

"What do you know, you stupid whore," Sarah said. "When was the last time you really felt anything for anybody?"

Daydee couldn't answer her. Sarah got up and walked off to her car and left.

\* \* \*

She was awake at two in the morning, feeling miserable and achy and alone again. If she went out to her father in the middle of the night, would he even recognize her? It would be too scary. She wandered around the house and thought of having a drink and cigarette and talked herself out of both. There was nothing on television. She ended up out in the garage plunking away at the old piano there. It sounded terrible. Like she was hurting it. Finally, returning to bed, she tossed and turned for what seemed like eternity. The sun would never come up.

The next night she let herself fantasize about him.

\* \* \*

Edward was coming out of the diner one morning as she was driving to the hardware store. She pulled to the curb next to him and rolled down the window. He leaned toward her like they were teenagers.

"Tonight at six? I'll pick you up?" he asked.

"Sure."

It was as if the last two weeks hadn't happened. Maybe he wouldn't eat her up.

# Chapter thirteen

They had a quiet dinner. They flirted. He talked about a court case. They were going to go dancing. That was the plan.

Daydee wanted to tell him about being afraid of him, but just couldn't bring herself to do it. You can't confess to the enemy. They did make it to the club where a band was playing, although she was feeling tired. He agreed to just a short visit. The dance floor began to make her woozy. His chest against her and his gentle hand on the small of her back. He nuzzled her neck. She was hotter than she could ever remember. The room was swirling.

"Let's get out of here," she told him.

Then she was spirited away to the car and taken to his house. It was all so quick and dreamlike. She was naked on the bed and on fire. He still wasn't hard. Everything he did was perfect. And she came and he brought out the silk neckerchiefs and they repeated the ritual from the last time. Then she was undone and they dozed. Sometime during the night, he awoke her and made love to her again with his mouth and she came again and then she passed out.

It was very late in the morning when she awoke. The sun was high outside. She was hung-over and unsteady and cold. She looked for her clothes but couldn't find them, so she borrowed one of his shirts and went out to look for him. He was stretched out by the pool with coffee and the Paris newspaper. There wasn't ever much to it. Usually only five or ten pages.

"You finally got up," he said.

"I don't feel so good."

"It was a wonderful night."

"Yeah," she said.

She started to pour herself some coffee and he handed her a glass of orange juice. She drank it and it seemed to help. Now she didn't want the coffee.

"Where are my clothes?"

"You really need them? I like you naked."

"It's hard to try to go anywhere naked, love."

"Take the day off. I'm just going to hang around here."

"I need to get some stuff done."

She stood up but grew dizzy. She sat back down.

"What's wrong with me?"

"You should go back to bed for a bit. Get some more sleep. You catching the flu or something?"

She tried to stand again but had to grab the table to steady herself. He was up and beside her.

"Come on," he said softly.

She hung on to him and he helped her back to the bedroom and back to bed.

"Man, am I fucked up."

He unbuttoned the shirt. She feebly protested.

"Edward, I'm not up for it."

Then he was on top of her. She didn't have the strength to push him away or get away from him. This was turning her on even though she didn't want to be. Why was this happening? He was as hard as a rock. He was inside. He had promised not to. She tried to hit him, but her arms were lead and all she could do was squirm.

"Edward, stop!" She was crying, but she was far away and it came out like a whimper.

He just went on and on forever and then he came. He was off her as quickly as he had gotten on.

"I'm sorry, baby. I couldn't help myself."

"You promised."

"It will be all right."

He tucked her in.

"Sleep a little. I'll call the doctor."

The room spun around and she thought she might throw up, but she passed out.

\* \* \*

When she woke up again it was evening. The sun was setting outside. She was groggy and sore all over. It seemed a big effort to just sit up in bed. She was dressed in a fluffy see-through baby doll nightie. She couldn't remember putting it on. Was it something Edward had given her? All she remembered was his love-making that morning. She hoped the baby was all right. Her crotch was tender. She couldn't remember it hurting that much or them going at it too long.

She made an effort to get her feet over the side and on to the floor. The wood was cold. The evening air was cool. The thing she had on offered no warmth whatsoever. She started shivering. She tried to pull the bedspread off to wrap herself in but it was too big and heavy for her to manage it. She could hear the television somewhere in the house. She tried calling his name, but couldn't muster much of a voice. She stood, rather shakily, and went to find him.

She had chills. He was sitting on the large sofa in his living room watching a football game. He was snorting a line of cocaine on the coffee table in front of him. She went in to him.

"Edward," she said weakly.

"You're awake."

"I'm freezing. Is there a robe or something I can put on?"

"Come and sit next to me. I'll warm you up."

"Seriously."

He got up. "Sit. You still don't look too good. I'll find you something."

He came back with large shawl. It was fancy and looked like a Mexican senora wrap, but at least it was warm. He put his hand over her hard nipple for a second. She pushed him away and he laughed.

"I'll make some tea."

She sank back into the couch and gazed at the television. The game was just noise. She felt like she was dying. She couldn't ever remember having the flu this badly. Maybe he would call a doctor for her or take her to the hospital.

He came back with the tea.

"Maybe you should take me to the hospital," she said.

"Have some tea and we'll go. You've not had any liquid since this morning. I don't want you passing out in the car." He held the cup for her and tried to help her drink. She shoved it away, making it fall from his hand and spill on the carpet. The cup didn't break.

"You are fucking drugging me!"

"You're sick," he said. "I think I'll just take you back to bed."

She shoved him away and got to her feet. She'd find her clothes in the bedroom and get out of here. He grabbed her wrist.

"Please," she said.

He pulled her to him and she couldn't seem to resist him, though she wanted to. He kissed her and stroked her forehead. She was sweaty. He parted the shawl that she held over her bosom and began caressing her breasts.

"Edward, please."

His hand was on her crotch. She had no panties on. He was massaging her gently there. It ached.

"Stop!"

He put his arm around her and walked her back to the bedroom. He pushed her down on the bed, and she was hitting him, but it had no effect. She was too weak. He tied her wrists to the headboard. He blindfolded her. She kicked at him. Then there was something else he was putting around her ankles. Metal. Her feet were shackled!

"God damn you! Let me go!"

"I'll leave you to think about things. We'll talk in the morning."

And he left her there.

\* \* \*

She slept badly. Every time she turned she was reminded of where she was. There were several times during the night that she would awaken, suddenly sit upright, sure that he was in the room. But he wasn't. Another bout with his body would make her try to injure him in some way. It was probably the reason he wasn't here sleeping. In the early morning hours she just fell asleep, exhausted, and didn't wake again until the sunlight was in the windows. She felt better. He was sitting nearby reading the morning paper. She pulled herself up to sitting. She slid her knees up and felt the shackles under the covers. She was still in the baby doll outfit.

"So what's the idea?" she asked rather feebly.

"You're awake. Good."

He got up and brought a bed tray with plates covered to keep them warm. And coffee and orange juice. She shuddered involuntarily when he sat it before her and brushed her arm.

"I thought it was a good idea to feed you. You haven't eaten in a day and a half."

"Why should I take any of this? You've been drugging me."

"Because you're hungry?"

He was right. She couldn't stop herself. She was ravenous.

"There's nothing in any of it, so don't worry," he said.

"I'm getting out of here."

"Relax. The circumstances might grow on you."

"You're nuts. This is kidnapping."

"You came of your own free will. Nobody is knocking on my door looking for you. The sheriff is on my payroll."

She ate and tried to think about a way out.

"I've got business today. So I thought I'd leave you here to let it all sink in. It could be very cushy here for you if you were willing to accommodate me a little. You could have anything you wanted. Your child will get the best of everything."

"What makes you think I want to be forced?"

"But you want it in some way or you wouldn't have allowed me to get this far."

"You drugged me at dinner."

"Perhaps I should have done your wrists too? Maybe stuck something up your ass?"

Daydee said nothing. She couldn't look at him. She would cry and beg if she opened her mouth. She was still achy and sore and hungover.

"Good. Well, I'll be home by five. We can talk more then. The housekeeper will be here at ten. You can hide from her or you can let her make you lunch. She will wait on you hand and foot, except for driving you anywhere or getting you out the gate. She doesn't have keys."

"You've done this before."

He nodded. He started to kiss her forehead but she jerked away. He left.

* * *

After she heard the car drive away, she forced herself to get up. She was very wobbly and almost fell over. The flimsy little nightie was just irritating and she was cold. She thought to get into his closet to see if she could find something to wear so she shuffled over to what appeared to be closet doors. The shackles were heavy and constrained her walk. The closets were all locked. She came back and managed to pull the comforter all the way off the bed. Then she had to sit down and rest and catch her breath. The blanket that was now exposed was just as large but wasn't as heavy or bulky. She managed to get it free and wrapped it around herself. It was a lot of fabric to trail, but at least she wasn't cold.

She was as weak as a kitten. She had to sit down and rest again. Damn him! She hoped the baby was still ok. She was ready to lay down again and sleep, but resisted the urge. She finally got to her feet once more and shuffled out to the living room. She made it to the couch and stopped to rest again. There had to be some way out of this. Maybe when the maid appeared, she could figure something out.

She finally got up again and explored the house, looking for the controls for the front gate or anything that could help. There were no tools to be found – no way to cut the shackles off. No keys anywhere. Nothing that could be used as a weapon, except for some smallish kitchen knives. Not even a telephone. The front of the house was locked up, but she could go out to the pool and there was a small gate that she could get over by getting on a chair. – that would get her out front. There was no way through the gate. She went back to the couch to rest.

A car came in the gate and parked in front. It was the maid. She came in the front and locked it behind her. Daydee hid her shackles under the blanket. The woman came into the living room.

"Good morning," Daydee said to her.

The woman looked away without answering. She was a short Hispanic woman in her forties. She looked so much like those illegal women Daydee had helped it was saddening.

"You know this is against the law, don't you? You could go to jail."

"No lo sé."

Daydee shook her head.

"I have money I can give you to help me get out of here," she said suddenly.

"No puedo eviter."

"A thousand?"

She hesitated but looked scared. "Sin dinero," she mumbled.

"I'm pregnant, for God's sake."

"No puedo eviter."

"Can you find me some clothes to wear. I'm cold."

"No lo sé."

Daydee waited until the woman was cleaning the bathroom off the master bedroom. She got up and shuffled into the kitchen. She found a waste basket and wadded paper towels into it, made a wand out of several sheets and then turned on all the burners of the stove. She took off her blanket and wadded it up on the stove top. Starting her wand on fire, she dropped it into the waste basket and carried it all out to dump on the couch. There was a good blaze going on the stove and a little one started on the couch. Smoke drifted out of the kitchen.

She went outside to the pool area, pulled a chair over to the gate and jumped up. All of this was in slow motion because of the shackles. Balancing on her bare bottom on the steel rail of the gate, she swung her feet and ankles over ahead of her. The shackles got momentarily caught, but she was able to get them loose. She tumbled down to the concrete on the other side, bruising her knees and hands. She got up as quickly as she could. The woman would be on her. She wouldn't be able to run away from her. Turning the corner of the house, she followed the walkway around to the front. She wasn't sure what to do now. If she tried the car the woman would probably spot her and grab her. She was naked for the whole world to see. The car windows were open. The keys were not going to be in the car, but there might be something in the trunk to cover herself with. The front windows of the house were filled with smoke. She waddled over and crouched behind the car and made her way on hands and knees to the driver's side. She found the trunk release and crawled back to it.

There were sirens off in the distance. The maid had called – she knew where the phone had been hidden. The blaze was winning. There was a dirty blanket in the trunk. She wrapped it around her and shuffled over to the bushes beside the gate. She got there and managed to hide just as the woman came running out the front door. The gates swung open. Daydee waited. The woman would see her. But she wasn't doing anything. The sirens blared louder.

Daydee stood and tried to make it out. The woman was letting her leave.

"You should have taken the money," Daydee called.

The sirens were upon them – just at the end of the drive. Daydee scrambled off the driveway as the tires of the big truck screeched by her. She fell on her knees in the grass and scrambled for the bushes. No one saw her, she hoped.

The firemen were out of the truck. Had they hit the woman by accident? It was hard to see. They were all crowded around her, either keeping her on the ground as a precaution or they were trying to treat her injuries. A stretcher was brought up and they moved her onto it and carried her out of the way. Smoke was rolling out of the house at this point. The trucks pulled on inside the gate and the firemen went to work on the house. No one had noticed Daydee.

She crawled away carefully until she thought it was safe to stand, and she began to shuffle out to the highway. The whole thing was too crazy to try to go to the firemen for help. The shackles would just fit in with the other rumors the town already had about her kinky sex with the accountant. The maid might be awake and would tell them she started the fire. Her word against Edward's maid wasn't going to fly in this town. She had a bit of a distance to go to get home. She would struggle to the next place that she could remain somewhat hidden and then look up and down the road and then try to hurry to another spot to hide.

A familiar car came down the road. She tried to hide, but it pulled up beside her.

"Deidra." It was Winston. "Come on, get in the car. I'll take you home."

She struggled across to him and climbed in. He looked at her as she pulled the blanket closer around her.

"Don't say a word," she told him. She was tearing up. "Thank you for showing up."

"I've been out looking for you since yesterday. I have the rest of the money for the plot. I told you not to get together with him."

"Guess what, you were right."

He helped her into her house. The front was locked, but she had hidden a key under a rock out by the street. Winston was kind. He found her a robe to put on and brought her a cup of tea and went to work on the shackles with the hacksaw. It was slow going, but he finally got them off after fussing about an hour. A hammer and screwdriver were needed too. He tried hard not to cut her or bruise her. After she was free, she went to take a shower and nursed her scraped knees and palms and elbows. She dressed and came out to find that he had made them some lunch – tomato soup and grilled cheese sandwiches.

They ate.

"So what do you think he'll do next?" she asked.

"He'll be over here. He will want you back."

"He's really sick. He wanted me unconscious to fuck me. What kind of fun is that?"

"It's like the first time," Winston said quietly.

"I tried to convince myself that it was something else. Butter wouldn't melt in his mouth." She wanted to make a wisecrack, but she couldn't think of any. She sighed.

"I guess it's a war now," she said.

\* \* \*

After lunch, she had Winston drive her to the dog pound where she adopted the biggest meanest animal she could find. It was a mongrel male German Shepherd. They went to a pet store and bought a dog house and chain and food and returned to install the dog on the front porch with chain that would let it get almost to the sidewalk. The dog did what it was supposed to do. A car driving by sending it running out, barking its head off. She hugged it and gave it treats. She knew she needed the shotgun out at the cemetery. And she suddenly realized that she hadn't seen her father in a couple of days. Shit! He was probably starving. Loading the dog into the back of the pickup, she had Winston drive her to a McDonald's and then out to the cemetery so she could bring him dinner. Winston waited at the car. The dog took to it like he had been riding around in the back of a truck his whole life. She was almost tempted to let him off the leash, but was afraid he might run off. She bought lunch for it and herself as well and walked it down to the grove of trees. Her father was just sitting on a log as if it was a bus stop and he was waiting for the bus to come along now any minute. Her father just accepted the bag being handed to him. He seemed intrigued by the dog. She unwrapped the other hamburger and laid it down for the dog and it was gulped down in one swallow. She put down the fries and those disappeared immediately too.

"Sorry, I couldn't bring lunch for a couple of days. I was under the weather."

"Sicky baby. Wail and tale."

"You like my new dog?"

Her father reached out and scratched the dog's head. The dog stuck its nose at her father's hamburger. He held it out of reach.

"Him sniff and sniff. Good sniff. I like good sniffs."

"We need to name him," she said.

"Sniffy."

"How about a boy's name," she said, laughing. "I'm starting to make no sense myself."

"Snuffer."

"Snuffer, it is. I think he likes you."

"He likes sniffs."

She and Winston took the dog back to the house to feed it a real lunch. It gobbled up a big bowl of food as quickly as it did the hamburger.

"Do you want me to stay tonight?" Winston asked her as she was putting the dog back on its chain out front. The dog was back at leaping about at the end of his chain.

"What are you expecting?" she asked.

"You know. Edward. I'm trying to make amends."

She looked him up and down.

"I'm sorry for what's happened to you," he said.

"All right."

\* \* \*

Daydee made him a bed on the couch. She didn't really expect to be able to sleep much anyway and wore her robe to bed just in case. The dog woke her up in the middle of the night. He was barking his head off. Grabbing the shotgun in the corner, she went out to the living room. Winston was awake as well. He looked lost like he wasn't sure what to do. Some protector. She snuck a peek out the front drapes. Edward was standing out front, just beyond the length of the dog's chain. She could shoot him now and get it over with. He didn't look armed. It was a warm night. He didn't have a jacket to hide a pistol in.

"It's him?" Winston asked, rubbing his eyes.

She nodded.

"What do you want to do?" he asked.

"Call the sheriff."

She opened the front door and went outside with the shotgun. The dog was leaping and barking at him. He wasn't even flinching.

"Winston is inside. He's calling the sheriff."

"You wrecked my kitchen. Do you realize what it's going to cost to fix it?"

"Edward, go away."

He reached behind his back and pulled a revolver out. Aiming at the dog's head, he squeezed the trigger. It collapsed, the top of its head opened and splattered.

"Christ!" she screamed.

She fired the shotgun at his foot. Her aim was off, it hit his shoe, but there was no blood. He jumped back.

"Drop the gun or you are dead!" she shouted.

He stopped, stared her down and put the gun away behind his back and then turned and walked across the street to his car. She could kill him now. Now. He drove away. She went over to where the dog lay. She bent down to stroke its side. God. This was her fault.

She went back inside to wait for the sheriff or someone to show up. Winston had called and got the night switchboard operator. About a half hour later, the sheriff himself drove up. He was out of uniform. And didn't seem to be in much of a hurry. Daydee and Winston went out to meet him where the dog lay. She told him what happened.

"There was a fire over at Edward's house. You don't know anything about that, do you?" he asked.

"No."

"Edward will just say the dog attacked him."

"The dog was chained up. It was at the end of the length right here." Daydee told him. "You really aren't going to do anything about this?"

"This is a small town. People get worked up. A mail box gets trashed. Somebody's tires get slashed. Lots of dogs get shot here. You want to file a complaint, come down to the office in the morning and we'll file it. It didn't work out between you two?"

"No."

"Well, if the smoke clears, I'd still like to take you out. I'm a good guy."

"You are kidding."

"Sorry about your dog."

He climbed back in his car and left. She asked Winston to help her throw the dog in the garbage can. They did it, but she couldn't sleep for the rest of the night. She got up and pulled her suitcase out of the closet. In the bottom was a ragged hardback copy of *Gone With The Wind*. It had sat on the top of her refrigerator in New Orleans for years. Men wouldn't touch it. Except John. He reached for it once and she quickly told him not to touch it, that it had belonged to her mother. Inside, in a custom cutout in the pages, was the little Ruger 38. It had never been fired. The bullets were in a velvet jewelry bag underneath the gun. She loaded it and figured out how to switch the safety off. The gun had been a present. From a big Italian who was probably Mafia. She put it under her pillow and tried to sleep. She dreamt of the dog.

## Chapter fourteen

Winston left after breakfast, saying he'd check in on her later in the day.

"The dog wasn't your fault," he said as he was out the door.

She called the doctor's office and made an emergency appointment. She lied about spotting, so they would take her and not send her to whatever they called an emergency room here. Whatever Edward had given her was a concern and the penetration wasn't a great thing either. She carried the shotgun to the pickup when she left to go, feeling a little foolish. To have to lock it in the truck while she was inside seeing the doctor now seemed odd. She never locked the truck anymore.

It was a different doctor. Older and seemingly a little absent-minded. He told her everything looked good. The baby had a strong heartbeat. The ultrasound was fine. She was floating in there as happy as a clam. Blood was drawn and they would let her know the results. She didn't repeat anything about spotting, so she guessed the receptionist hadn't bothered to write it down for him. She was sure he would call her later and lecture her about drug use.

There was a fleeting glance of what she thought was Edward's car on her way home, so she circled the block but didn't see any trace of him. She would shoot to kill next time. The phone was ringing when she came in. It was Winston. His wife had died that morning.

"God, I'm so sorry," she told him.

"We knew it was coming."

"When do you want the funeral?"

"I guess next Saturday. We don't have to wait. There isn't any family to wait for."

"I'm so sorry," she said again.

"Hey. I have to go."

So, she needed another burial vault. Winston hadn't thought about buying one and it had slipped her mind as well. But it was expected. She would worry about the expense later. He would need a marker as well, which they hadn't discussed either. If it had been anyone else, she would have called them back. She called the place in Terre Haute and ordered one for pick up the next day. Who was going to help her unload it? There was Sean. It was going to be too much for her now. She called him as well.

\* \* \*

This was a big to do. Winston's wife had been a teacher at the high school for years. Everyone had known her and loved her. The plot was close to the drive that circled around the cemetery so she wasn't too nervous about screwing up the lawn. She wouldn't have to go very far off the drive. This would be the first one without anyone helping. She had hired Sean to come over and unload the vault and get it into the ground. He had offered to do the grave as well, but she would be damned to let him play told you so and lord it over her about how he was the goddamn expert. She had practiced some more after they had unearthed the last of the Mexicans. So she was up early, chugging down the lane to open the grave. An hour later, it was done, a perfect hole. All the soil piled on a tarp a discreet distance away. She chugged back to the shed in time to meet Sean. They drove her pickup back down and he grunted over the vault and the railing and the winch to lower the casket as she set out folding chairs. Winston had said to expect fifty people.

She left Sean and walked back over to the office to rest and draw up her marker order. She was sweaty and dirty and was generally feeling like the Goodyear Blimp. Edward's car pulled up in front of the office. She grabbed the shotgun from the alcove and lay it across her desk. He came up to the screen and knocked.

"All right, come in!" she said.

He stepped in.

"Yes?" she asked him.

"I came to see if you had any second thoughts?"

"You killed my dog. I have lots of thoughts. None about being nice to you."

"Well, maybe there would be a better time to talk. The damage to my house was a lesson well taken."

"Edward, go away."

"Who is the old man you stashed away down the hill?"

She picked up the shotgun.

"Excuse me, Miss Deidre," Sean said from just outside the screen door. "You all right?"

God bless the asshole.

"I will kill you, Edward. You leave well enough alone."

"I'll come back at a more convenient time."

"Go buy a blow-up doll and paint the eyes closed. That's all you need."

"That's not true."

But he turned and left. Sean came in after he was climbing in his car.

"You all right, missy?"

"Not at all," she said. You go fuck yourself as well, was what she wanted to say, but didn't. "Thanks for your help today."

\*\*\*

The service started at the funeral home on Saturday morning. Winston asked her to go with him, but she felt that was going to be too much. And she wanted to make sure everything was in order at the cemetery when the casket arrived. All the ladies of the church were going to be there. It would be enough that they came and whispered. She was out at the grave site when her father wandered up the little road and came to look over the scene. She went over to him.

"Daddy, there's going to be a lot of people coming here very soon. You understand?"

"Of course, we zoo everything and have many hands."

"You want to go back and I'll go bring you breakfast in bed? It's Father's Day."

She didn't think it really was, but she wasn't sure. She just thought it might get through to him somehow and get him out of the area.

"Paddy's day, day? Way way. I'd like a cake that big."

"Ok, you go back and I'll be right there."

He seemed to get the idea and ambled back down the road. She climbed in the truck for a McDonald's run. The hearse was just arriving by the time she returned. There were several cars parked nearby and about twenty people already assembled near the open grave. Her father was standing in the drive waving his arms at them. Everyone was politely ignoring him. She parked and brought the McDonald's bags over to him. He grabbed them both as if he was starving and was digging in the sack for something to pop into his mouth. Daydee took him by the arm and he jumped. But he didn't pull away. He let himself be guided back down the hill and through to his burrow. He ate all the way.

"Now you stay here," Daydee said. "Please understand."

He nodded and sat down on his log. By the time she got back up the hill, the minister was beginning the service. Winston was in front. She didn't feel up to being the center of attention which was what would happen if she tried to join him, so she just stood in the back. The ladies from the church were there and were whispering snide remarks about her to each other. She didn't have to hear what they were actually saying – their eyes and the phony smiles gave it all away. She was hot and sweaty and sat down when she got to the outside row of chairs. She wished she had stayed home. The preacher spoke on and on it seemed. Jack! It hadn't registered with her that it was him preaching at them. The whole day was a distraction. An angel wouldn't have anything on Rev. Jack. He acted as if he was as pure as snow. His wife and Sarah were there, but neither of them looked in her direction. Winston was crying. Edward wasn't around, thank God. As the service went on the sheriff wandered over and sat down beside her.

"Who was that homeless guy?" he whispered.

"I don't know his name," Daydee said. "I give him some work once in a while. He just shows up from time to time. He usually comes in from the front entrance."

"Well, if he gives you any trouble, give us a call."

"Edward is hassling me."

"I can speak to him, if you'd like."

She looked at him. He just looked back without blinking.

"Excuse me," she said, getting up.

She moved to sit next to her sharecropper and his wife. They, at least, nodded to her.

The service was finally over and people began to leave. She couldn't because she had to lower the casket and fill in the grave. Jack and his wife walked out without looking at her. The ladies from their church were snooty about walking by her. Sarah offered her hand. Daydee stood up.

"I hear you've been having adventures," Sarah said.

"You were right, what can I say? I always manage to do the wrong thing."

"I'd like to invite you to a quilting bee we are starting."

"You are serious?"

"It had been bantered about to make one for your baby... before all that stuff about Mat. Well, the urge to hang out and drink and prick our fingers until they bleed is still a driving force. The idea is that if we invite you, then the women we don't want to see, won't show up."

"I don't know how to sew."

"Neither do I, but what are you going to do? I don't want to hang out in bars."

"All right."

Sarah squeezed her hand. Daydee finally decided that Winston was going to stand there forever so she sat down again. He finally turned and realized she was there. They were the only two left. He came over and sat down beside her.

"Thanks for being patient with me," he said. "You need some help finishing up?"

"Don't you have family to go to tonight?"

"No, she had no relatives alive. My brother in California hasn't spoken to me in years. We had no children."

"Won't it be odd, cleaning up after your own wife's funeral?"

"Nothing much is odd anymore."

She handed him her truck keys.

"If you'll bring it down, that will be a big help."

While he was doing that, she cranked the coffin down into the grave and took apart the frame that had held it. He was back.

"We need to load all of this into the truck along with all the chairs."

They began carrying things over.

"I think your presence is aggravating my daddy," she said.

"I imagine it would. He was always extremely jealous of your mother and it just got worse the crazier he got."

"How long was this thing with my mother going on?" Daydee asked.

Winston stopped and looked at her.

"Before you were born," he said quietly.

He turned and went after the folding chairs. It was a few minutes before they were back at the truck at the same time.

"I often wondered if you were really my daughter," he said.

Daydee stared at him.

"You gang raped your own daughter?"

He turned red.

"I didn't know who you were."

"Winston, the whole fucking town knew who I was! I didn't realize it then. But there's hardware store clerks in this goddamn place that are still drooling. You have to be the most incompetent evil man I know. I'm not your frigging daughter, all right!"

"I guess I'm stupid."

"You can say that again and again." Then she caught herself. It was his wife's funeral.

He went back for more folding chairs. They worked in silence. After the truck was loaded with everything, they drove it back up to the shed and unloaded it. She thanked him for his help.

"What else is there to do?" he asked.

"I need to go close the grave."

"Would you care to go to dinner after? My treat?" he said.

She shook her head and he looked crestfallen.

"All right, your treat. Why don't we just do Bob's Big Boy. I'll meet you there. At five?"

He smiled. She climbed in the backhoe, still shaking her head at herself.

\* \* \*

By the time she filled in the grave and parked the backhoe by the shed, it was well into the afternoon. She walked down to check on her father before going home to clean up. The earlier funeral hadn't drawn him up to the grounds. It was Winston. There is just too much shit that has gone on here to figure it out. His shopping cart was gone from its usual spot.

"Daddy!" she called.

Nothing. There was a trail through the weeds made by the cart. He decided to hide further away? Or he had decided to leave? She walked along the trail he had left. It wandered over a hill and came out on a paved road. She looked both directions, but there was no sign of anything. One way was into town, the other was just out into the farmland. She decided he would head for town. There would be dumpsters and people to panhandle. She hurried back to her truck. This was ridiculous. This whole day was just too much work.

As she slowly went up Main Street, she spotted Edward coming out of his office and walking toward his car. She thought of stopping to confront him about her father, but thought better of it. He wouldn't have bothered with the shopping cart if he had something to do with his disappearance. And if he didn't know, she wasn't going to be the one to tell him. He did spot her driving by though. Stupid move, slowing down.

She went up and down the streets, but didn't find any trace. Then she circled through the alleys. And around the grocery stores' back entrances. Around the dumpsters. Still nothing. It was getting into dusk. She wondered if he had gone the opposite direction on the road after all, out into the farmland. Then she found the shopping cart. It was laying on its side behind a drugstore – the blanket she had given him, hanging out of it like a dog's tongue. She stopped and went through the stuff in the cart. It appeared to be his junk. If she left it, somebody else would probably pick through it, even if it was mostly garbage. She quickly threw it into a pile in the back of her pickup and covered it with the blanket. God, did it smell. She could steal him another cart if need be. There were a couple of teenagers down the alley, sitting on the curb, smoking. They might have seen something. When she stopped beside them, they quickly hid the joint and started walking away.

"Guys, I'm looking for a homeless guy, not you!"

"We don't know anything," the taller one said over his shoulder.

"Twenty dollars?"

They looked at each and stopped. She dug in her purse.

"I'm trying to find the old homeless crazy guy that had the shopping cart back there."

"Yeah, the cops took him. In the back of their patrol car."

She handed the boy the twenty.

"Was it the sheriff or the Paris Police?"

"It was a sheriff's car."

"Thanks."

\* \* \*

Shit. She hurried to the jailhouse. God, how she hated jails. There were just too many lockups in New Orleans when she was young. Too many ham-handed officers and guards. Too many quickies to get out of being taken away. She parked and went to the front desk.

"I understand my father was picked up this afternoon."

"What's the name?" The girl was in uniform.

"Donald McIntire, but you wouldn't have gotten that unless you found some ID on him. He's really crazy."

"You have ID?"

Daydee handed her the Louisiana ID, not thinking. She had a driver's license from Illinois now. She handed over that as well.

"You have something that says who he is?"

"Nothing handy. There might be a birth certificate in my mother's records. But that might take a while to find."

"I really don't know how we can help you. We need proof of relationship."

"Is Sheriff Turner in?"

"He won't be able to help you anymore than I can."

"He knows me."

"Please wait," she said and disappeared with her ID.

Daydee wandered around the little reception area. This was not going well. This meant more payback. More dates? God. The sheriff came out.

"Hello again," he smiled. "So, what's this about this guy being your father?"

"He is."

"That's not what you told me this morning."

"I've been trying to take care of him and figure out what to do with him. He's really crazy. I figured it was better if no one knew about him. He's been living in the woods behind the cemetery and I can't get him in the truck to take him anywhere better."

"Your father is dead, Deidre. He's buried out there beside your mother."

"I don't know who you people put in that hole, but this is my father."

The girl at the desk looked away when Daydee glanced in her direction. The glance wasn't lost on the sheriff. He ran his big hand over his scalp.

"Deidre, you don't want to start a big ruckus."

"So you know who is in that grave?"

He eyed her.

"Release him to her," he told the girl. "Bring me the release form, I'll process it myself." He smiled weakly at Daydee. "Nice to see you again."

She sat down to wait. About forty minutes later, a guard escorted him out to her. Her father was wild-eyed and trembling all over. There was a good chance that he would just run down the street once they got outside. Could she get him in the truck? She took his arm and directed him out the door. He wasn't resisting. When she opened the passenger door, he climbed in. She locked him in and ran around to her side. Driving away from there as quick as she could, she wasn't sure where to take him. This was her chance. It would soon be too cold for him out there in the woods.

She took him through McDonald's and handed him the bag. He was eating cautiously, as if he was afraid the bag might be grabbed away at any second. It was almost comical. He was Charlie Chaplin throwing glances her way, scared like a puppy might be.

"You are coming with me today," she told him.

He let her take him by the arm again as she got him out of the truck in front of the house. Beneath the big oak tree, he stopped dead and looked up into its bare branches against the night sky.

"Come on, Daddy."

"Such a place to nest!"

She tugged on his arm and he looked at her.

"Pretty."

He came in. All right, he was a child, she told herself. She would treat him as one. Leading him into the bathroom, she started undressing him. His clothes were stiff and dirty and oily. His socks were glued to his skin. She was afraid of pulling skin off with each sock. His body was bad, liver spots all over his feet and ankles. Scratches and scars on his back and arms. Skinny. Slack and sagging tummy and butt. She had never seen an eighty-year-old man naked. Never had a client this old.

She turned on the shower and tested the water and pushed him. Soaping him up and rinsing him left her soaked herself. She shampooed his scraggly hair. She pulled him out and dried them both off and gave him her white robe to wear. He let himself be led to the living room where she plopped him down on the couch in front of the television. Cartoons seemed to be the best bet. She made sandwiches in the kitchen. He seemed resigned to his fate.

He ate again.

"You are going to stay here tonight," she told him.

As he didn't appear to be interested in resisting, she left him and threw his clothes in the washer and brought a blanket and pillow back. He wrapped himself up and snuggled down on the couch on the pillow she had fluffed up for him and fell instantly asleep.

There was knock at the door. Winston! She opened it, thinking to herself that she was being stupid, it could be anyone. Winston was standing there with a bag of Chinese take-out.

"God, I'm sorry. Come on in. My father wandered off and was picked up by the cops. I just got him here."

He came in and sat the bag on the kitchen table.

"That's why I brought take-out," he whispered. "I figured something came up. We can still eat."

She didn't have the heart to tell him she had just eaten. They took out the boxes and opened them up to dish out on plates. Daydee picked at hers. It actually tasted pretty good.

"You sure you don't know who is buried in my father's grave?" she asked quietly. "I just blackmailed my father out because the sheriff apparently knows who is buried there."

"Honestly, I don't."

"Who would you guess it is?" she asked.

"I think you better leave well enough alone."

"Winston, I'm going to have a hard time proving that this is my father if he is legally dead. How do I get him treatment?"

"It's probably Edward's father," he whispered.

"Really?"

Winston nodded.

Suddenly, her father jumped Winston and knocked him to the floor. He had Winston under him and was beating him with his fists. Winston cried out. And tried to protect himself. Daydee pulled on her father but couldn't get him off.

"Daddy!"

She grabbed the spray nozzle from the sink and turned on the faucet on all the way and spayed him in the face with water. He released Winston to cover his eyes. He was moaning. She pushed him over and got Winston up to his feet. Her father was squirming on the floor trying avoid the cold water.

"Go," Daydee screamed at Winston. "He remembers you!"

Winston ran out the front door. She let up on the sprayer. Was he going to attack her now? The kitchen was a mess. Chinese food and water everywhere. She backed away to the sink, with the spray gun in hand. Her father scrambled up to his hands and knees and crawled back to the couch and wrapped himself in the blanket again. He was shivering and looked soaked to the bone. After catching her breath, she replaced the nozzle and went to close and lock the front door. Her father seemed over his rage. She cautiously moved past him to go get towels. When she came back, she threw one towel over his head as she went into the kitchen to sop up the floor.

"Thanks," he said.

Such a damn normal thing to say! He hid in his blanket with the towel still over his face.

# Chapter fifteen

There wasn't a lock on her bedroom door, so she took a kitchen chair in to lean it against the knob. It wouldn't really stop him, but she would hear him try to get in. Locking up everything she could, she took the keys to bed with her and slept with them under her pillow. Her dreams were odd and dark and scary. Gunshot wounds, maggots in some homeless guy's wrapped up legs. She didn't want to remember them. Do you give your unborn child nightmares? She finally got up about five, giving up. He was snoring on the couch. She locked him in and went for a walk around the neighborhood.

There was not a soul around. It was still dark and chilly. Her little area didn't seem to have children about. No toys in yards. No fences to keep them from wandering off. No dogs to speak of. Occasionally, one would bark from inside a house. One kitchen light came on and a grandma type was making coffee in her house robe. The young families must be in the newer houses. She'd have to look. She wanted hers to have other kids around to play with. Not like her childhood. The sky began to grow light. A diehard cardinal was busy in a bush.

He, at least, won't be freezing his rear off out there. She came back and found him still knocked out on the couch. Checking the dryer, she looked at his clothes. They would have to be washed again with lots of bleach. She threw them in the trash. The Goodwill was open now.

She'd chance it leaving him alone. Locking him in, she went off to buy him new clothes. It took a while. Once she was there, she decided she might as well buy him several of everything. When she returned at noon, he was up and pacing back and forth from the living room to the kitchen and pulling on his hair. The McDonald's lunch helped. He sat and gobbled. She brought in her bags of clothing and then gathered up the stuff from his shopping cart that was still in the back of the truck and carried that in as well, leaving it in its bundle in the blanket on the kitchen table.

"I've brought you some new duds. Your clothes were too old. You know how to dress yourself?" she asked him.

She threw underwear and a pair of jeans at him. He managed them ok. The shirt was a problem. He let her help with that and a belt. He actually looked pretty good. Tempted to try running a comb through his messy strands of hair, she decided it might freak him out. She would have to sneak up on him with a pair of scissors to trim him when he was asleep. Then she suddenly realized his beard stubble was hardly there. Had he been shaving all this time? Weird. You'd imagine he would slit his own throat or something. She had shoes and socks, but she didn't give them to him. She was afraid he might get the idea to run away.

"You look good. Almost like I remember you."

He was quiet.

"Cat got your tongue?" she asked.

"Thumb got your tongue?"

Ok.

"I brought your stuff from your cart."

He just looked at her. Bringing the bundle from the kitchen, she put it all out in front of him on the coffee table. There was a lot of trash. She put the blanket on the floor and tossed the empty bottles there. The cans as well. In a bag, she found a cigar box. He was interested in that. Inside were some photos and some postcards. The photos were of Paris, but there were no people in them, only store fronts and houses and a tree.

"Did you take these?" she asked.

He shrugged. The postcards were not written on or mailed. Five of them were of the French Quarter in New Orleans.

"Where did you get these?" she asked. "Were you in New Orleans?"

He shrugged again. It would be too weird if he had been there. She decided that maybe these were things he had just taken out of people's trash or found lying on the street somewhere. In another bag was a camera. It looked like there was an uncompleted roll in it.

There were a lot of odd bottles, medical prescriptions, hand lotion, a small ketchup: all empty. She added these to the throw away pile and then retrieved the one prescription bottle that had a pharmacy name from Main Street in Paris. It had her father's name on it. It was dated from December of the previous year. It was Chlorpromazine.

"So I know this one is yours," she said.

"Snowy mommy snow mama," he told her.

She called the pharmacy. They gave her the name and number of the doctor that had prescribed it. In a few minutes she was on the phone with the doctor. Small towns.

"Oh, yes," he told her. "I treated him. Your mother had brought him in. He didn't keep his follow up appointments, or request refills from the pharmacy. And your mother died. I guess I thought some other arrangements had been made for his treatment, or something else had taken place."

"Can I bring him in?"

"Certainly. Let me give you back to my receptionist. I'll ask her to get him in this week."

And she made an appointment for the next day.

"You were hanging out with Mom?" she asked her father.

"Snowy mama."

"Snowy mama," she repeated back to him. "Why are you making sense suddenly?"

\* \* \*

Her father was amazingly docile the next morning when she loaded him in the truck to go to the doctor. There was no conversation between them. His responses were all just one or two words that didn't make much sense, so she just got tired of trying to talk to him. What did he know? Did he understand she was getting him help? There had to be something to his calm cooperation. He followed her direction out of the car and into the waiting room and then into the exam room without any hesitation.

The doctor was her age, gray hair tousled. Overworked probably. The examination went quickly. He ordered blood tests.

"It's good to see you again, Mr. McIntyre," he said after the exam. "Bring him to my office next door, when you have him dressed."

He patted her father on the shoulder.

They were seated in overstuffed chairs in front of his large desk. There were medical records and journals in piles all in a small mound on the side where her father sat. She wanted to move her father over so he could see the doctor as he spoke, but the chairs looked immobile.

"So, I'm renewing the prescription for the Chlorpromazine. You should see quick results on that front in just a few days. We had his hallucinations under control before your mother passed. Deidre, I want you to understand that your father has terminal acute lymphocytic leukemia. We had guessed that he might have another year, but he is well past that prediction. When he was cognitive, he declined all of the more drastic forms of intervention, such as radiation or chemotherapies. I can give you options for care." He handed her a booklet. "Please look at this and call me with any questions you have. Bring him back in two weeks."

"Ok," was all she could get out. She wanted to cry.

They stopped at McDonald's before she took him home. Locking him in, she ran back to fill the prescriptions.

This was making her dizzy. Her old bitch mother had taken him in and was trying to help him? Why would she do something like that?

\* \* \*

She kept watching and waiting to see what was going to happen to him. It appeared he was having trouble talking. She would try to get him to say something, but he would stutter and say something she couldn't understand and she would ask him to repeat it and he would just shake his head. The television was perpetually on and he seemed content to be parked in front of it. He did whatever she directed him to do. The second day brought his ability to stand in the shower and wash himself without her help. The third morning he dressed himself.

The pamphlet about the leukemia was helpful, but depressing. He was going to die. Pretty soon. There was a list of symptoms and she racked her brains trying to remember if she had noticed them. Shortness of breath. Nosebleeds. Easy bruising. It had been difficult to see anything under the grime of living out there in the bushes. Why hadn't she looked through his stuff earlier? Wasted time. Why hadn't her mother left a letter or written her in New Orleans? Or told someone else besides the doctor he was here?

She was going stir crazy. She didn't feel right leaving him. The nagging awareness of the body buried out there under his marker didn't make her happy. Edward and Jack and probably the sheriff were in on it, with Winston as an accomplice. So this was just the new version of what she encountered upon arriving here. Except it was now a murder instead of a rape. Her father was proof of the crime. They hadn't been aware he was alive and here. Now they were. She needed a project.

She brought him into the garage and sat him down in a cleared circle and began unpacking the boxes before him. Maybe recognition of something from the past could quicken whatever the pills seemed to be doing. She would ask him about clothing and ceramic elephants and books. He just shook his head. Handing things to him just made him more confused. It could be that all this stuff was collected after he disappeared. She had been seven. Thirty-two years. She was asking him to remember things he had never seen.

When the boxes uncovered the front of the old player piano, he got up unsteadily and climbed around things to sit on the bench before the keyboard. He began to play, a little slowly, tentatively at first and then he got braver. The piano was horribly out of tune. But he was all right. She had forgotten he could do this. He played an old rag time song. Then a Frank Sinatra tune. She found herself wanting to sing along. On and on. He was smiling. And getting fancier and faster. He looked happy!

She jumped at the knock at her front door. It was loud. She ran out to answer, but stopped to peek out the window. It could be the fucking sheriff. It was Sarah. She opened the door.

"Thank goodness," Sarah said. "I thought you were dead or something."

"The piano," Daydee told her.

"I can hear it. It sounds really bad."

"It's out of tune. Come see," Daydee said.

They went to the door to the garage. Her father didn't even look up.

"Who is this guy?" Sarah asked.

"My father."

Sarah eyed her.

"You sure? I thought he was out there in the cemetery."

"Yeah." Daydee didn't know what to tell her. But she trusted her. "Winston thinks Edward's father is buried out there."

"Jesus."

"Well, it was after your divorce, right?"

"I try to think of myself as a good person," Sarah said. "I'd like to think that I would try to stop bad things from happening."

"He's a sociopath. He can lie and make you believe it," Daydee said.

"It was before the divorce. I warned you."

"This town was a cesspool when I ran away," Daydee said.

Sarah took her face in her hands and gave her a long gentle kiss. Daydee didn't resist.

"Anyway, the quilt party is tomorrow night at six. We're going to do it in my real estate office because there's more room. I'll come get you if you want."

Daydee told her ok, thinking that her truck left parked out front would make it look like she was home. It would only be for a few hours. He seemed content in front of the television.

She walked Sarah out. As she started to close the door, she realized that Edward was standing, leaning against the door of his car across the street. Sarah was parked several yards in front of him. Quickly closing the door, so they wouldn't know she was watching, she went to peek from window curtains. Edward stood to confront her friend. They exchanged angry somethings. Sarah shoved him. He almost went after her as she walked away, but glanced at Daydee and then climbed in his car instead. It started but sat there. Sarah opened her trunk and took out a baseball bat, turned and walked back to the front of his car. Swinging, she took out a headlight. Nothing happened. Sarah walked back, replaced the bat and climbed in. The black sedan pulled out ahead of her. Sarah waved at Daydee in her hiding place before she drove off.

The piano played on and on.

# Chapter sixteen

The next morning, the coffee was already made when she stumbled out to the kitchen. He was snuggled on the couch in front of the television with a cup in his hand. She was a bit frightened. She joined him in front of the morning news.

"Good morning," she said.

"Howdy."

"Are you sane?" was all she could think of to say.

"It's being as heavy as a whale and some fella holding you down to the bottom of the sea. But everythin' around now is the room and you."

"Can we turn that off or turn it down?" she asked. This was so bizarre.

He obliged by turning it off.

"Do you remember the last six months?" she asked.

It seemed to take him a while to put the words together before he said them. He had a five second delay in answering everything.

"Yes, ma'am. You been good to me. I'd be dead or someone would have run me off if you hadn't showed up."

"My mother was helping you?"

"That she was. I was up in Chicago. They told me I had hardly a year. So I called your mama and asked her if I could. This was where I was raised. It's home, even though it wasn't most of the time."

"It's hard to believe," Daydee said.

"She hardly could speak of you. There was that Christmas card. You were in New Orleans?"

"All of my life," Daydee said.

"I'm sorry I missed out on it."

"I didn't know where you were. I just imagined you living out on the street, crazy, just like I found you. She wouldn't talk about you," Daydee said. "She was such a fucking bitch!"

"I was in a home up near Davenport for the first piece of it. Then the state sent me to this halfway house and I was out on the street after that went belly up. I could manage well enough to find food and a little money, but I got locked up for scrappin' with a cop. That's where I got real treatment. When I was in prison."

"I wish I had known," she said.

"How could you? New Orleans a rough place?"

"I survived. It wasn't always easy. But it can be a beautiful place. I was thinking of going back."

He started to cry.

"I'm so sorry," he finally said.

"I never blamed you. You were crazy."

"It was a long life?" he said.

"You play what you're dealt," she said. She retrieved a box of tissues for him. "Hey, you feel up to a picnic today? It's still ok outside in the daytime. We just have to dress warm."

"I was staying out at the cemetery office before some fool locked it up. I was hiding out. Do you know about the marker with my name on it?" he asked.

"More than you do maybe. There's a property that Mom still owned out on a lake on the corner of the land that belonged to Aunt Eunice and Great-Grandma. Nobody would see us out there."

"I probably need to vamoose before your mother's friends find me."

"They already know you're here," she said. "You know, I just had an idea."

\* \* \*

The sun was high in the bright blue sky. They parked and walked about at the edge of the lake, but it was too cold to sit out and eat lunch on a blanket. He was shivering, something she had never seen him do before. Returning to the truck, she started the engine and turned the heater up. They had coffee in a thermos.

"Do you know this guy?" her father asked. "The Chief of Police?"

"I've met him a couple of times. He was always hanging around after the sheriff left. I looked him up in the phone book. We can go to the downtown office or try to talk to him at home. We go lay our cards out and ask for his help."

"If he's in with them, they'll know you are going to make trouble," he said. "It would be easier for me to just drift on out of here. Chicago was all right."

"You owe me for a hell of a lot of Big Macs. I'm expecting you to work it off," she told him.

"You want to go up there together? You have the money?"

She unwrapped the sandwiches she had made and handed him one.

"There's stuff here, Daddy. The farm and the house and it's all still in probate. And the goddamn cemetery. I'd have to come back for the court stuff. Edward would certainly know when I'd have to show up here again. Who's going to run the cemetery? My doctor for the baby is here. I'm not going anywhere. And neither are you."

"You don't owe me nothing."

"What about those Christmases when I was little," Daydee said.

"I don't remember. You recall that far back?"

"You were the only one that ever cared about me. To the rest of them I was an inconvenience. I was a stray dog that they would have taken to pound if they thought they could get away with it."

"I was crazy back then."

"We didn't have Christmas any more after you left," Daydee said.

"Your mother had me put away."

"I wish it could have been different. But it wasn't." Daydee smiled at him. "Why on earth did she decide to help you?"

"I'm not sure. I was dying. Maybe she figured it was going to be a short and sweet fix. Maybe her ass was covered if I died here, so she could cover it up by hiding my corpse after. I think she knew she was close herself. That card you sent was sitting on the desk out at the office forever."

"What happened to it? I didn't see it."

"It's in my stuff somewhere."

"There were postcards from New Orleans in your stuff. Did you get down there?"

"Nah. I must have found them somewhere and thought they were pretty."

\* \* \*

Daydee and her father went to see the Chief of Police. The office was a tiny brick building attached to the Paris Fire Department and the fire truck garage. There was a big flag pole out front on its little lawn. Not a big department. She had called ahead and made an appointment. They seemed friendly enough. Just being close and talking to them made her edgy. Sleazy cops were out there everywhere, a whole lot of them in New Orleans.

But this was a small town, and she was hoping for the Boy Scout type.

As they were walking up the sidewalk, Rob came out the front entrance. She was just going to ignore him, but he stepped in front of her.

"I tried to make you feel welcome in this town, but you continue to screw things up."

"I don't have anything to say to you," she said. "We are here to see the Chief of Police."

"Good luck with that!"

Suddenly her father was in front of her, poking his finger at the sheriff.

"You leave her be," he said.

He looked like a hound dog growling at a grizzly bear. His hand was shaking. Rob hit his own open palm with a fist.

"Give me an excuse, old man."

"You have plenty of excuses," Daydee said. "Really? Out here in front of the world? A pregnant woman and her feeble father?"

Rob looked around. Daydee grabbed her father's elbow and navigated them around him.

Rob scratched his head and walked away.

\* \* \*

They found their way to the chief's office. She had met him before. The chief, a small guy, with muscles and a goatee, came out to greet them and brought them back to his tiny office. He was probably about thirty-five, probably with a wife and kids and a little boy who he was teaching to play football. Daydee hadn't really looked at him closely before. There was no decoration or any pictures in the office. No papers on his desk.

His name was Ted.

"What can I do for you?" he asked after they sat down.

Her father was shivering a little.

"Well. We've come to get your help," Daydee said. Boy, did that sound strange to her. "This is my father, Donald McIntyre. I know because I knew him up to the age of ten before he was committed. He knows me. There's someone out in the cemetery that was buried next to my mother that was identified and buried as him. We think it might be Edward Stills' father. I don't have any proof of any of this, but I think my father is in danger."

Ted grimaced. Opening a desk drawer, he took a few sheets of paper that were stapled together, like it might be someone's book report for school. He looked at it and then handed it to her.

"It may be against procedures to show you this, but you seem to be willing to cooperate with us. I received it in the mail. The sheriff and the editor of the Beacon got copies in the mail as well. For all I know you and Mr. Stills may receive it too. The sheriff has already been in contact with me. I understand you know Mr. Stills and the sheriff socially."

She looked at the papers. At the top was typed in capital letters: THE CONFESSION.

"Read it," he instructed.

It was all neatly typed up.

*It started with the night we won the state championship. Those two boys I had bet on, encouraged, cheered for. I knew we could win that year. They both could have played pro ball. I thought after they made it into college football that they would make that next step, and I could have the bragging rights. Who would've thought one would become a lawyer, the other a minister. I had nursed them through school. Neither of them were too good at their studies then. I had to cajole passing grades from several of their teachers in their senior year. Maybe that's where it started. To get to that last game of the season in Springfield. And to carry home the title. They would be graduating in June, they already had offers for college. They all drank anyway. It wasn't like I was encouraging that. We had started out having a fancy dinner and bragged and were applauded. We all drank too much. I went back to school to double check on the gear lock up and noticed their car on the hill above the school. I went up to shoo them home. There were other kids out there. My headlights caught them.*

*Edward on top of Deidre inside a car. You couldn't help but watch. She was the cutest, sexiest girl in the high school and in the whole town. There wasn't a man in town that could have resisted watching. Deidre looked really drunk or really in the throes of passion. Her clothes were halfway off and Edward just went ahead on her. She didn't protest or fight or do much. Then Edward and Jack came after me. They told me I had to. They both were beside me, dragging me back to the car. They pushed me in and somebody kicked my shoe to get me to draw my leg in and the door was slammed. Deidre was unconscious. She was a mess and smelled of Rum and sex and that sweet stuff they were all smoking then too. And how was I supposed to refuse this. Her body was as open as a door. I did it quick. I was gentle, but I knew she wouldn't remember a thing the next day, so it didn't really matter, did it? I was the fucking coach of the State Champions! After that, it gets a little fuzzy. I do remember getting out of the car and getting patted on the back by Edward and Jack. Jack tried to take a turn, but she bit the bejesus out of his ear. I was the one that bundled her up and took her home. The boys and the rest of them had disappeared. I thought what had happened might be some kind of powerful dream you know, like in one of those Shakespeare plays, where you wake up not knowing if it was real or not.*

*The affair with Mary McIntyre started shortly after that. She was alone and Deidre had disappeared and she seemed to need me around. It was easy to cheat on my wife. I was a coach. I had to be at training sessions with the boys in the evenings. And we were traveling to neighbor towns for games and didn't make it back at night if it was too far away and the game ran late. Mary would drive and meet me. My wife never cared for football. I'm not sure what she saw in me other than I was gone a lot. We went on for about six months and then Mary asked me to deliver a package for her on one of our game trips. I knew what it was. Then there was a few more deliveries asked for. I joked about getting gas money for all this running around and she started giving me a split. There were one or two good sized packages a month to make it somewhere around the southern part of the state. Where it came from and where it went after I delivered it, I didn't know then and didn't want to know. It was pretty simple to open and snort a line and then wrap it back up no worse for wear — nobody could tell. The guys I gave it to were mean looking sons-of-bitches. They were distributors, I guessed. It wasn't until later that I found out about the coyotes and the wetbacks that were coming up. The coyotes were the mules bringing the cocaine across the border and they would drop it with Mary when they delivered the farm workers. The farmers would drive in to pick what they could from her safe house. The one Deidre lives in now. The sheriff knew all along about the whole set-up. Mary cut him in. There was no way you could bring twenty bodies into a little town in the middle of the night without everyone knowing it. The good citizens just looked the other way. God knows the farms needed cheap labor. The bodies that were buried out behind the cemetery were the ones that tried to run away. Nobody heard a thing. Nobody saw a thing. And nobody cared. Mary called me one night to help hunt one of them down. She thought since I knew where all the teenage football players hung out when they were doing something they shouldn't be doing, I might know where to find a desperate wetback. I found him. He was no more than a boy himself. I coaxed him back to the house with a revolver. I didn't realize the coyote needed an example. I took the kid to his death. The guy shot him in front of all of them. And it was my job to carry the body back down behind the cemetery so it could be bulldozed over. Jack was home for the summer and needed money. His father had taught him the backhoe.*

*Then Edward graduated from law school and came back to set up shop. He immediately started a turf war with Mary over who had rights to what in town. He was always into the kinky stuff, so he had a little syndicate over in Terre Haute for the prostitutes and he had a lot of money deals which made some rich and others not. There's a lot more. But that's probably enough for one session.*

*Things kind of went on for a few years. I got addicted to heroin and the affair ended when Mary got married again. I did love her, but she no longer needed to keep me in with the sex. I needed my fix. It wasn't free. The football team pretty much went down the tubes. My heart wasn't in it any more. I was just treading water. The boys knew it. The school and the town knew it. Mary needed sole proprietorship of the properties and the cemetery and no one could find her crazy ex-husband. Mary wanted her husband dead, so she came to me and Edward to find her a body. Edward wanted his father gone. So we coaxed him out to the farm and the old barn and we ran him over. Mary identified him as Donald and the sheriff ruled it an accidental death and we buried him in Donald's grave and everybody was happy. Edward told everybody his father had moved to Florida for his health and he just took over everything his father had.*

*My wife saved me. She drove me to a clinic and checked me in and left me. In six months, I finally got free of it. But it left its mark. All the things I had done dragged me down like so many lead weights. I tried hanging myself, but the rope broke. Don't laugh. It wasn't funny.*

Winston had signed it and dated it.

"Jesus," she said. She looked at Ted incredulously. "Should I give it to him?" she said, meaning her father.

"You can tell him what was in it, later," Ted said. Daydee handed it back to him. "Do you know where Winston is?"

"No, I've not talked to him since his wife's funeral."

"We need to question him about this. If he contacts you, tell him he needs to come see me immediately. For his own protection."

"What about us?" she asked.

"Well, as far as I know you and your father haven't broken any laws and you are cooperating. We will need to get a search warrant for your house and the cemetery, or you can give us permission to search without it."

"You can come home with us right now if you want," Daydee said, wondering if she had emptied the ashtray of pot ashes.

"Is everything in the letter true?"

"As far as I know. I don't remember the rape. Winston told me that he didn't have anything to do with who is in the grave, but I guess that wasn't true."

"I need to have one of my officers come along. I need some more answers from you until we find him."

They sat and explained to him the story about her father, Donald, returning to Paris and her trials with Edward and Jack. She left Winston and Sarah out completely. And the money that was no longer in the house anyway. The sheriff was not mentioned by anyone including Ted.

When the second officer arrived, they went out to the house.

* * *

They spent most of the time looking through the things in the garage. Daydee had gotten rid of almost all of her mother's personal belongings when she moved into the house, so this was all that really remained. Her father offered to play the piano while they searched. Ted, the police chief, eyed her with a grimace. She shooed her father out to go watch television.

"So according to our police report, your burglars said they had women with them," he said as they were rearranging the boxes.

"I didn't see any," she told him.

"There wasn't another vehicle outside?"

"Not that I saw."

"You were pretty rough with them."

"What?"

"Where did you learn to handle yourself? Were you a marine or something?" he asked.

"New Orleans can be a rough place when you're young. I got there at sixteen."

"They were deported without charges being filed against them. Did the sheriff mention that to you?"

"No. I guess I forgot about it. I've been busy with the estate and my father. Those things seem like they take years. I guess I thought I'd be contacted to come and testify when you all were ready and just forgot about it."

"You know anything about the fire at Edward Stills' house?"

"Was there a fire? When did that happen?"

They didn't really find anything. The police chief asked about what might be out at the cemetery. She offered the accounting log book that she had given to the sheriff.

"I've been through every record out there, trying to make sense of her bookkeeping, but it's pretty much a mess. I keep thinking some family is going to show up and I won't have anything that they paid for."

"Well, I'll call you and arrange to come out and take a look."

"You know Edward Stills will be after my father pretty soon. He's proof of somebody else buried out there in my father's plot."

"It's doubtful that he has seen it yet."

"If the sheriff has a copy of the confession, then Edward has seen it."

"I'll assign a patrol to check in over here. I will tell Rob that you are a cooperating witness in the case and that he is to back off and, if available, he should assign a deputy over here. That should keep him from trying to help Edward."

"You read the letter," Daydee said. "He is much more involved than you think."

"This is a small town. I need to proceed carefully."

She wanted to tell him off. He was just another fucking dick. But she only nodded. This was all she had other than her mother's shotgun. And her little toy gun she kept for safekeeping.

## Chapter seventeen

She knew she hadn't asked the right questions. What was involved in digging up a grave? She owned the cemetery. Did she have the right to dig up anything she wanted to? That was a question for the new lawyer. Would the chief have to go to a judge to exhume a body? Was he even going to do that? If she was in Edward's situation, she'd go get Jack and dig up that casket in the middle of the night and drive off with it to dump in Lake Michigan or somewhere. And if her father disappeared, it would just be her word against the sheriff about the death certificate. Was the chief going to investigate or was he going to just ignore it all? He hadn't acted like he was going to ignore it. She just couldn't trust the cops. They all were self-appointed judge and juries. And they never explained anything.

She called the lawyer. It took him a day to get back to her. Since the casket was legally considered her family member, it was legal to dig up the body and move it. The chief was next. She told him what the lawyer had told her and invited his department to be in attendance. She only needed to know when he wanted to do it. He told her to wait. He finally said, after a long pause, that he wanted a

Criminal Court Judge for the county and the mayor to be in agreement to go ahead before he would be ready to do it. Fucking cops!

\* \* \*

She had seen the chief on the sidewalk walking towards Edward's office yesterday. Was he going to see him? She had a moment of panic. She had made a mistake going to him for help. They were all the same. There wasn't a cop in New Orleans that wasn't on the take. Or a mob boss that didn't send Christmas presents to everyone that could look the other way. And she had agreed to wait. She wanted to cry.

\* \* \*

The quilting bee that Sarah had invited her to was tonight. She told her father that he could go with her or stay locked in the house with the shotgun beside him. Those were the only options. He chose to stay home. They had been going for walks around the neighborhood. Until now, she hadn't been willing to let him out of her sight. They had grown accustomed to being around each other without much being said. She missed the gibberish chatter sometimes. He seemed to have developed making funny noises with his mouth when he got up or sat down. A sigh or a little groan or something in between. His illness was showing. It took him a long time to get dressed and out the door. He had mentioned a couple of times that the 'crazies' did seem to wipe away body pain. Or at least he didn't remember it.

He seemed to enjoy the way his boots crunched on the snow-covered sidewalks. This was Daydee's first snowy winter since her early teens. It wasn't bad, if you could bundle up and stay dry. The city didn't seem to be in much hurry to plow the streets in their part of town, so the streets were so many ruts through the snow that were slowly growing wider and darker. There really wasn't anything to do at the cemetery. No one seemed to care if the markers were covered. She wished Winston was around to ask if she was expected to clear the drives around Christmas time. Did families come out to put flowers up? But there had been no word from him.

\* \* \*

The quilting bee was at Sarah's business office. She had pulled the desk back against a wall and put out one of those big folding tables and put folding chairs around it. There was plenty of fabric and scissors and thread to go around. Hanna was there and a teller from the bank that had her mother's accounts. And about four other women she didn't know. Almost all were younger except for Sarah and Hanna. They all seemed to know each other and they all seemed to know how to make quilts. Sarah gave her a basic hand-sewing lesson and started her off on one square for the quilt. She kept sticking herself in spite of the thimbles she soon had on three fingers. She sucked the blood until it stopped and started sewing again. So far no blood on her square.

The beer was served around and most of the women took one. No glasses, which Daydee took as a good sign. She declined, patting her belly. Then one of Sarah's friends told her it was good for the baby, so she decided one would be ok. It tasted good.

That started one of the women on a long story about her pregnancy and her old German doctor who prescribed good German ale and hot baths for whatever the pregnant ailment might be. It turned out that two other women had had at least one of their children delivered by this doctor.

She was slowly picking up the knack of this. There were two done for each one of hers but she didn't mind. They started gossiping about some women, primarily from the church, that they had not invited. She didn't mind that either, since two of the women had come with Jack's wife to arrange to get rid of their plots at the cemetery. She wondered what it would be like to live here forever and know as many people intimately as these women did? It seemed very strange. She had never had more than a couple of friends at a time in her whole life. These gals were kind of fun.

The talk turned to complaining about the men in their lives. Dirty boots tracked across newly mopped floors. Dirty clothes, mostly socks left lying about like leaves blown by the wind. A lot of the men here took no responsibility for being adults. They were picked up after, fed and clothed much like a child in this world, much like she had done for her father. She kept asking why and they would shrug at her as if it was the way of the world and nothing could be done to change them.

Sarah was the exception because she was the 'fallen woman' – a divorced soul set adrift. It was a little in-joke between them. They all knew Edward and understood completely why a woman would leave him. It turned out that Sarah had a 'boyfriend,' a contractor from the next county over where Sarah spent some of her weekends and 'he' was on 'his' best behavior almost all of the time, which made Sarah the object of great envy. Daydee knew why the 'boyfriend' was so perfect.

Hanna talked about how her husband did bring her fresh meadow flowers one Valentine's Day. He had stopped in the middle of fertilizing to pick them for her and nursed them in his thermos with his drinking water in his pickup all afternoon. She was proud that he gave up his drinking water on a hot spring day to bring her flowers. Daydee was surprised that Sean could be nice.

The one beer had turned into several.

Daydee talked about a little Easter basket she found on her kitchen table upon rising late Easter morning. It was full of daisies and chocolate bunnies. John's doing. There were little things that they all did that were endearing, despite the non-responsiveness and clumsiness and immaturity. Daydee found herself talking about John's one memory of his mother who died young. He used to gather colored leaves to take home to her from school as a bouquet. He would search out the best colors. She was in the ground by his third birthday. Why on earth was she telling these women these stories?

"He wasn't a dishonest man," she heard herself saying. "He and a friend broke into a dry cleaner's shop to steal money. The dry cleaner was a big-time bookie, they figured that they would make a killing. John's partner worked with him in the print shop. He had seven children. They didn't pay him what a white man would make. He had a sick mother who didn't leave the house. Not John, his negro friend. In New Orleans, the electric company would extend credit to you in the hot summer months so you could run your air conditioner, but you were expected to pay it off through the winter. This guy never got caught up. John turned himself in for the robbery so they wouldn't find and arrest Wilbur as well. John told the police that he had done it by himself."

They all wanted to know when he was getting out. He still had six months, it would be after the baby was born. Was he coming here? Was he happy that she was doing well? Did they write, or call each other? Daydee looked around. They all thought this was terribly romantic. They hoped they would meet him.

Daydee thought of his hands suddenly. He was a printer, the fingers on both hands were stained black from the ink. When they saw his hands would they still think the same way? Twelve months might be long enough for the ink stains to be slowly washed away, if they didn't have him running a press in the prison. Would they all think the same thing, once they realized he was a drunk?

She was really wondering if he would show up. She had written out a list of rules he would have to follow if he was coming here. She had started it in seriousness and then it turned into pure silliness. She hoped he would get a laugh out of it if he ever saw it.

"We laughed a lot," she told them. "Most of the johns weren't..." she stopped in mid-sentence, realizing what she had just said.

The women looked at her curiously. No one said a word.

"How about some music, ladies?" Sarah spoke up. She went to her shelf for a record. "Rod Stewart?"

"I was raped here before I ran away," Daydee said.

Sarah looked at her. "You all right?"

"I guess so. The beer has gone to my head, I think."

"Is that true?" Hanna asked.

"I guess so. I had an abortion in New Orleans. I couldn't remember how it had happened. I was usually stoned out of my mind the last year I was here. I thought it could be anybody. When I came back, Edward and Jack and Winston freaked out – they were sure I was going to try to hang them."

The women looked at Sarah.

"It's true."

"The holy of holiest is up there every Sunday telling everybody how to live their lives," Hanna said. "And his wife is worse."

"Edward, sure. But Winston?" asked one of the women.

"He's asked me to forgive him. He's actually been very kind to me. But he's very crazy, I think. Deep down inside. He's afraid of going to hell."

"We ought to do something about this!" Hanna said, probably feeling the beer as well.

This turned into a very large expression of indignation and all the women suddenly seemed bent on somehow humiliating all three men. Jack became the easiest target. They could protest outside the church with picket signs. Write mean letters to the town newspaper. Rent a billboard.

\* \* \*

They had been at the house. The minute she turned her key in the lock, her father opened the door and pulled her inside. He looked scared and disheveled. They dead bolted the door.

"Are you all right?"

He nodded.

"Right after you left there was a great pounding on the front door. They said they were with the sheriff's office and to open up. I hollered back that we were under the city police's protection and if they tried to break the door down I would shoot their brains out."

"Did you see them?"

"Nope, they tried that back window that's all rotted out, but it looks like it was glued shut. I couldn't see nothing 'cause it was dark out, so I shot out that window. A car sped off a few minutes later. I don't think I got any of 'em."

She went back to look. He had upended the kitchen table against it. The window itself was covered by a garbage bag that he had taped to the sill.

"You've been busy," she said.

"They didn't seem ready for a shootout."

"They probably thought you were in that state you were when you got picked up off the street."

"Ha on them."

"I'll get somebody to come fix the window tomorrow. You had dinner?" Daydee asked. "I'll make you something."

"I could probably put new glass in it. I used to know how to do those kinds of things."

"Maybe it's time for a whole new window," she said.

"You look a little happy, you all right?"

"Too many beers. I said some stuff I shouldn't have."

"I don't know much about the way women talk. Don't they always say too much?"

"Maybe," she said. "I don't know much about the way they talk either."

Over dinner, Daydee told him about her life in New Orleans.

"Jesus Christ," was about all he could say. After the third time, she asked him to stop saying it. He stopped.

"It was my choice," she heard herself going on. "I didn't want to be a waitress. I was too young to be hired at any kind of regular job. Ringer was just right up my alley. Drugs and cool clothes and a warm place to sleep at night. He treated me better than Mom ever did."

"You're lucky to still be kicking," he said.

She could see the sorrowful look in his eye, all about his regret. She didn't want that. All she wanted was for him to know who she was.

"It was just a year after I got there that I woke up one morning and was tired of being stoned, tired of not seeing what was going on around me. It didn't seem like much of a big deal. You just passed when it was offered. You had a little taste of the bottle to be polite and then you left it. It's harder to quit smoking cigarettes."

"You've got a whole caboodle of backbone."

"I don't know. I had nothing to have a party about. Nothing at all to celebrate. I got rid of Ringer and did my job to make money. I liked the down time. Reading a book. Watching television. Going for a walk. I didn't need anyone at all. It was like I was tired of people. Tired of all the fucking agendas."

"You're not like that at all."

"Something changed when I decided to keep the baby. I pretended I wasn't pregnant for a while, thinking it might disappear on its own. Then I wouldn't have to be disappointed if it wasn't real. It's just hormones. I guess it will all change again after she comes," Daydee said. "And then there was you sitting out there in the weeds."

"I gets to be a grandpa."

She felt like crying again.

"Go take a load off," he said, patting her hand. "I'll do the dishes."

She curled up on the couch with a cushion under her head and watched the television. When he finished, she made room for him on the couch and then put the cushion on his lap and lay her head back down.

"You mind?" she asked.

"Not in the least bitty bit."

He stroked her hair. About midnight she awoke and got up to get him to stretch out, covered him with a blanket and went to her own bed.

\* \* \*

Sarah knocked on her door on the next Sunday morning. Everything outside was bright blue and white. A few of the ladies from the quilting bee were waiting in the car. Sarah told her she had to come. Daydee really did not want to confront anyone this way, but Sarah pointed out that she was out voted and the women were bound and determined to do this with or without her. Hanna waved at her from the car. Sarah asked her if she really wanted to miss the occasion. Put that way, she decided she would regret it if she didn't go. Maybe they could all do it for her and she could just watch. Hanna had some old grudge against Jack which she refused to talk about. Sarah thought it came out of some craft fair they had held at the church years ago, and her handicraft had been slighted by the good pastor and his wife and she never forgave them and had actually quit the church because of it. Daydee was growing to like this odd slender boy-woman.

All of them were dressed for church. So they had to wait for her to get ready. She also checked the shotgun on the way out and told her father to stay put. Daydee thought it strange that two of the women that she had only just met –she would be pressed to remember their names – were out here on her behalf. Or maybe it was something else. They were early, despite Daydee taking time to get ready, and all had agreed they wanted to be up front. So they filed in twenty minutes before the service was to start. Sarah was grinning. She was having a great time. Jack's wife and her friends were whispering furiously in the corner, but it lasted only a minute and they grew silent and stern and they separated to be with their husbands and children. Jack was oblivious until he mounted the stage in front to begin the service. And there they were. He was suddenly nervous. He began with a hymn and everyone stood and sang. Then everyone sat down. Hanna took a folded piece of paper out of her purse and unfolded it and held it against her bosom for Jack to see. Only Sarah and the woman next to her on the other side could read what it said. This wasn't planned or discussed. Daydee and the others were not sure of what they were doing. Jack turned very bright red.

There was a pause.

"Ladies, I want you to feel welcome here. Please stand so I can introduce you to our congregation."

Daydee wasn't sure if that was supposed to embarrass Hanna into putting her sign away, but she didn't. As she turned, Daydee read 'Rapist' on the paper she held on her chest. The congregation could now read it as well.

"Please introduce yourselves," Jack said.

The women did. Just first names. Daydee felt silly. Everyone knew who they were.

"Please welcome our newcomers with a round of applause. We want all who have come seeking salvation to be welcome in our place of worship."

They sat down again.

"We are children of Jesus. Children. Children will make mistakes, sometimes grievously wrong mistakes. Jesus does not desert his lambs. All that is required is confession and regret and allowing the Son of God into your heart. A new life can be found. And an entry to heaven…" And on and on for the next fifteen minutes. A long tale with a few parables thrown in about Jack's redemption. It felt improvised, and he seemed to lose his train of thought here and there. Daydee wished Winston could have been here. It might have made some sense to him. Daydee had never felt any shame about her life. She didn't need anyone to tell her she was forgiven. How was he going to explain the sign to his wife? To be honest, she was more pissed off about his attempt to steal the backhoe shovel than anything else. He finished and they sang a couple of hymns and he read from the New Testament and they sang another song and the service was done.

Jack, pulling on a coat and muffler, went out front to shake hands with the people that wanted that. His wife remained over at the side in back of the pews, so Daydee and her friends, in filing out, would come nowhere near her. The women purposely lined to shake Jack's hand before they left. He looked nervous. Daydee went last. She hadn't really heard what any of the others might have said to him.

"Thief," she said, smiling.

"Today you will be with me in Paradise," he replied.

She knew that was probably a quote.

\* \* \*

She spent the day on the phone while the guy replaced her window. The police chief told her that the investigation was ongoing and that the sheriff had denied that anyone from his office had been to her house. It took the handyman all day, with the cold air flooding the house. It was something to watch. The entire window came out, frame and all and a new one was popped in. All in one piece. She made her father and the window guy grilled cheese sandwiches for lunch. Suzy homemaker. All she was missing was an apron. She called Sean about ploughing the roads through the cemetery. He didn't have anything to do it with and he didn't know if her mother owned a snow plough blade that could be put on the back hoe. He said he could probably put it on if there was one. Jack had handled all that before her mother died. Daydee told him that she would go look. She tried calling Winston, but there was no answer. There was a guy at the newspaper that she had met with his wife at the doctor's. She called him about what the cemeteries here do for Christmas holidays. So people were expecting to be able to go put flowers on the graves. But he didn't think she was required to clear off the headstones. Which was good, because she wouldn't last very long out there in the snow with a shovel and broom. The baby would surely come out of spite.

When the handyman finally finished, she paid him, locked up and took her father along to Walmart. They picked out a tree in a box. And some lights and ornaments. If the baby came before, it would be her first Christmas. She tried needling her father about what present he would like. He couldn't really think of anything but nice warm socks. They went to dinner at the local Denny's and then headed out to the cemetery. Daydee wondered if this was smart, it was already dark, and was beginning to snow again, but she needed to get this figured out and she hated leaving her father alone to go run errands.

Was there a car following her? It turned off. She drove very slowly and carefully. The roads were slick. Up ahead was a snow plough truck heading toward them. As the truck passed, she caught a glimpse of the driver. It was Jack. He waved. And then he was gone. They turned into the cemetery gate and she realized that the drives around the grounds had all been ploughed – recently. That was dumbfounding. Did the road crews just include her just because? Why did she think it was Jack? Maybe he just did it every year when he worked the plough truck and he forgot this year that she was the enemy? Or he just did it to be nice to the old folks who bring flowers. Jesus could be helpful.

She pulled down to the shed to go look anyway. Grabbing the flashlight from the glove compartment, she got out. The snow was falling quietly. Flashing the light around the shed didn't expose anything that looked like a snow plough. Well, there was a reason. They didn't need it. Then there was a sound, a crunch in the snow behind the side wall of the shed. Movement. Someone walking. There was another dark figure walking down from the office. She ran for the truck. Grabbing her purse off the seat, she pulled out her little Ruger.

"Dad, lock the doors after me."

She slammed the door and he climbed out of the other side.

"Dad!"

The first one came out from behind the shed. Edward was the one walking down to them. She faced Edward. Twenty feet away, she could see him well enough to shoot him. He was still coming. Over her shoulder, the other man had stopped.

"Stop!" she screamed.

He just kept coming. She fired at his feet. He went down in the snow.

"Goddamn it! You shot me," he yelled.

She put the light in his face, afraid that he might have that gun he shot the dog with. His hands were empty. She turned on the guy behind her. In the light, it was no one she knew.

"Who the hell are you?" she demanded.

"Jeremy Turner." His hands were up. "Sheriff Turner's boy. I don't want a gun fight, ma'am."

He sure sounded like his dad.

"Come up here with your friend."

He took a wide path around her and walked up to where Edward was sitting in the snow. His hands were up. There wasn't a uniform or a holster as far as she could see. She slowly approached them. It wouldn't be good if she slipped and fell. Her father's feet were crunching the snow behind her.

"Dad!"

Edward was trying to take off his shoe. It looked bloody. It looked like it hurt too much to remove it. She fired into the ground beside the two men. They both jumped.

"Dad, get back into the truck!"

She had no idea if he was going or not. Edward's gun could be in a pocket. She couldn't look away.

"Ma'am, Mr. Stills asked me to come along and help corral you and a crazy old bum. And escort you both to Chicago. Nobody was going to get hurt he said."

"That's a plan?" she asked. She looked back and forth between them.

"I wasn't going to hurt him or you," Edward said.

"Neither of you were trying to break in the house the other night?"

"No," Edward said.

She fired the pistol at the snow about two feet away from Edward's wounded foot. He jumped and covered his head with his arm.

"Christ, don't shoot me, please," he said.

"Are you afraid, Edward?" she asked.

"Yes."

She fired again at the same spot.

"Are you afraid, Edward?"

He looked up at her and smiled.

"Turn your pockets out!"

"They won't pull out. I didn't bring my gun."

"Help your friend up and get him back to wherever you left the car," she told the sheriff's son. "I'm waiting until you disappear."

Jeremy nodded, and helped Edward get up. It looked painful for him to walk. She watched them until they were up near the office. Turning, she found her father right behind her.

"Let's go," she said. "You need to listen to me when I talk to you."

After this, she started carrying the pistol in her coat pocket.

# Chapter eighteen

She spotted Ted at the grocery store. He had his young daughter in the child seat and was slowly shopping, stopping to check his list. Daydee sent her father to go get fruit and wheeled her cart down the aisle of cereals. Ted's daughter was eating grapes.

"Hey," she said.

"Oh, hello."

"So I saw you and wanted to find out what was happening."

He looked at her.

"I have to do this by the book," he said.

"What is that supposed to mean?"

"You know, sometimes you look at someone and you just know who they are. What they are made of. I understand you hate cops. I may know why, but that's neither here or there. You know me the same way I guess. Why else would you go against everything you know to come to talk to me? I need to do this by the book. Sorry."

"Ok," she said. "Do you tell fortunes? Read Tarot cards or something?"

He smiled.

"Not at all."

"Edward and Rob's son tried to kidnap us, you asshole!" she whispered.

"Your father and you?"

"Yes."

"You didn't call me."

"Now you know."

"You want me to arrest him?"

"If you want."

"Let me look into it."

"You are going get us killed," Daydee said.

"Just give me a couple of days."

"You better hope he doesn't show up in front of me again," she told him.

\* \* \*

They put the tree up and tried to decorate it. It really didn't look like much. Neither Daydee nor her father could ever remember doing it before. Her mother had never wanted the fuss of it. His father's parents were fallen Jews and they hadn't done anything to celebrate Hanukkah either. Daydee had never met them. Daydee could recall going to her mother's parents in Indiana one year and her grandmother had a tree and a cardboard fireplace. But those two grandparents died in their fifties under circumstances that were never talked about. Her father had already been taken away by that time, so he didn't know what had happened to them.

They tried. The ornaments she had bought were all hung evenly spaced and the little lights blinked off and on. It needed a star on top and some garlands or something else. She reminded herself to look again when she went back to buy him those warm socks he wanted. She covered the stand at the bottom with a green shawl she had kept from her mother's things. Maybe a real tree would be better. That would be something for next year. God. Next year. The baby would be here. Maybe John as well. You needed a man to pull a live tree into the house. Fuck, she could do it herself once she was mobile again.

She kept waiting for the cops to show up about the shooting, but no one did. She called Ted, again but he was too busy to take her call. So Edward and Rob's son hadn't reported it. She wasn't going to either. Ted was turning out to be a dud. It was an attempted kidnapping, wasn't it? Edward would have to explain why they were at the cemetery. She didn't quite understand what they were trying to do. Take them to Chicago and hold them captive? Or just toss them out on the sidewalk and leave? That plan made her think that Edward didn't know that her father was under medication and conscious. Now he does. He wasn't with the guys that had tried to grab her father when he was here alone. The whole thing was too weird. Why would Edward want them out of town for however long it would take to do something? And what did he want to do?

\* \* \*

Daydee came out in the morning to find her father sitting on the couch in his bathrobe, crying.

"Daddy! What's wrong?"

"I'm a dead man. With nothing to show for nothing."

"Oh, come on. We're warm and inside out of the cold. We've got a Christmas tree."

"The drugs keep the sprites away but I weigh three hundred pounds. I can hardly lift my arm. And when I go, they'll be there to meet me and carry me off. They ain't ever gonna let me go!"

"You don't know that. What if they disappear when you die?"

"This world ain't been kind to me. Why would I expect it any different in the next? And I don't have anything for you or your little one."

"Daddy, don't worry about that. I'll be fine. The sale of the farm should set me up for the rest of my life."

"I'm so sorry for your life. I should have been there."

"Hey, that doesn't matter. We did what we had to do. Can I make you some breakfast? I thought we could go Christmas shopping today. That would cheer you up."

"You go. I don't want nothing. Not hungry."

"Why don't you lie back down and I'll tuck you in and bring you a little toast and jam."

He complied without answering her and she turned the television on for him. The news told of another snow storm coming. When she returned with the toast and coffee, he was asleep. She sat around for a bit, watching the news. And then grew restless. His episode made her think that she might need to take him back to the doctor. Things were probably going to get worse for him. Would she even be able to take care of him when he couldn't get out of bed anymore?

She decided to go Christmas shopping on her own. She wrote a note for him, telling him that she would be back in a couple of hours and would bring home lunch. And he was not to go out. She bundled up and locked him in and went off to Walmart again. For those socks he wanted. She bought some Christmas candy as well. And some beer.

There was a music store downtown. She headed there next. Somewhere in her early memories of him, she thought he had played a harmonica. She'd see what she could find. Driving past the diner in the way, she found Jack and Edward out on the sidewalk in front. They looked really angry with each other and Jack was poking him with a finger. They were so involved they didn't even notice her driving by, which was just as well. What was that about?

She found the shop and went it. The choice of harmonicas was confusing. She talked to the owner for a long while before he decided what she should buy. All with a promise that they could return it if it was untouched. He couldn't take it back with someone's spit in it. She had it gift wrapped. By the time she made it out of the drive-through at McDonald's it was noon.

She turned the corner on her street and immediately spotted the sheriff's car out front. He was standing in the front yard with his gun drawn, looking up into her tree. Her father was up in the tree standing on a branch. He had his coat and wool cap on, so he must have gone out on a walk. How the hell did this happen? She honked as loudly as she could. The sheriff looked over at her.

Her father leaped from his branch. He landed on the sheriff and they both went down. Her father rolled across the icy street. She jammed on her brakes and slammed it into park and climbed out, running to her father across the slippery pavement and almost fell. He was motionless. His legs were both twisted in strange positions like both were broken. She got down on her knees. He wasn't breathing. There was a big gash on his head which was bleeding.

The sheriff was on his back, writhing with pain. He was conscious.

"I can't move!" he yelled.

Daydee ran to his car and got on the radio and told them an ambulance was needed and that the sheriff and her father were seriously injured. She ignored Rob and went back to her father. He wasn't breathing. She tried giving him CPR, but she was sure it was hopeless. She kept on breathing for him until the ambulance came. It seemed like forever. The paramedic took over with oxygen and tried getting life signs. He tried the defibrillator twice with no result. She got to her feet by pulling herself up on the gurney. Another sheriff's car arrived. It was a dream. Unreal. How could this happen?

They covered her father and put him on the stretcher. Rob must have been moved as well. He was gone when she turned. The deputy came over to take her statement. She looked at him and very slowly tried to tell him what had happened. He walked her back over to the open door of her pickup and had her sit down while she told him everything she saw. The smell of French fries were all around her. She handed the bag to the deputy and asked him to take it away.

She recalled the deputy said they would give her a call when her father's body was to be released. That right now it was criminal investigation. Did she need help parking the truck? Did she need a hand into her house? She just shook her head. He left her there. Someone must have turned the engine off. The ambulance had already left. When the deputy drove off, she pulled the truck up to where she usually parked it and, leaving the presents on the seat, she carefully walked to the front door. Her knees were skinned. The door was locked.

* * *

The snow was falling softly when she got to the cemetery. Sean had offered to help, but she turned him down. She did accept a loan of the electric blanket thing he owned for digging in the frozen ground in the winter. The plot was down the hill from the office on the back edge of the grounds. It overlooked the clump of trees where she had found him camped out. As far as she could tell it wasn't owned by anyone. She drove her pickup down to where she had laid out the five by fifteen blanket. It had been some work to clear the snow and lay it out and then run a power cord down here from the shed. She lifted one corner and tested the ground. It had thawed overnight. She unplugged it and rolled it, and by climbing into the bed of the truck, she could pull it up. Walking back up toward the shed, she rolled the extension cord over her forearm as she went. She tried unrolling it out again up to where her mother was buried, but it wasn't going to reach. Then she realized that running it from the office to her mother would work. Unplugging from the shed and running it from there to her mother was a bit of trudging through the snow, but she had a mission. She drove the blanket up and rolled it out again, this time over her father's first grave. She had cleared that snow the day before.

A break in the office to warm up and a cup of coffee from the thermos she had brought, was enough get her going again. The baby kicked as she went down to the backhoe. It was odd to watch your belly jump. She drove the backhoe down and opened the grave for the funeral on Saturday. It was still a couple of days away. Maybe she would hire Sean to close it after. It was nearing lunch time when she finished and drove the backhoe up by the office. Sarah arrived.

"I've been looking all over for you," she said. "You couldn't hire someone to do this?"

"Come on in the office. There's coffee."

Sarah followed her inside. She handed Daydee the morning's newspaper. The headline read: *Sheriff Turner Seriously Injured*. The article talked about how he was attacked while in a criminal investigation and had broken his back. Surgery was scheduled in two days. A specialist was coming in from Springfield. He was in intensive care and was in a serious condition. His attacker had died at the scene. No name of the attacker was given. Nor any explanation of the investigation.

"They released his body to me yesterday. I had the Templeton Funeral Home go and get him. So I guess the investigation is closed."

"Why didn't they give more of the details? Everyone in town knows it was your father."

"How did you find out?" Daydee asked.

"From Hanna."

"Oh, well that's hardly the whole town. I called Sean for his help."

"How are you?"

"I'm ok," Daydee said. "Just really pissed at this fucking town. My father took Rob out to help me. I hope he dies as well."

She told Sarah the details.

"Jesus Christ. What a horrible thing to watch."

"It still feels like a nightmare. It just doesn't feel real."

"You had lunch? You want some company?" Sarah asked.

"I can't eat. I need to return the presents I bought him."

Daydee began to cry. Sarah hugged her and Daydee laid her head on her friend's shoulder.

"I bought a goddamn harmonica," she said.

Daydee wiped her eyes and withdrew from her friend's arms.

"He was going to die in another few months anyway. He wasn't feeling very good."

"Anything you need, love?"

"You want to come back here in the morning? I could use some help with the old grave that my father's name is on. The ground should be thawed by morning and I want to take up whatever is in that grave."

"Is that legal?"

"I own the graves and the cemetery. And the backhoe."

"Ok. What time?"

"Early. 8:00?"

Sarah nodded.

"Don't mention it to a soul, please," Daydee pleaded.

"My lips are zipped."

They locked up and left.

\* \* \*

She had a sleepless night. Why hadn't anyone figured out her father was the one that died? Wouldn't Edward think, if he found out, that her father's first grave would probably be opened? He had to know. Why was he arguing with Jack? Rob's son would tell Edward the details. Or Rob himself if he was able to talk. She just knew that she would show up in the morning and the blanket would have been removed and the ground would be too hard to dig in. She was supposed to hang out there all night long with the shotgun? She knew that's what she should have done, but she was too tired – too discouraged. The presents were still sitting on the seat in the truck. She couldn't bring herself to touch them. This was to be her first Christmas.

She dozed on her moist pillow and dreamed herself back out to the cemetery. With the shotgun in hand. And the figures all standing around the open grave in the dark. You couldn't tell who they were or why they were there. If she ran for the backhoe, would they chase her? The hole had to be bigger. Why had she dug it so small? Like it was for a child!

She stirred, not knowing how long she had slept. It was still dark outside. The clock said 5:15. Getting up, she showered and dressed and drove out to the grounds, certain of what she would find. But the blanket was intact, not unplugged, not moved. The ground underneath had thawed.

Bringing the backhoe up, she began to dig, being as careful as she could. She didn't want to smash it. If it was in a burial vault, it would not be so worrisome, but she had no record of the grave or what was in it. The whole thing was really stupid. She had no intention at all of burying her father next to her mother. She suddenly realized what Edward had been trying to do. He was trying to get her and her father out of the way, so he could come out here and do the same thing she was doing. Except he would haul it off somewhere and it would never be found out. No evidence, no witnesses. This grave was just something buried, everyone hoping it would never turn up again. Just like her.

She hit it. Climbing out, she approached the hole. The casket looked intact. It was still covered by soil on the top. She swept one end and found the handle. She went off to the shed for the chains she had noticed hanging there. This was going to take a little bit of effort to get down in there and wrap the chain on it to pull it out.

Sarah drove up.

"Just in time!"

"I should have gotten some strong guy to come along," Sarah said.

But she looked ready for duty in her jeans and boots. Sarah climbed in the hole. A couple of tries were needed before the chain was securely attached to the casket and backhoe well enough to actually pull the casket out of ground. Daydee dragged it to an open spot. They brought crowbars from the shed and tried prying it open. Daydee wasn't much help. She didn't have any way to put her back into it. They were both nervous about what they would find.

Sarah finally cracked the viewing door and they pulled it open. There was the remains of a man in it. The body was pretty decomposed. This is what we look like? Daydee asked herself. There was some smell, but it seemed to dissipate quickly in the brisk winter air. They were sweating with their work.

On top of the chest of the body was a jacket.

"It's a football letterman jacket from Paris High," Daydee said.

"This is Edward's father, I recognize his wedding ring," Sarah said. "Shit. Edward said he died in a nursing home in Florida. So, what now?"

Daydee explained to her about Ted, the Chief of Police. They went to the office to give him a call. He called back almost immediately, telling them not to touch anything and he would be right there. They broke out the coffee Sarah had brought and waited.

The wind came up. Outside the office window there was a small twister of snow moving across the grounds and then it feel apart. No clouds at all. Just sun. The Paris City Police car came in the entrance and pulled up at the office. Daydee and Sarah went out to meet him.

"It's over here," Daydee directed him.

They walked around the backhoe to the casket.

"I thought I had asked you to wait," Ted said.

"It's my plot and my cemetery. My father is dead because you wanted to wait."

"Your father shouldn't have resisted arrest."

"Oh, fuck you!" Daydee said.

"It is Edward's father," Sarah interrupted. "It's his wedding ring and it looks like Edward's Letter jacket from Paris High was buried with him."

Ted didn't say anything and knelt in the snow to look over the body. He got up without touching anything.

"I'm trying to conduct a proper investigation," he told the women.

Edward walked out to them from behind the backhoe. His foot was in an injury boot. He limped toward them. Daydee jumped.

"Motherfucker," she said to Ted. Her hand was inside her coat pocket already. She gripped her little revolver there.

"Morning, ladies. Ted."

"So, this is your father?" Ted asked him.

Edward nodded.

"Mr. Stills, you are under arrest." Ted pulled his cuffs off his belt. "Hold your hands out."

"What the fuck?" Edward said. "You are joking? You are supposed to be helping me!"

"The money you handed me has been put into evidence and I have our conversations recorded."

Edward backed away and pulled a gun from his coat pocket. Ted tried to pull his revolver out, but Edward shot him. Ted fell.

"Well ladies," he aimed the gun at Sarah. "It looks like you get to help me."

"Fuck you," Sarah told him.

"How about I shoot our favorite pregnant cow?"

"Edward, it's all too late," Sarah said.

"I'm not going to jail."

Ted was moving, trying to pull his revolver from its holster. Edward bent over him to grab his police revolver. Daydee followed him. Her pistol got caught in her pocket. Shit! Edward had Ted's gun. She ripped hers free and shot Edward twice in the back of the head before he even straightened up. He fell on top of the police chief. She tried rolling him off, but couldn't manage it.

"Help," she cried at Sarah.

Together they both managed to get him off the chief. Ted was alive. But there was blood and it looked like he had been hit in the chest.

"Go call for help with his car radio," Sarah told Daydee.

Sarah was down in the snow beside him. She pulled off her scarf and was using it to try to stop the bleeding.

"They are sending an ambulance," Daydee said when she came back. "This was real stupid."

"I thought I could take him by surprise," Ted said.

"Real stupid."

Then she felt a little pop and her jeans were all wet.

"Shit!" she said. "Stay with him. I need to go to the hospital. My water just broke."

"What?" Sarah said. "Wait!"

"Stay. You know where I'll be!"

She walked carefully up to her pickup and climbed in.

"Hold on, kiddo," she told the baby. "Take a deep breath." Then she laughed at herself.

## Chapter nineteen

She drove to the little hospital and checked herself in. They called the doctor and he came. The delivery wasn't going anywhere. She wasn't having the baby any time soon. After dilating half way, she ran out of steam. The contractions just seemed to fade away. She was exhausted. They let her nap for twenty minutes and then started her on the Pitocin drip and the baby was born about four in the morning. They let her hold the baby briefly before she was whisked away to the heat lamp in the nursery. Daydee didn't want to give her up, but she was exhausted.

She awoke at dawn. There was not a soul around. There was a little chirping of the sparrows outside her window. She was sore and miserable. She tried the buzzer, but no one responded. Sitting up slowly, she put her bare legs down and stood, holding on to the bed until she thought she was ready to walk. The IV came with her. It helped to steady her. The night nurse was asleep on her desk, her head on her arms on the blotter. The intern that was the doctor on duty was snoring on a gurney. Daylight was peeking in the windows.

There was one patient she glimpsed as she passed the room. It was Rob. There was a guy in a white coat with him, changing his IV. The sheriff was in bed facing the door. He was in a body brace that had rods coming out of it to hold his head and neck immobile. His face was purple. But their eyes met. Daydee kept walking. The guy in the white coat hadn't noticed her.

She found her way slowly to the nursery. The nurse there was asleep in her chair, her head drooped. Daydee's little daughter was the only baby there. She was curled up in a little gown and blanket with a little cap on her head. The lamp was over her. She looked content. Daydee stroked her cheek.

This was so amazing. How did she rate being given this little soul to take care of. All she wanted to do was pick her up and hold her against her breast – for the rest of her life. But she was asleep and warmed up, so she thought it better to leave her in the crib.

"We got a ways to go yet," she murmured.

She pushed the rolling crib ahead of her with her other hand bringing the IV along and slowly made her way back to her room. She rolled her daughter up next to her bed and got back in. Propping herself up, she put her right hand in with the baby, so she could touch her and stroke her. The baby had the cutest button nose she thought she had ever seen. She watched the window grow brighter and brighter as the day began.

\* \* \*

There was a very small and quick service for Daydee's father. She had Sean do it all for her. Sarah had Edward buried in another cemetery without a service. The son didn't come home.

Things changed. Sarah was around a lot to help with the baby.

The local paper had reported the shootout, superficially, without naming her or Edward. A little later, they reported that the sheriff had back surgery and was indicted for filing false papers regarding the burial of Edward's father and for covering up the illegal migrant workers that had been smuggled through town. One of his deputies testified against him. Not a word in the paper about Jack or Winston.

Jack continued to plough the cemetery for her. And his name was still on the sign at his church. Winston never came back from wherever he went. She hoped he went somewhere. She couldn't believe he had done himself in. By his sights, he couldn't get into heaven that way. She hoped he was doing good things wherever he was.

Ted recovered. And came to see the baby the day after New Year's Day.

Daydee roused herself out of the house finally, and with the baby bundled twice over, took her to cemetery and gathered and threw away the frozen and brown decorations left over from Christmas. People started saying hello to her in the grocery store and cooed over the baby. The newspaper editor crossed the street to see her and the baby. His baby girl had been born on Christmas day.

And in early March it was spring and the snow melted and her daughter began sleeping through the night. It looked like the probate proceedings on the estate might finally be closing.

\* \* \*

Two months later, Daydee and the baby in a stroller were on the sidewalk waiting for the bus. It was the same spot where she had stepped down when she had arrived here. She glanced to see she how she looked in the window's reflection. She needed to diet. The bus pulled up before her. The bus driver came out first to open the baggage bays and in a moment John stepped down. He was thinner, and older. There was no drunkenness about him. He seemed a bit nervous and offered his hand to Daydee in an awkward attempt at a greeting. Daydee hugged him. He didn't know what to say. His fingers were still a little gray, but much better looking than with the black stains. He claimed his suitcase and handed the driver a couple of bills for a tip. Then he turned to bend over the stroller to look at his daughter.

"Boy oh boy," he said.

He put his finger down to touch the baby's hand and she held on to it.

"Jill?" he asked.

"It won't ever turn into something else."

"I was thinking I'd call her Jillie-bean," he said. She looked at him in disbelief. "Thanks for having me," he added.

"How are you at cutting grass?"

"Sounds like paradise after being in for so long. Grass, think of it."

They walked toward her pickup.

If you enjoyed this book, please let others know by leaving a quick review on Amazon. Also, if you spot anything untoward in the paperback, get in touch. We strive for the best quality and appreciate reader feedback.

editor@thebookfolks.com

www.thebookfolks.com

DISCARDED BY
HAZELTINE PUBLIC LIBRARY

44252937R00152

Made in the USA
Middletown, DE
01 June 2017